UNVEILED

UNVEILED

Danielle Leneah

Donnelly Bootcamp Series

Book One

Boettcher-Tuufuli Publishing LLC

Editing by: Krystlynne Muscutt

Copyedited by: Rebekkah Wilde

ISBN: 978-1-7325461-1-0

Printed in the United States of America

First Edition: July 2018

10 9 8 7 6 5 4 3 2 1

Authors Note

I started writing this book while on a family camping trip with: my husband, children, parents, siblings, nieces, and nephews. I could have never imagined at the time, that it would be my last trip with my nephew. Ripped so tragically from our lives, it's has brought new meaning to the phrase 'The most important time, is family time.' Family is precious; love them, hug them, kiss them, and talk to them as much as you can because you never know when it may be your last chance. I would like to dedicate this book in loving memory of:

Timothy Jacob Reeves
January 18, 1999 – July 17, 2017

Acknowledgments

First, I need to thank my husband and children. My dream of publishing this series impacted them the most. So many hours spent writing, editing, designing, and everything else that goes along with it. I love you and am grateful for all of you.

To my mom and dad. They groomed me to be the person I am today, even when it meant letting me read Stephen King books when I was still in elementary school. Thank you for all your love and support.

To Krystlynne who stuck by me in this whole journey. It was not easy and there have been so many setbacks, but she pushed me back on track countless times and deserves so much credit for helping me get this off the ground. I know I say it all the time, but thank you so much for everything!

Last, but certainly not least, to all my fans. This book is a product of your support. From the ones that were there from the beginning, pushing me to keep writing, to those who came recently and have cheered me on. This started as just a passion that I never intended to go anywhere. A special thanks to each and every one of you; we made it!

UNVEILED

CHAPTER ONE

(Saturday, May 30th)

THIS SUCKS!

I'm sitting here in a holding cell waiting to get my final visit with my family after my fate was sealed. All I can do is think about everything that has happened in the last twenty-four hours. Why couldn't they have just sent me to juvie for a few months? It's not like it's the first time. I know I've always had anger issues, and I tend to take it out on other people, but damn this just isn't fair.

In the past, it has always been the same thing; get in trouble, get arrested, do a few months in the local juvenile detention center – or as most of us call it 'juvie'. Then, after I served my time, I got to go back home. All three times I've been in, it was for the same thing – assault. I don't do well with people bossing me around, or people touching me.

People tend to blame my parents for my behavior, but they're not horrible people. They raised my three sisters, our brother and me the best they could. My dad kills himself working construction and mom always worked those little meaningless jobs that helped out while trying to keep us out of trouble. Living in Chicago, there is only so much a parent can do to prevent their kids from getting into trouble. Honestly, compared to most families in our neighborhood, our family was better than most.

My oldest sister had a problem with drugs in high school, but she graduated, turned her life around. She is now off at college with our perfect sister who has never once gotten into any trouble. Despite being the good one in the family, she has an 'I don't give a fuck what other people do or say' attitude that I envy. I also admire the fact that she can hold her tongue; something I have yet to master.

My other sister and I were closer being that she is only one year older, but she fell in with the wrong crowd, getting deep into drugs and dropping out of school. A few months ago, she got arrested and is now doing time for identity theft. Once in that kind of life, you have to find a way to support the habit.

Even though my sister and I are close, my younger brother Evan and I have always been the closest. He is a good kid, and no matter what, we look out for each other. He is one of those rare guys that continually treats women with respect, and is extremely protective. I suppose having three older sisters will do that to you.

He does sell pot from time to time to make a bit of extra money, but he has never been in jail, and he is a good student. He plans on getting out of Chicago no matter what it takes and currently, football is the ticket.

The expression on his face yesterday when I went in front of the judge, is what crushed me the most. Of course, it was her, the same judge I somehow get every time. I thought for sure it was going to be like every other time, but boy was I wrong!

As I went in front of Judge Renee, she started out the same way she always does.

Flashback

"You have been charged and convicted of assault. Again. This is your fourth conviction and to be honest, I am tired of seeing you in that seat. You are turning eighteen in the next few months, so it will no longer be my concern, because next time, you won't be receiving a sentence to Juvenile Detention. You will be in adult court, and it's going to be real jail time for you."

"Yeah, I'm aware of that." She pauses. *Crap, did I just say that out loud?* I've got to stop speaking my mind out loud.

Ignoring my comment, she continues, but not with the words I expected to hear. "Dealing with the current issue, it is evident Juvenile Detention isn't working. So instead, I am sentencing you to four months at the Donnelly Bootcamp in Cle Elum, Washington."

End Flashback

She kept talking, but that was when my world turned upside

down, and her voice lowered to a dull hum buzzing in the background. She continued to say something about them having a high success rate turning troubled teens around, and a deal made to send some kids from Chicago. Hopes of starting a similar camp here. *Blah, blah, blah.*

Only a few parts of her speech got through as my attention turned to my brother's face. It was hard to not physically shudder at seeing the angry and helpless look that appeared almost as quick as I could turn around. His thoughts clearly plastered across his face: 'How do I protect her there?' He has always been there to help me. His extracurricular activities have gained him many friends in many places, which is often to my benefit.

I have a quick mouth that tends to get me into trouble, and while I'm not terrible at fighting, I'm far from great at it. I've won some and lost some, but none of that matters in juvie because no one fights fair anyway. Either you're in a group, or you spend most of your time in the infirmary; in some cases, worse.

Unfortunately, with my attitude and demeanor, making friends is difficult. My brother always has contacts on the inside to make sure that people leave me alone. That doesn't help me now; he is small time, and his connections don't reach beyond Chicago.

The only upside that makes its way into my head is that I won't have to deal with the dumb asses in juvie. Sadly, it only gives me a little relief—this place could be just as horrible. The people aren't the only thing to consider.

It's going to be hard to get used to the fact that they are sending me all the way to some hick town in Washington. To make matters worse, I'll be spending my entire summer there. *Can this get any worse?*

The holding cell door opens, and a guard escorts me to the visiting room.

CHAPTER TWO

(Saturday, May 30th)

IT'S SIX FORTY-FIVE in the morning, and a guard leads me into a room where my parents and brother sit patiently. He tells me we have ten minutes as he turns around to give us some privacy. Naturally, the first thing out of my dad's mouth is, "What did you do that for?" His lips are pressed in a straight line as he pauses to give me a minute to let the words sink in. Right away I know what he means. Although he's only said six words, the implications run deep.

My dad is a man of few words. He believes that attitude is the difference in life and he was always able to say so much in so few words because his actions and expressions said enough on their own. He only said six words, but I know he really meant: 'Why did you do this again? I'm so disappointed in you! Why are you putting us through this? I thought you had learned your lesson.'

All the small, quick remarks made to me over the years come flooding into my mind, just as he knew they would. Immediately, I feel like shit for letting him down yet again.

I've always loved and appreciated my dad. He's a respectable man and tries hard to provide for his family. He is the only person I never mouth off to.

"Sorry, Dad."

He shakes his head keeping his eyes trained on me and continues, "Now you have to pay the consequences. I hope this place they are sending you to teaches you something useful. We all have anger issues, but you need to learn to control them. You're not a kid anymore Nadalynn!"

Funny coming from him, since I know he has let loose a few times himself. Although, he was lucky enough never to be arrested for it. I glance at Mom, but she is staring at her hands with a with a solemn look on her face avoiding my eyes.

I get my anger from her too, but she is more controlled than my dad or me. My uncle told me once that some lady was trying to pick a fight with her at the bar, and when my mom sat down, the woman swung her purse at her head. Mom simply ducked, grabbed the woman's head, slammed it on the table. Unfazed, she went back to drinking her beer like nothing happened while the unconscious woman's boyfriend dragged her out of the bar. She didn't have room to lecture about anger issues either.

I suppose it's not the point though. Mirroring my mom, my eyes fall to my hands. I fucked up, and my embarrassment is undoubtedly showing on my face. I've never been afraid to admit when I'm wrong and this is no different.

Satisfied that he got his point across, Dad gets up and gives me a firm hug, kisses me on the top of my head, and walks out of the room. Although it has only been a few minutes and he didn't say more than a few sentences, the weight of our exchange feels like he's been lecturing me for hours.

He always knows how to talk to me. It's those short, intense conversations that sink in better than going on and on. If he used that method, I would most likely just tune him out like I do my mom. Quickly following Dad, my mother gives me a hug and kiss, says she loves me, and that I need to listen to my father. She shuffles out the door to catch up with my father leaving just Evan and me.

We only have a few more minutes before our time is over and he doesn't waste any of it.

"Dammit! What the hell were you thinking?" He yells as he gets up and starts pacing the room.

Never one to back down, I look him straight in the face. "What? That prick grabbed my ass and got what he deserved. He put his hands on me and then tried to kiss me! What was I supposed to do?"

He doesn't slow, and the anger is still glowing brightly on his face. I continue before he can start yelling again.

"I know he's the one who got Karen pregnant! He's a Senior, and she's a freshman! So, what—he fucks her, dumps her, and then thinks he can just get all touchy with me and I am going to let him? He should've known better to keep his damn hands off me!"

"And you think that justifies breaking his nose and giving him a concussion? Jesus, if I weren't there to pull you off him, you probably wouldn't have stopped until he was dead. Seriously, if he wasn't so shocked, I doubt you would have had a chance to do that much damage. He's almost twice your size!"

The implication that I was supposed to back down just because of his size pisses me off, and I'm on my feet. "Yeah, that crossed my mind. Which is why, when he went down after that first punch, I jumped on him, and started banging his head on the ground. I wanted to make sure he didn't have time to get up. That is, until you pulled me off him. You know I could have handled it!"

My words only infuriate him further. "That's what you always say, but I'm always the one that has to deal with the aftermath! Do you know how much it costs me to protect you when you're on the inside? And now what am I supposed to do? You're going half way across the country to some town that I have absolutely no connections in." *I knew that's what he was thinking yesterday.*

His voice morphs into a threatening low tone. "You need to be careful, and more importantly, you need to be smart. Get your irrational emotions in check, because there is nothing I can do this time." It drives me nuts that he's able to control his emotions so much better than I can.

He sounds utterly defeated, and it's enough to calm my fury. Dropping my stare back to my hands, I begin twisting them in knots. "Don't worry about me. I'll be okay. I'm your older sister remember. You don't always have to be there to protect me."

The corner of his mouth twitches up slightly. "Well you may be older, but I'm bigger and much more handsome." My angered lips turn up into a smile; he knows just how to calm me quickly.

"Whatever jerk. People thought we were twins until you grew six inches taller than me. Don't forget I used to kick your ass too!" His laughter effectively ends the argument. Our fights never last long.

"Seriously sis, please be careful. I don't want anything bad to happen to you."

The guard enters cutting off our conversation; my time is up. My brother gives me a giant bear hug and kisses me on my head just like Dad did. *Fucking tall people.*

"See you in four months, *little* sis." Trying my hardest, I glare at his words, but my heart isn't in it.

"Later Evan. Take care of shit around here while I'm gone. Love you."

He smiles and shakes his head as he walks out. "Love you too!"

The guard walks me back to my small cell and lets me know the bus will be leaving in an hour.

CHAPTER THREE

(Saturday, May 30/Sunday May 31)

AN HOUR LATER I'm loaded onto a bus with eleven other teenagers. I'm the last one to board, so they take me to the very last row. Irritated at myself, my head hangs low; not in shame, but utter frustration.

As I drop in to my seat, I give myself a moment to take in my surroundings. They've seated us in separate rows on alternating sides, presumably to keep us from talking to each other. The bus is barely big enough and has just enough rows. Three guards post themselves at the front of the bus, two in each of the front seats and one in the driver's seat. My escort heads off the bus prompting one of the guards in the front to rise, moving into the aisle he starts speaking.

"Good morning. My name is Tim, this fella next to me is Matt, and the driver behind me is James. This little trip is going to take about thirty hours so get comfortable. You are not to move from your seats or talk to anyone unless told otherwise." Pausing, he takes the time to glare at each of us ending with me. A small shiver of irritation runs down my back. It goes unnoticed as he continues with his well-rehearsed speech.

"We will be making regular stops for fuel and bathroom breaks, but on our schedule, so don't bother me with the 'I have to piss' speech. Go when we stop or don't go at all. We will provide you with brown bag meals on this trip, and you're expected to clean up your own garbage. Fail to comply with these rules, and you'll be sorry. We've been kind enough to remove your cuffs, but I have no qualms about putting them back on." He gives us all one last hard look of warning before turning to fall into his seat. "Let's get this show on the road James."

Shakily, the bus pulls out, and we are on our way to Washington. Heading to some camp outside a hick town named Cle Elum. *This sucks!*

For the first few hours, we're all completely silent, mostly looking out of the windows as Chicago disappears behind us, then Illinois. Signs flying by out the window are the only indicator of where we are as the surroundings grow less and less familiar. Just as we pass one that says, 'Entering Warrens,' Tim rises and announces that we are finally making a pit stop for gas and bathroom breaks. *Thank God, my bladder is about to explode!*

As we pull into the gas station, Tim stands, bringing his attention back to us. "Matt and I will be escorting you to the bathrooms one at a time while James is pumping the gas. I expect to be in and out of here in fifteen minutes. Ladies first, who needs to piss?"

My hand is in the air first, and he motions for me to get off the bus. The fresh air hits me the moment my feet hit the ground. I pause to stretch my limbs and enjoy the clean air after being cooped up on the bus for so long. Tim impatiently grabs my arm and tries to move me forward.

His actions aren't aggressive, but I've always had an issue with people touching me. I jerk away violently, but quickly freeze when I'm free of his grasp. The last thing I need is to get into trouble already, and the idea of wearing handcuffs the rest of the trip doesn't sound appealing.

I've reacted to people touching me like this for a long time — ever since I was a nine to be exact. When anyone lays a finger on me other than a select few, I freak out, which is usually what causes all my troubles. A few years after my aversion to touch first started, my reactions transformed, and I began lashing out physically when people invaded my space. The only time I feel comfortable is with my family and a few very close friends.

Tim's body is in high alert mode as he assesses the situation. Matt is on his feet just inside the bus watching us with Keen attention. Taking a deep breath and trying to relax a little, I take a half a step back toward him so I'm next to him but not touching him. Quickly I attempt to explain in a discreet voice. "Please... I don't like to be touched."

I'm not sure if it's my tone or the look on my face, but his tension ebbs away, leaving only mild irritation. Giving me a wary look he murmurs, "Fine. You stay right next to me and don't try anything funny."

I nod, letting out a deep sigh of relief, and start with him inches behind me. It's a miracle I just got out of that so easy. We head to the restroom on the side of the building, and he moves stepping in front of me so that I stop short of the door. "You have two minutes."

"That's it... really?"

A satisfied smirk erupts on his face. "Be happy with what you've got. If you were a guy, you would only get one. Now hurry up, time is ticking." My feet move swiftly into the bathroom, and the heavy metal door slams closed, leaving me alone with my thoughts.

I feel so much better once I've emptied my bladder, but by the time I finish, wash my hands, and splash some water on my face, Tim is beating on the door yelling that my time is up.

A whining noise from paper towel dispenser alerts me it's empty forcing me to give my hands a shake and allow the air to dry them as I open the door to exit the bathroom. Tim reaches to grab my arm again, but when I flinch he pulls back and gives me an odd look. After a moment of hesitation, he resigns, putting his hands down by his sides, and we make our way back towards the bus.

As I am boarding and heading back towards my seat, Tim

starts calling out for the next person until a familiar voice breaks through his words. "Oh shit, it's Nadi!" I freeze, and my head snaps up. Only people who know me call me by my nickname.

A familiar face is sitting just in front of me. It's Jeff, but that wasn't whose voice I heard. As my eyes continue to search, it is only another moment before they land on the face that matches the voice. Patrick's beaming smile is a ray of sunshine lighting my dark mood. *How did I not notice them until now?* Jeff moves to hug me as I pass but Tim pushes me forward and shoves Jeff back down in his seat much harder than is necessary.

"I said 'no talking,' and that sure as hell means no touching!" Smiling at both boys, I head to the back of the bus and settle into my seat letting just a hint of joy escape me. No one can sour my mood now, not even the grumpy guards who are all exchanging glances between each other with an indication of caution.

Matt hands us all bags for lunch as soon as we get going again. The plain PB&J sandwich, apple, box of raisins, and bottle of water is nothing special. It's a basic lunch, but much more tolerable than the disgusting food they serve in juvie. Chancing another peek, I spy Jeff and Patrick both smiling at me despite both of their mouths being full. It's unbelievable that they are both going to Donnelly Bootcamp too. *What the hell are the odds?*

My head falls back to rest on the seat, and I gaze out the window. The boys and I haven't been close friends for a few years, but there was a time when we were best friends. We met in elementary school when Patrick lived in an apartment downstairs from me, and Jeff lived down the street. In no time we were inseparable and did everything together.

Once we got to middle school, they both fell in with a group of kids who were heavily into drugs. The obsession, addiction, and danger that surrounds drugs isn't my scene. I've seen people go down that dark path—including my closest sister—and wanted nothing to do with it.

It caused me to begin distancing myself from them, not wanting to follow that same path; but it also caused me to become more withdrawn. My neighborhood is overflowing with gangs and drugs which makes it hard to find good friends who aren't into those things. Yes, I had some friends, but not close friends like Patrick and Jeff, which only caused further isolation.

By the time we reached high school, we didn't talk at all anymore. Patrick and his parents moved to an apartment complex across town, so I rarely saw him around the neighborhood. Occasionally I would see them at school, but our school was large, with over forty-five hundred students; the sightings were few and far between. My heavy load of advance placement courses only decreased the chances of seeing them even more. In the last three years, my classes with either of them have been limited to one. I don't think they ever got as heavily into drugs as my sister did, but then again, I didn't see them enough to know.

A warm feeling begins to rise in my chest, and it's becoming clear how much I miss that close friendship we shared. Unfortunately, things change, and I'm sure they're not who they used to be. *People change.*

They both are seventeen like me but look a little different than I remember. Jeff's black hair that used to sport a short buzz cut has given way to a fade—longer on top, tapered at the sides. His face has thinned a little bringing out a more masculine angular jaw line. From what I can tell, he is now several inches taller than me and a lot more muscular than was. Just a hint of facial hair is peeking through giving him a barely perceptible shadow and making him appear a little older than he is. The one thing that hasn't changed is his eyes. They are the most beautiful honey brown eyes that you could easily get lost in.

Patrick appears to be a little taller too, but he was always about the same height as me, and I doubt he beats me by much now. He has also become more lean and muscular over the years. His short blond hair and blue eyes are boy band gorgeous, but it is his heart-stopping smirk that always attracted the girls. It used to drive me nuts how bubbly the girls would get around him. Jealousy was something I dealt with the entire time we were friends—even though I never thought of either of them that way. They were my friends, my best friends. *Boy, do I miss those days!*

❋ ❋ ❋ ❋

I'm startled awake. I must have fallen asleep from boredom. Tim is standing at the front of the bus calling out to see if anyone needs to pee. Out the window, I take note that we are again in some small, rinky-dink town. There are no city signs, so I have absolutely no idea where we are or even what time it is.

This sucks! No cell phone, no watch, and no idea what's going on! After a few minutes, I'm a little more awake, and I search for something that will ground me a little. Glancing inside the gas station, a bright light gives me my reprieve. A vintage neon-clock on the wall reads five o'clock. *Wow!* I slept for almost four hours. Maybe it was more than just boredom.

Tim gets back on the bus and makes a last call for the bathroom. I don't need to go, but I know it will be hours before I get another chance, so I raise my hand, and he beckons me forward. As I'm passing Patrick, who is sitting on the edge of his seat, he reaches up and discreetly pinches my thigh. Other than my lip curling up into a half smile, I don't react. It's his way of saying hello.

Jeff's eyes are laughing as they find their way to me, letting me know he saw it too. It was our thing; we used to do it in school, so we didn't get in trouble in class for talking. They are the only two friends who I ever allowed to touch me without getting pissed off. A sense of relief spreads over me knowing they will be there with me.

The next few hours are dreary as hell. My ass is beginning to hurt, and I just can't get comfortable. Every once in a while, I glance at Jeff and Patrick. The few times they are peeking round at me, I smile my knowing smile, and they do the same in return.

The other people occupying the bus look dreadful. There are eight guys and four girls, including me. Most of the guys are kind of cute, which is a big plus. While I have an aversion to touching,

I'm not afraid to talk to guys. Having so many sisters, I'm put off by girl drama, so I'm glad there are twice as many guys. The chance that I will probably have to share a room with one of these girls, or all of them, is not exactly something I'm thrilled about.

The brunette sitting two seats ahead of me is staring out of the window, and her shoulders are shaking with silent tears. Another girl with black hair turns to look at me, maybe feeling my stare. Her eyes are red and have been rubbed raw; she's been crying too, not a good sign. *Can't they just suck it up already?*

All of us look similar in age, around sixteen or seventeen. I overheard Matt talking to James earlier about how this was a "last chance" boot camp and that we were all in for a treat. His voice was oozing with sarcasm, so I can just imagine this is going to be a huge pain in my ass. If it is indeed a *"last chance"* boot camp, I'm probably right that we're all close to being eighteen.

Darkness sweeps slowly into the bus as the sun sets in the distance. Many have fallen asleep, and as much as I wish sleep would find me too, my earlier unplanned nap prevents it. Once or twice I consider trying to speak to the guy in the next row up, but James has already gotten pissed about people attempting to talk, shouting for them to keep their mouths shut, so I decide to just stay quiet.

The brown bag sitting next to me still holds most of what comprised our sorry excuse for dinner. I pull out the string cheese that is still in there and slowly pick it apart. I braved my way through yet another PB&J sandwich when we got them, but it killed the rest of my appetite. The only difference from lunch was we were given a cheese stick instead of raisins. *How original.*

＊ ＊ ＊ ＊

By the next day, my body is itching to be there already. The thought that it is in middle of nowhere is no longer a factor; I'm just tired of being on this rickety old bus. Our morning continues the same as the previous day, stopping every four or five hours to use the bathroom. For breakfast, we get a muffin and fruit cup, which is a relief. I'd begun to think we were going to get PB&J sandwiches throughout the entire trip. A little while after we eat breakfast, we cross into Washington State, and I know we we're close.

Our last stop was a few hours ago; or so I think, since I have nothing by which to tell the time. We stopped in a place called Moses Lake; it seemed like a beautiful little town. People were relaxing on a beach next to the lake, and it depressed me that my summer is going to be a far cry from theirs. I've been daydreaming what it would be like to be relaxing on that beach. Tim gave us another brown bag for lunch, but as soon as I saw it was PB&J yet again, I tossed it aside. Instead, I focused on the canyons passing by out the window and resumed imagining myself in that happy place on the lake shore.

The bus exits the freeway, pulling me out of my daydream. I'm ecstatic to see the sign that says, 'Entering Cle Elum,'—not what I was expecting to feel on our arrival. We drive through a small, one-stoplight town. It looks like something straight out of a western movie, with the quaint storefronts that line the main street, and there are nothing but homes and trees nestled behind them. As we enter, I even see a little cafe called 'The Cottage.' *How Quaint.*

As we reach the other end, we go to the right at a fork in the road. A Safeway Grocery Store sign beams at us from down the left side of the fork as we turn, but besides the Safeway and a Dairy Queen, there is no sign of city life. My previous thoughts of this being a 'hick town' are not so far off.

As we head to what I am guessing is the outside edge of the little town, all I see are trees. It looks like this is going to be an all-out camping type of camp, with woods, chirping birds, and everything. Several minutes later we start to go down what seems like a long, rough, dirt driveway. We pass under a sign that says, 'Donnelly Bootcamp.' *We're here. Finally!*

CHAPTER FOUR

(Sunday, May 31st)

THE FIRST THING my senses pick up through the open windows is how much different the air smells. I suppose I was oblivious to it until now. The smell of grass and trees is refreshing, making you want to take a deep breath. No hint of smog, sewers, or disgusting garbage; it's just – clean. Out the window, a fast-moving river runs just beyond the trees. So many beautiful green trees, plants, and flowers. I marvel at the sight in front of me. It's nothing like back home in Chicago. In the city, we don't have anything like this. It's beautiful.

The bus comes to a stop in a large round driveway with a flagpole planted at the center. At the top, the iconic American flag sits above a black flag, but the lack of wind is hiding most of the red symbol that peeks out in spots on the black cloth. Four identical square buildings line what I'm assuming is the front of the property, and running between the two middle buildings there is an immaculate dirt walkway lined with logs.

Posted at the beginning of the path are two good looking men standing with their feet shoulder width apart and their hands behind their backs, piquing my curiosity. They both look similar with short brown hair and matching uniforms, though one is a few inches taller than the other. I can't help but grin as I take in their well-fitted black pants and tight black tee-shirts that show off their muscular upper bodies and flat stomachs. *Nice.* Even if this sucks, at least I have a little eye-candy.

The taller one gets on the bus, his eyes sweeping back and forth, taking in each of our faces. The hard look on his face says that he's all business. I give him another once over; he's damn good looking. The small gauges in his ears and that eyebrow piercing are extremely hot. *Wow, those eyes!*

Suddenly those eyes are staring straight back into mine; I stiffen and feel my face flush as I realize I've been caught checking him out. His gaze is so intense it's impossible to look away. After a second he breaks our exchange and starts talking in a quiet but robust voice that resonates throughout the bus.

"Well, well, well. Don't you guys look like a sorry bunch of maggots." *Well, hell.* I was hoping for prince charming. *Why do the hot ones always have to be jerks?*

He continues without taking a breath, "I'm Aerick, and I am one of the instructors here. You will all follow me off this bus, grab the bag next to Brand with your name on it, then walk quietly down the path until you're standing in front of the stage at the edge of the courtyard." I glance at the other guy and see the bags that I hadn't noticed before all lined up neatly near his feet. *Did he just call that other guy Brand? What kind of name is that? Must not be a "Brand" name kind of guy.*

He turns and exits the bus; we all look around at each other, a little confused about what's happening. When we don't move immediately, Aerick shouts 'Move!' and it breaks us out of our trance. Jumping up, we all start shuffling toward the front of the bus. As I exit, Tim and Matt mutter something to each other and laugh, which just makes me more uneasy about the whole situation. My mouth twists into an irritated scowl; glad they think it's funny. *Assholes.*

I move at a sluggish pace and grab a black duffel bag that has "Nadalynn" printed on it in bold, red letters. I don't particularly like people calling me by my full name. Back home, the only person that calls me Nadalynn is my dad, and that is reserved for when he's upset.

Everyone else just calls me Nadi, a nickname I got when I was young, and it stuck. I roll my eyes, letting out a heavy sigh as I move in the direction of the courtyard. Patrick and Jeff slide in front and behind me. Patrick chances a whisper to me, "Hey Nadi," as we walk.

The guy who introduced himself as Aerick looks irritated; we must not be going fast enough for him. As if he were reading my mind, he looks at me and shouts. "Hurry up; I don't have all day."

We walk into the courtyard, and there's a wide but short stage to the right of us that sits in front of a weirdly shaped building. The building looks like three long rectangular buildings that all connect at one end to a circular room in the center. Four more square buildings that mirror the ones we just walked between sit in front of us and to the left. There are a further two long, rectangular buildings sitting end to end. All the buildings are a matching log cabin style that seem to blend seamlessly into the trees behind them.

The pentagon shape of the courtyard reminds me of a crosswalk sign, with the buildings lined all around it. The walkway we came in on connects to another path that runs just inside the edge of the buildings, all the way around the courtyard. Except, instead of following the weirdly shaped structure behind the stage, it is in a straight line across the front of the stage, creating a square pathway. Small, uniform logs line the path all the way around on both sides with short walkways that lead to the entrance of each building. Other than the pathway, the rest of the courtyard ground is luscious, green grass cut to perfection; you can even see the meticulous, straight lines from the lawn mower.

This place is quite beautiful. The difference between here and city life is extraordinary. It's looking like this place will be marginally better than four months spent in Juvie. But I'm not stupid; I'm sure they call this 'boot camp' for a reason. Despite the awesome scenery, my anxiety and unease grow, and I'm not the only one. Several of the guys and all the girls have the same unsure look plastered on their faces.

Standing on the stage is an African-American man that looks slightly older than the other people, but he's wearing the same black pants and tight black tee-shirt. Beside him is a tall, slender Asian woman dressed in a tight black pantsuit who seems to be sizing us up as we walk towards them. A group of people line the front of the stage with the men to the right and the women to the left.

They all look young, maybe in their early twenties and stand with the precision of a military squadron. Their hands are stiff at their sides, and their faces are seemingly emotionless as their focused eyes stare straight ahead. I'm starting to think this is going to be like military training only they're not wearing camo clothing; they're all wearing black pants and tight black tee-shirts instead. The only difference in the uniforms is the women's tee-shirts are V-necks instead of crew necks. Their clothes show that all of them are incredibly fit and muscular. The teenage girl inside of me starts to awaken as I get giddy at the sight of so many good-looking guys.

Our group stops, loosely scattered in front of the stage; Jeff and Patrick come to a stop on either side of me. The two instructors that escorted us here fall in line next to the guys in front of the stage, and the man standing on the stage begins talking, abruptly bringing me out of my thoughts.

"Good afternoon ladies and gentlemen. You are here today

because you can't seem to follow the law like everyone else in society. You've been sent here to learn how ordinary citizens should act and that is what we plan on teaching you. Starting today, you are all considered cadets, and we will address you as such. We use first names here as this is not the military and in the real-world people use first names, not last names." *Okay, not what I was expecting.*

"I first want to introduce myself. I'm Luther, and this is my camp, so if you mark it up or destroy anything, you will be answering directly to me. Next to me is my operations manager Ayla. When I am not here, she is in charge." His voice tightens as he is talking about his camp but then lightens up as he introduces the woman standing beside him.

"The people standing along the stage in front of me are our capable staff." He begins with the end of the girls' line and starts to introduce them. As he calls their names, they step forward, nod and then step back.

"The young lady at the end is Tia. She mainly teaches in the classrooms, but she will also be helping our instructors in the field from time to time. Next to her is Andi. She is the one who cooks our fabulous meals, so I would suggest being nice to her. Terrie here is our resident nurse. If you have any medical issues, she is the one to see."

With another pause, he turns to the men's side. "Over here we have Brayden, who is our maintenance hand and groundskeeper. Next, we have Jake." As Jake's name is said, he doesn't step forward but bends down, grabs a small bag and walks over to us.

"Jake here is our tech guy. He is going to put a tracker on one of your wrists. With these trackers, our staff can locate you at all times." Jake begins putting thin metal bands on everyone's wrists.

When he secures mine, I notice there is no clasp. One end slides into another, and when it is tight, he removes a weird pin. I examine it closer once he has moved on. It looks more like a bracelet than a tracker. Once when I was on house arrest, I had a home monitor on my ankle. It was bulky, and it irritated the shit out of my skin. This band is different; it's much thinner, and is only about half an inch wide. It displays the time and date on it in big bold numbers. If there was a design on the band, it would almost make it pretty, but it's just plain metal. I try to move it to see how much play it has, but there's no give. There is no way I'm going to be able to slide it off; at least it seems comfortable.

As I inspect my tracker, Luther keeps talking.

"These are not those shitty trackers you get when you're on house arrest. These are top of the line titanium tracking bracelets. Don't bother trying to remove them, because even in the unlikely event you can get it off, they have security measures, and we will undoubtedly know. These also double as your watches. Your days here are planned out by time, and you are expected to be on time at all times. So now you have no excuses." Jake finishes up and goes back to his place. He picks up a small tablet computer from the edge of the stage and starts messing with something on the screen.

Luther walks over to the end of the stage where Aerick and three other guys are standing, and with a slight smile on his face starts talking again. "On the end here are your primary instructors. You have already met Aerick; he is the senior instructor, so if there are any issues with other instructors you are to go to him. If you have a problem with him, you come to me. Beside Aerick are our other instructors; Brand, who you have also met, and the two at the end are Paulo and Trent."

I give the two new instructors a once over. Both instructors have the same solid physique as Aerick and Brand. *Wow, they sure know how to pick 'em here!* Paulo looks like he might be an islander, with his tanned skin and coarse black hair. Trent's African-American features are strong, like Braden's but Trent is a good six inches taller and stands with much more confidence. I'm still trying to wrap my head around all these good-looking guys around here.

Ayla brings my attention back as she steps forward, Luther taking a comfortable stance behind her.

"As Luther said, this is not the military. We are not training you for war. Our job is to rehabilitate you in the hope that you will not fall back into your lawless ways. This program has been tremendously successful in the past. As a matter of fact, most of our staff are graduates of this camp."

Seriously... I'm wondering which ones she's talking about and what crimes they committed.

"Don't get me wrong; this camp is no cake walk. While we

may not be the military, that does not mean we don't use the same tactics. We will test you and push your physical and mental limits." She pauses as she looks out at our group, letting her words sink in.

When she starts talking again, her tone is sterner. "You are expected to be respectful at all times, and you are expected to follow the rules at all times. You are expected to learn and uphold our camp values at all times. These values are in the handbook that we will provide to you, and you are expected to memorize them by tomorrow. If you follow the rules you may be rewarded, but if you break them, there will be hell to pay. Consider this is your one and only warning."

My mind is still stuck on the previous graduates' part. Looking at our instructors, I would be willing to bet several of them were in for assault like me. A wry smile plays across my lips and I shake my head a little at the thought.

Before I know it, Aerick is standing right in front of me, my face just inches from his chest. "Is there something funny cadet?" His voice is low and intimidating.

My eyes pull up to him, and his expression is less than pleased. I stop smiling and try to reign in my irritation about him being so close to me. Although he isn't touching me, he's too close for comfort. Taking a moment to collect myself, I answer him in a steady voice with a smirk as I look up into his eyes. "Nope." *His eyes are a vibrant gray!*

"That's weird because that smile on your face suggests

otherwise." He has not moved an inch, but his intimidation doesn't scare me.

I pull myself up a little taller. "Just because I smile, doesn't mean I think something is funny. I could have just had a happy thought." My head tilts slightly, and I half smirk as I finish talking.

His face fills with confusion for just a second, and then just like that, it immediately hardens. "We will see how happy you are when training starts." His voice is much lower, slightly threatening.

He turns around and starts walking back to his place when Jeff lets out a small laugh. I'm sure he's amused that I still have a problem keeping my mouth shut—or maybe it's because I still have that sly smirk on my face.

Aerick whirls back toward us and gets in Jeff's face. "That goes for you too asshole. You better watch yourself, or I am going to make your stay hell. You got me?"

Jeff looks a little stunned, but answers in a steady voice. "Yeah, I got you."

His answer just infuriates Aerick even more. "When you answer a question, you answer me with 'yes,' not 'yeah,' and next time you address me, it will be as 'Sir, or Aerick, Sir.' Do you understand, cadet?"

"Yes, sir," Jeff's voice drops, and all the amusement has disappeared from his face. I immediately feel bad, knowing I got him into trouble. Aerick joins the other instructors who are now forming a square around the outside of our group.

Jake hands the tablet to Luther as he begins to speak again like the whole exchange never happened. "You will all be split into four groups. I will now be pairing you with an instructor who will be your lead instructor. When I call your name, stand next to your instructor. Royce, Leann, and Joseph; your lead instructor is Trent. John, Steven, and Karen; your lead instructor is Brand. Nadalynn, Jason, and Michael; your lead instructor is Aerick." *Fuck...* I had to get stuck with Prince Charming.

"Tara, Jeff, and Patrick; your lead instructor is Paulo."

Once we are all situated around our instructors, Luther continues. "Behind me are the main dorms. If you are with Paulo or Aerick, you will be in dorm A. If you are with Brand or Trent, you are in dorm B. Your instructors are in dorm C, on the back side of this building."

In a rush, the girl with red hair standing next to Trent speaks up in a high voice.

"Wait, we are sleeping in the same rooms as the guys?"

Luther eyes everyone as he takes a step closer to the front of the stage obviously not amused at her sudden outburst, he gets a very stern look on his face.

"These are co-ed dorms. We do not differentiate between sex here. You are all one team, and you will do most things together as a team, including sleeping in the same room as your team. However, sexual contact is strictly forbidden, and if you break this rule, there will be hell to pay. Guys, you will not look down on the women; you will see them as nothing other than your equals, and vice versa. There is also a strict policy of no harassment, so keep your unwelcomed comments and actions to yourselves, and girls, this goes for you too."

The guys standing around me, whose eyes were filled with glee a moment ago, suddenly look a little somber. They apparently don't like these rules, and it makes my smile return. "It's just after fourteen thirty now. Your instructors will now show you into your dorms. I know you have been in the same clothes and on a bus for more than a day, so you will have two and a half hours to shower, change, unpack your things, and begin learning the rules. I expect everyone to be in the mess hall at seventeen hundred for dinner. Dismissed!"

I turn and follow Aerick, who is already heading toward the door with an 'A' above it.

CHAPTER FIVE

(Sunday, May 31st)

ONCE THE SIX people in dorm A get through the front door, Aerick stops and faces us. Paulo comes from behind and joins him. The closeness of everyone makes me move toward the front; even as much as I don't want to be near Aerick right now, there are too many people standing too close to me.

"Okay, listen up. Everyone pick a bed. Here is where you will be sleeping for the next four months. You will not switch spots unless authorized to do so and you will keep your area clean at all times. Beds will be made every morning when you wake up." Not stopping to wait for questions, he continues walking to the other end of the room. Another door sits in the center of the wall, but he doesn't proceed through it; instead, he stops and turns to face us.

"Laundry is collected on Sundays and Thursdays. You put

your dirty laundry in the laundry bag provided to you and hang it here." He points to the pegs on the wall next to the door. "It will be picked up, cleaned, and returned to your bed. I do not like smelly, dirty laundry." He mumbles. Personally, I hate laundry, especially doing laundry. Another point on the list of pros of being here. Something tells me there won't be much more added to it.

We walk into a bathroom that is peculiar; shaped in a perfect circle. Three frosted glass doors including the one we just walked through, are the first thing I notice. My guess is that they go to all three dorms, but they also divide the bathroom into sections. In one, four showers are separated by full-length wall dividers and, I'm glad to note, have real doors on them. *Thank goodness.*

Four toilets are separated in the same fashion as the showers in another section, and again thankfully, they have real doors on them. The only difference is the showers are slightly wider. *At least you can't see through doors.* The last section has four sinks, with mirrors attached to the wall. Good thing there aren't a bunch of girls here or we would never be able to wash our hands. In the center of the room, a round wooden dresser with drawers sits with towels and wash rags neatly folded in stacks on top of it.

Aerick looks at us with a smirk on his face. "This is the dorm's bathroom. You all share this with the other two dorms. All the dirty towels and wash rags will go in the laundry basket under the sink there." He points to a square basket that sits in between the two middle sinks. "There will always be clean ones on the dresser. When you change out of those ridiculous orange outfits, put them in the garbage. I don't want to see them again after dinner."

He lays his hand on the dresser. "Each one of you has a drawer with your name on it where you can keep all your toiletries. Your drawers already contain a toothbrush, toothpaste, a brush and a comb. The showers stalls each have shampoo, conditioner and body wash in the dispensers on the wall. If you run out or need anything else, take it up with Ayla and if she feels it is a necessity, she will provide it for you."

Interested in testing his patience and also to get back at him for standing so close to me earlier, I decide to embarrass him.

"Aerick, sir—" I try to keep my face as straight as possible, "—are tampons considered a necessity?"

Most of the guy's faces turn red, but Aerick doesn't miss a beat as he takes two strides, so he's right in front of me again. His expression is entirely unchanged, and he speaks in such a quiet voice that I'm sure only a few people near me can hear. "Are you currently on your period?"

I'm floored, not only by his words but his sudden coolness. Actually, I don't think I've ever heard those words out of a man's mouth. "Not just yet." I try to play it cool, but my voice betrays me as it falters. *How the hell did he do that with a straight face?*

He steps back allowing everyone to hear him. "For the women, feminine products are considered a necessity and can be requested from Ayla. Are there any other questions?"

He pauses and looks pointedly at me. I shake my head no along with a few others. "Good. Now go back to the dorm, pick a bed, unpack the contents of the bag provided to you into the chest at the end of your bed, shower, and change. There are a handbook and map on the desks next to your beds; I suggest you start reading them. You are to be in the mess hall no later than seventeen hundred hours."

With that, Aerick and Paulo walk through another door, which I suspect leads to their dorm. Slowly looking at each other, we file back into ours. Jeff puts his stuff on the first bed to the left, I take the second, and Patrick takes the third. The other girl from Paulo's group drops her bag on the one across from Patrick, and the other two guys move to the remaining beds. *That was easy, too easy.* No arguing, no talking even, everyone is just going with the flow. Also something I am not used to. In Juvie, you typically have to buy your way into a bed.

My body collapses on the bed; I lie back and take in my surroundings. The beds are a warm wood which goes well with the dorms' interior, and the headboards are set flush to the wall. Above each bed is a six-panel window that lets in the natural light, but is too high to see out of if you're standing on the floor. On one side of the bed, there's a wooden desk with one drawer that spans the entire length, and a simple matching chair. A nightstand with a basic desk light and an alarm clock is set up on the other side of the bed. Nestled under it is a square laundry basket with a linen bag inside it. All our areas look the same, the two sides mirroring each other.

Just as I'm about to get up and start unpacking, Ayla walks in. "I will be issuing your name tags to put on your laundry bags, clothing chest and uniforms. Is there anyone who does not go by their listed name? I will only do this once, so speak up now." *Do we get a choice?*

I do so quickly. "I go by Nadi, N-A-D-I, not Nadalynn."

She takes note of the spelling as a boy with sandy blond hair calls out, "I go by Huck."

Ayla raises her eyebrow and Huck looks annoyed. "My middle name is Huckleberry, so people just call me Huck. There are too many people with my first name." He explains quickly.

"And I go by Mike, not Michael," brown-haired boy pipes up.

She writes it down and continues. "Anything else you would like to request right now? Nadi, Aerick mentioned you needed something." *Shit.*

Warmth creeps up my cheeks. Despite what I told him, I'm not due for several weeks, so I just shake my head no. Damn him; he won this round.

"Okay. I will be back in an hour," she nods and walks out, her posture beaming self-confidence.

Almost an hour, later I've gotten my clothes put away in the chest. I'm not sure how the camp knew our sizes, but they've provided me with pants, V-neck tee-shirts, tank tops, socks, cotton underwear, and sports bras. Everything is in sets of seven.

They also gave me three shorts/camisole pajama outfits, three zip-up hoodies and a pair of boots. All the clothing is black with a red stripe running down both sides; except for the hoodies which also say, "Donnelly Bootcamp" in red on the back.

Patrick and Jeff are also unpacking, and I see that the boys have boxer briefs, crew neck tee-shirts, and ribbed tank tops with their pajamas instead of the camisole the girls received. All the clothes look like the same thing the staff was wearing, except their clothing doesn't have the red stripes. It must be their way of keeping us separate.

Once we finish putting our clothes away, we just sit on our beds and talk. It turns out we're all seventeen. Mike and Huck seem like pretty nice guys. Mike apparently knew Patrick before back in Chicago, but they weren't friends. Funnily enough, Mike, Patrick, and Jeff are all here on possession of drugs charges.

Huck just moved to Chicago and was sent here for burglary when he tried to get some money he claims he desperately needed. And after a bit of coaxing, Tara tells us she is in for shoplifting. I didn't think that was severe enough to warrant this, but then Tara explained it was an expensive diamond bracelet that she got caught lifting. She made quite a bit of money selling them on the streets.

I'm in the middle of telling my own story when Ayla walks in and starts handing us our name tags. "The nameplate goes on the square on the front of your chest; just tear off the back and stick it on. You should attach the small name pin to the top of your laundry bag. The larger name pin should be attached to your shirt or hoodie any time you leave this dorm. There is a spot on the top, left-side of all your t-shirts, tank tops and hoodies to attach it. Do not lose these or there will be consequences." With that said, she turns around and leaves.

After talking for a little while longer, I decide it's time for a shower. Tara, Huck, and Mike have already traded off taking showers while we were all talking earlier. I jump up from my bed, grab out a pair of pants, tee-shirt, bra, underwear, and tell no one in particular that I'm going to take a shower. In the bathroom, several people are already showering, but there is still an open stall. Before going in, I am sure to grab a towel and wash rag. The last thing I need is to come back out butt naked, trying to cover myself with a dirty old jumpsuit in search of a clean towel. A small shelf is affixed to the back of the door and a hook on the bottom to hang the towel, giving me a place to put my things.

I neatly put my clean clothes on the shelf, hang my towel, and turn on the shower. The door completely closes off the shower stall so other people can't see inside. I'm far from shy, except when it comes to my body. I have never been one for skimpy clothing. I don't have a big chest or a big butt; my body is plain. My stomach is not super flat, but it isn't fat either. My frame is more that of an athlete—without the well-defined muscles.

My thick, dark-brown hair falls to the middle of my back and has a bit of a natural wave. It can be a pain in the ass to do when I dress up, which thankfully isn't often. The one thing I happen to like about myself is my eyes. They're a dark forest-green with subtle hints of brown in them. Many times, I've had guys tell me how beautiful they are.

A sound from somewhere in the bathroom startles me out of my thoughts and realize I've finished washing my hair and body.

Sighing deeply, I turn off the shower, grab my towel to dry off and pat dry my hair. I'm not about to get dressed in front of other people, so I grab my clothes and put the towel on the floor so I can stand on it. It's a bit of luck that the shower is big enough to get dressed in without touching the sides, and I manage to get dressed without getting my clothes wet.

Once I've finished putting on my new clean clothes, I gather my nasty ones off the floor where I'd tossed them along with my towel and wash rag. I pitch the wet towel and washrag in the laundry basket, place my old clothes in the garbage, and look for my designated drawer in the dresser. Sure enough, the sticker on it says Nadi and not Nadalynn. *Yes!*

Inside, there are all the things Aerick said would be in there. Digging around, I find what I am looking for—black hair ties. In my hurry to embarrass Aerick, I forgot to ask if we would get any and considering what I expect we'll be doing, they are going to come in handy. Grabbing the brush and a hair tie, I quickly run the brush through my hair and braid it down the side. Patrick and Jeff come in just as I'm leaving, Jeff giving me a reassuring smile; I miss that. Even something as simple as a smile seems to calm me from the inside out. Many times in our younger days, that smile was the only thing that kept me sane.

Back on my bed, I slip on my socks and boots, and put the name pin on my shirt where there are two small stitched holes for it to go through. The handbook and map are on my desk as Aerick said they would be, so I grab them and sit cross-legged on the bed. We have thirty minutes left before dinner; better to use my time wisely. Besides, if I'm studying, people will be less likely to ask me questions. I was reluctant enough to talk about what got me here, but I figure it may let people know to keep their distance.

The map shows the square buildings we entered between are numbered one through four, and are labeled: Main Office (Luther & Ayla Offices), Staff Office, Supply Building, and Infirmary. The four square buildings on the other side of the courtyard are the staff cabins. One of the long rectangle buildings is the gym. It appears to be the entire building, which means it is a pretty good size. Maybe somewhere to go work off frustrations that are going to inevitably arise. The other building has the mess hall, and classrooms A and B. A red line goes around the whole property, and above the line, it says 'DO NOT CROSS THIS BOUNDARY' in big, bold letters.

The map should be easy enough to remember. I put it down and look at the handbook. The first few pages are titled "About Us," which gives a quick history and some statistics on their success, so I skip through most of it. The next section is the camp values. I vaguely recall Ayla saying something about them.

It goes more in-depth, explaining why each value is

42

significant, the ways we are expected to behave, and how our behavior corresponds to each value. The section on the rules follows. It's been made clear that breaking them is not a good thing, so I take my time reading though them. The text goes over a lot of what was covered earlier such as why we are here, and our tracking bracelets. The part that really interests me is where it informs us that if the boundary line is crossed, the bracelet's security measures will go off. *Hmm...I wonder what that is supposed to mean?*

My heart jumps as someone suddenly puts a hand on my shoulder. Spinning around quickly, my fist finds the person's arm. *Shit.* I realize too late that it's just Patrick.

"Sorry." I give him a half smile hoping it is enough. "I haven't been used to you guys being around much."

He rubs his arm and smiles back. "Wow, I think you hit harder than you used too."

I glare at him, "Ha, ha, ha, very funny."

His smile gets marginally wider, "Come on, we have ten minutes to get to dinner." I get up off the bed, and Jeff is behind me. Tara, Mike, and Huck also get up, and our group heads to the Mess Hall. Most of the kids from the other dorm are not far behind us as we head outside. When we get to the mess hall door, Tia is standing there, and she instructs us to sit at the tables once we get inside.

The Mess Hall is a large, open room. Two long wooden tables run parallel to each other and are spaced several feet apart. Each table could comfortably sit at least eight on each side. The hall seems a little empty with only the two tables; they could comfortably fit several more in here.

Taking a deep breath, the aroma of food mixes with the smell of wood. After the crappy brown bag meals we have been eating for several days, I am starved and ready to eat a semi-decent meal. At this point, I wouldn't even mind the food from Juvie. As basic and almost tasteless as it is, at least they rotate what we eat, but from the mouthwatering aroma that is pounding my senses, I have a feeling this will be much better.

We stay together as a group and sit at the end of one of the tables. The other dorm comes in and sits at the end of the opposite table, where several of the staff members are already sitting. All four instructors sneak in quietly from a door at the other end of the hall and sit down at our table. Luther walks in and stands at the head of the room; the clock on the wall reads precisely five o'clock. *Very punctual.*

"Listen up." He pauses for a minute until the hall is quiet. "Meals are served at zero seven hundred, twelve hundred and seventeen hundred hours. You only have thirty minutes to serve up your plate and eat, so if you are not here, you don't eat." He waves to the wall behind him. There is a long counter between the room we are in and what is presumably the kitchen. The girl, whose name I think is Andi, is standing on the other side of the counter where a buffet is laid out.

"You serve yourself, and you clean up after yourself. Cadets, you will each be assigned to clean up after one meal each day. The list will be posted next to the mess hall door every Sunday by dinner time. These cleanup groups will change weekly, allowing you the chance to work with all your fellow cadets, so make sure you check the list every week. The only exception will be today. After dinner, the camp staff will be cleaning up and showing you how we do things as well as getting you familiar with the kitchen. After this place is properly cleaned up, your lead instructors will give you a quick tour of the grounds. Then you are free to go back to your dorms for the evening. Lights-out is at twenty-two hundred, and I strongly suggest you get a good night's sleep. Tomorrow, we start the hard stuff."

The rest of the evening is quiet and uneventful. I'm getting a little more relaxed being here. We clean up after dinner, and I find out I'm on lunch duty tomorrow with Joseph, Karen, and Mike. The schedule rotates each day from breakfast to lunch, to dinner. Aerick shows us around the buildings; the classrooms are rudimentary but sufficient to fit fifteen people comfortably. The gym is the most interesting; it's enormous. It has a boxing ring, punching bags, weights, mats, and just about everything that you would want. With the way everyone looks around here, I can only assume it gets a lot of use.

Aerick tells us we are permitted to use the gym whenever we have free time, much to my joy. He walks us past the staff cabins, stressing to us that cadets that we are not allowed to be in them, and we're also not allowed in the supply building. Aerick seems to look at me a lot; while his expression doesn't change, it seems that he is waiting for my smart mouth comments—almost daring me. I use my better judgment and keep quiet, probably to his dismay. From his earlier actions, I've come to the consensus that he's arrogant and takes unusual joy in putting us in our place. He shows us the other three buildings and then release us to go back to our dorms. As we are walking, I glance back to see him heading towards the gym.

All the guys in our dorm are jokesters, although Mike is much quieter than the others, and he's always smiling at me. Tara still seems withdrawn. She just sits on her bed most of the time with her short black hair hanging in her face, and fiddles with her shoelaces or whatever she has nearby.

While washing my hands in the bathroom, I talk to the redhead girl from the other dorm for a minute. She introduces herself as Leena and unfortunately, she's very peppy. I noticed in the mess hall at dinner she was also very flirty and continually wanting all the attention. She seems to be that typical cute me-me-me girl, with her perfectly curvy body and big chest. I tend to stay away from these types.

There isn't much else to do except sit around talking which as long as, I'm not the topic, is not a terrible way to spend our time. I've changed into my pajama shorts, which I did in the bathroom, but decide to sleep in a sports bra and tank top instead of the camisole that goes with the outfit. In the morning, I'll be able to throw one of my tee-shirts over it and not have to worry about changing in front of the guys. I think I'll be okay changing into my pants in front of them as it doesn't show much, no more than a bathing suit would anyway.

As soon as the clock displays ten o'clock, Aerick comes in. "Lights out. The dorms are locked down from twenty-two hundred until zero-five hundred. Do not leave this building. If there are any problems during the night, you are to come into the instructors' dorm and wake one of us." The lights go out, and he exits back through the door leading to the bathroom.

I slip under my covers, and am glad it's summer because they're not very thick. My choice of clothing seems even better now. A dim glow comes from the bathroom door even though it seems those lights have dimmed significantly as well, but other than that it's dark and quiet; much quieter than back home. By contrast, silence is unnerving.

What I wouldn't give for my iPod, so I could fall asleep to music blasting in my ears. Music has always had a calming effect on me. After a little while, everyone's breathing has softened, but I can still hear someone sniffling. It's probably coming from Tara, but I'm not sure. The long day has left me exhausted. Not so much in my body, but my mind has been on overload since we got here. I turn over in my bed and try my best to sleep. Just as I'm almost out, my eyes flutter open, and catch a small blinking red light coming from the corner of the room. I think nothing of it and close my eyes one last time, falling asleep.

CHAPTER SIX

(Monday, June 1st)

I'M STARTLED AWAKE by all the alarm clocks going off at the same time. If it were only one of them, it wouldn't be too loud but all six of them at once is too obnoxious to ignore. I turn over and try turning it off. The irritating red numbers read five o'clock in the morning. *What the hell? You have got to be kidding me!*

Fumbling around in my daze I try to grab the clock, but quickly find out that it's attached to the nightstand, so my chances of throwing it across the room are non-existent. I also find there are no buttons to turn it off. Letting out an annoyed sigh, I sit up and look around in confusion. I'm not the only having this reaction; almost everyone is sitting on their beds seemingly a little irritated. After several seconds of just staring at one another, a sweet silence fills the room.

Aerick's stern voice comes through the speaker on the top of the clock. "This is your wake-up call. You have five minutes to be out in front of the stage. Do not be late!" I roll my eyes and let out another sigh. I'm starting to really hate him.

Scrambling out of bed, Patrick is still in bed sleeping, so I throw my pillow at his head. "Get up already!"

He opens his eyes with a groggy look on his face. "You have five minutes, now come on." I have no idea how he slept through that infernal racket.

I change into my pants in record time while the guys are still dragging themselves up and not looking at me. Pulling my tee-shirt over my tank top and pinning my name tag to it, I'm still way ahead of the others. Even after putting my socks and shoes on, the boys are still dragging on their clothes, so I undo my braid, brush out my hair with my fingers, and tie it back into a ponytail.

As I look around, I can't help but roll my eyes at Huck, who is watching Tara as she strips down to her bra and panties and puts on her shirt and pants. She doesn't seem to have a problem with guys looking at her. Then again, it's no different than having a bikini on in summer.

We file outside to the stage where Trent, Brand, and Paulo are standing. They immediately start moving us around. As Brand goes to grab me, I quickly jump back and put up my hands, palms facing him. "Don't touch me please, just show me where I'm going." I keep my voice quiet but stern.

His eyebrows pull together, but he walks about two feet to a certain point in the field and motions for me to stand there. Within a minute, we're put into three lines of four, all equally spaced apart. I'm standing at the very end of the front row. The other three instructors line up in front of the stage, when Aerick exits the dorm and makes his way onto the stage, stopping at the center.

"Well, wasn't that pathetic. I said five minutes, not eight, and I told you to make your beds every morning. Apparently, you guys don't know how to listen—but we will fix that. There will be an extra fifteen minutes of morning PT." I suppress my groan as everyone else just stands there looking confused.

"You will be up every morning at zero-five hundred. You are expected to make your beds and be out here in five minutes. You are given one additional minute to get into formation, and you should be lined up exactly like this when I come out that door. Failure to comply with these rules will result in punishment. Today, that means fifteen extra minutes of physical training, which means your standard thirty minutes of free time before breakfast is now fifteen." We all groan in unison.

"That will be another five minutes! I don't want to hear your complaining either." His expression says it all; there is not a trace of amusement which only furthers my irritation. *How can the look of someone irritate me?* "Physical training will be every morning until zero-six thirty, and then you will have thirty minutes until breakfast. Well, that is if you can manage to get your sorry asses out here on time. Now let's get started. You will copy my moves exactly." *I want to smack that smirk right off his face.*

He starts stretching his arms and legs and we mimic him exactly. The other instructors mirror him without looking back to watch; occasionally they shout comments to someone not doing it right. After we stretch, Aerick tells us we're going to follow him and run a mile on the dirt path. He then jumps off the stage and begins running; several groans sound from behind me.

I fall in right beside him. I'm fairly athletic, even played soccer for several years. Although regular exercise isn't my thing, I'm still very active. Aerick glances at me with a raised eyebrow and then looks away as we continue running, with everyone else running behind us. The other instructors can be heard shouting at the cadets telling them to "move" and "hurry up." Other than the occasional shout, we continue in silence, and once again I find myself missing the music. It would make this run almost enjoyable. By the end of the four laps, I've fallen a little behind Aerick and am breathing hard. Aerick, on the other hand, is breathing normally like that mile run was nothing to him. *Man, he must be in good shape.*

We all line back up as Aerick once again takes the stage and waits impatiently. When the stragglers are finally lined up to his standards, Aerick continues to guide us through exercises. Jumping jacks, up-downs, running in place, leg lifts; even being athletic, I'm dying. I want to give up, but I don't want to give Aerick the satisfaction, as he continues to antagonize us to see who the first one to 'give up' will be.

Weakness is not in my vocabulary, and I will not let him break me. It hasn't gone unnoticed that he tends to look my way quite often and I'm sure he's just waiting for me to throw in the towel. Not to mention that anytime someone starts slowing down or stops altogether the other instructors get in their face, and I don't want that either. It's important for me to avoid things that might get me into trouble.

Aerick looks at his watch. "Alright, it is zero-six fifty. You have ten minutes to get to breakfast. Dismissed." He jumps off the stage and walks away. I drag myself into the dorm, as I move without thought to brush my teeth. Now this feels like bootcamp. It's something you watch on TV or see in movies but think to yourself, 'Oh it wouldn't be that bad' — boy, was that wrong! Once finished, Mike is the only other one still here. Everyone else must have already gone to breakfast.

"You want to walk with to me to breakfast?" Mike asks timidly.

Sweat is still dripping down my back and I would love a shower, but with our time cut short, I don't have time for that. "Sure, but can you turn around for just a second while I change my shirt?" He blushes a little but thankfully turns around.

I grab a clean shirt and peel off my sweat-drenched tank top and tee-shirt together, trying to be as quick as possible. Just as I throw my sweaty tops on my bed, Aerick walks in. It startles the shit out of me, and I grab the clean shirt, holding it to my chest, trying to cover myself. His lips turn up a little as he starts setting a sheet of paper on each desk, his eyes focusing on his hands instead of me. "Don't let me stop you." *He is so cocky.*

Irritated, I turn around, feeling slightly violated even though he isn't looking directly at me. I pull my shirt on quickly and grab my name tag off the other shirt before hurrying to the door. "Let's go, Mike."

Mike turns around and shuffles over to me. His eyebrows raise, and I just shake my head, making my way out the door. As I glance back, there is something close to irritation on Aerick's face as he continues what he was doing. *Maybe that wasn't the reaction that he expected from me.* Good, I'm not letting him bait me again. My brother told me to be smart and it was good advice.

Breakfast is the typical eggs, potatoes, bacon, and fruit. I'm not one to eat much in the morning, so I just get a little fruit and a cup of coffee. At least they don't deny us caffeine. *Thank goodness for small favors.*

The mess hall is quiet; everyone must be as exhausted as I am. Once we are all sitting down, Max stands up. "Instructional time begins every day at eight-thirty. Your schedules will be put on your desk every morning, and you are responsible for being on time for each class. Most of your days are planned with specific activities, and you are expected to behave during your free time, or you will lose it. You will have free time thirty minutes before and one hour after each meal, unless you are on mess hall duty. Now, finish your breakfast and prepare for the day."

Once finished, Jeff, Mike and I walk back to our dorm. Patrick has to stick around for clean-up. When we get inside, there is indeed a paper on my desk. I'm curious as to what my day holds. I skim over the typed piece of paper:

Lead Instructor: Aerick
Nadi - Monday, June 1st:

05:00 Wake-up
05:05 Morning PT
06:30 Free Time
07:00 Breakfast
07:30 Cleanup/Free Time
08:30 Self Defense - Gym
10:00 English - Classroom A
11:30 Free Time
12:00 Lunch
12:30 Cleanup/Free Time
13:30 Knife Throwing - Gym
15:00 Math - Classroom A
16:30 Free Time
17:00 Dinner
17:30 Cleanup/Free Time
18:30 Evening PT
19:30 Free Time
22:00 Lights Out

Wow. They're actually going to teach us to throw knives. Awesome! The other things are much less exciting. English and Math... I moan just thinking about having to do school work. *This sucks!*

"Dude, we're going to learn to fight?" Jeff says as he walks up to me with his schedule and I take a peek. It's essentially the same as mine but his afternoon activities are at a different time.

Jeff goes over to Patrick's desk and looks at his schedule. "Patrick's is the same as mine. They must organize it by our lead instructor."

"Mike, can I see yours?" He walks over and hands it to me. "I think you're right because mine and Mike's are the same." I give Mike his schedule back, and he smiles broadly at me.

"Well, hopefully they'll rotate it so we can have different classes with each other," I say turning back to Jeff and ignoring the uneasiness I get from Mike's smile. Jeff and I sit down on our beds while Mike sits on the end of my bed, and we start to talk about nothing in particular.

Patrick and Huck join us a little while later, and I'm grateful when Patrick sits in between me and Mike. I swear he keeps moving closer to me, and I didn't want to have to do something about it.

We all head over to the gym since we all have our first instruction period together. When we get there, Aerick and Paulo are already standing by the mats so we go and stand in front of them.

"Cadets, each day you will be attending four instructional classes. You will have two classes in the morning, one educational and one physical. Then two classes in the afternoon, again, one educational and one physical. Educational classes include English, Math, Social Studies, Science, Nutritional Health, and Technology. You will attend each class twice a week. Tia will go over this more when you see her for your next class."

An urge to groan in complaint wells up inside of me at the thought of having to do school work, but thinking of what happened this morning, I decide it's in my best interest to keep my mouth shut. I'm all for pushing limits, but I'm too exhausted already, and I don't want to have to do anything extra.

He pauses for a moment before starting to pace in front of the mats. It's as if he was waiting for someone to say something. After a minute or so he continues, "Your physical classes include Self Defense, Knife Throwing, Archery, and Hiking. Everyone will be taking the Self Defense class daily and all the other classes twice a week.

My shoulders slump forward. *Man, this seems like a lot of work.* It's like being in school and the military at the same time. It's not like I hated school, but I didn't particularly like it either.

"These are taught by your lead instructors. Each class will include six cadets that are based on the Lead Instructor's groups and rotate throughout the week, so you will get to know all your fellow cadets." At this I brighten a little; at least I'll get to share some classes with Jeff and Patrick!

Aerick and Paulo step up on the mat. "In this class, we will teach you how to defend yourself. You will learn a variety of styles that will teach you to protect yourself at all times. I know some of you are in here for assault. It is NOT my intention to teach you so that you can beat up people. It is my intention to teach you control, strength, and discipline. One aspect of learning self-defense is mental training. Learning not to panic, learning to channel your anger, learning to curb your fears, and learning to act without thought. All these techniques are not just helpful in self-defense, but also in life. Emotions are one of the biggest drivers in your everyday living. It will benefit you to learn to control them." As Aerick stops talking, he looks at me.

"Gather around the mat. I am going to show you some basic techniques; then you will pair off and practice them."

He and Paulo demonstrate some basic ways to get away from attackers both standing and being pinned on the ground. I try to observe carefully, but I have a hard time concentrating knowing I will have to practice these. I'm not sure how I'm going to cope with others putting their hands on me.

After showing several moves multiple times, they get to their feet. "Alright maggots, pair off."

Jeff is quick to stand next to me. "Well, what are you waiting for?" Aerick shouts, even before everyone can get paired. "Get on the mats and start practicing. Start with the standing moves."

Jeff and I go to the far mat. Jeff stops me by grabbing my wrist, causing me to turn around. "Are you okay with this?" His voice is small, so no one else can hear.

"Yeah, I'll be okay, let's just do it. I'll attack first." *I have to stay in control.*

I stand behind him, and after a few seconds, I smack his shoulder. He glances back, smiling at me, and I raise my eyebrow. He's too tall, and there's no way for me to grab around his shoulder. He bends his knees until I can put my arm around his shoulder and under the opposite arm.

"Alright, try to get free." It takes Jeff about three seconds to grab my wrist, twist his hip to the side and flip me over his arm.

I land hard on my back, and he quickly helps me up. "Nice, now it's my turn," I say in a rush. I don't like looking weak, and right now that is exactly how I feel.

Jeff looks at me. "You sure?"

My irritation spikes. First he flipped me, and now he questions me. "I can handle it."

Hesitantly, Jeff moves to stand behind me. I look up and see Aerick is standing on the mat next to us, but instead of watching the people in front of him, he's looking at us. Jeff suddenly grabs me with the same hold I did to him, but he leans back so I can't spin out of it. I feel a tightening in my chest, but I quickly push it down. *It's okay; it's just Jeff.* Once I have my bearings back, I remember what we have just been taught and work to repeat it. I'm able to kick my feet in the air and then bring them back down just as quickly; I throw all my weight forward, and the momentum is enough to flip Jeff over my shoulder onto the mat.

Aerick's lip curls up just slightly and he turns to stand at another mat. A huge grin spreads across my face. *I can do this!* We each take another turn with the standing moves.

"Alright. Now practice the pin moves," Paulo bellows.

Jeff lies down. "You can be the attacker first." His face is tight. Clearly he isn't comfortable with this.

I ignore it and move to sit down on top of him so that I am straddling his legs. "I know you're stronger, but you know, you can at least pretend that this isn't too easy," I laugh still smiling over my accomplishment.

His face still shows a hint of stress, but he tries to joke with me to lighten the mood. "What I can't pretend is that I'm completely enjoying the fact that I have a pretty girl sitting on top of me!"

My hand is punching him playfully in the arm before I can stop myself. "Don't be a dick!"

He finally smiles. If it was anyone else, that would have pissed me off, but I know he's only joking. He doesn't like me like that. I reach down and grab his neck with both hands. "Go," I tell him calmly, trying to center myself and concentrate.

He pulls both arms to one side of mine, and with the inside one, he wraps it around mine, pushes my shoulder with his other hand, and thrusts his pelvis up as he pushes my other shoulder with his free arm. Then he drives the whole side of his body to roll us over. When he's on top of me, he jumps to his feet with lightning speed. He executed that perfectly. Jeff has always been smart, a fast learner. When we were young, I always thought he would be the one to get out of the neighborhood.

"Okay, now it's my turn," I say, refocusing my thoughts and lying back on my propped up on my elbows. He kneels next to me and looks around causing me to do the same. No one is watching us.

"I know you hate me asking, but are you sure about this? We can just keep practicing with you as the attacker." His voice is so quiet I can barely hear him.

"Come on, Jeff; I'm going to have to do this anyway, so I might as well try, okay? It's better that it's with you; I think I'll be able to handle it that way." I lie back, but he still hesitates.

Pausing a moment longer, he straddles my legs, not allowing any of his weight to be on me. "If this is too much, you tell me." His voice is full of concern, and I can already feel the ache in my chest, but pushing it away, I give him a nod.

However, he doesn't move. The worry in his eyes is enough to alert anyone who might have been watching us. I put on my 'just fucking do it' face and he sighs deeply, then slowly starts to get into position. As soon as I see him starting to cooperate, my irritation subsides, but the tightness in my chest does not. I try my best to breathe through it.

All of a sudden I feel his hands lightly around my neck, and my breathing immediately gets shallow. Not because he is holding my neck tightly, but because I feel like I have a ton of bricks on my chest. I close my eyes and try to push it away, but it's just getting worse.

I can do this; I can do this! I try to tell myself, but that isn't helping either.

Breathe, breathe...

Fuck, fuck, fuck...

I can't do this; I can't breathe!

I open my eyes; my chest is heaving as I'm trying to breathe, and spots begin to cloud my vision; my control is, lost. Jeff quickly removes his hands and starts to get off me before I even speak a word.

"*Stop, stop, stop...*" I try to push him away even though he's almost off me already. I scramble out from under him and get up, stumbling over to the wall, turning away so no one can see me. I can feel the tears trying to break through as I try to calm myself.

I'm okay; I'm okay, I am okay. I repeat this to myself, bending over with my hands on my knees.

Heavy boots start walking toward me.

"What the hell is going on?" Aerick's tone is forceful, but he isn't yelling.

"She just needs a minute, let her be," Jeff says in a rush.

Aerick lowers his voice. "I was not speaking to you cadet. Now get out of my fucking way." Jeff must have stepped in front of him.

In less than a second he's standing next to me. "What happened?" He barks in my ear. It's a good thing he didn't try to touch me because I don't think I could handle it right now.

I turn toward him, pissed at myself and still struggling to breathe. "I just need a fucking minute." His irritated face instantly becomes pissed. I know my own must be showing extreme anger and panic; I'm barely keeping the tears at bay.

This is too much. I need to calm down before I lose it completely. I take another shallow breath as panic overtakes all other emotions, and I lower my voice to a whispered plea, "Please."

I think a flash of concern crosses his face, but I'm not sure - it disappears quickly. "Step outside. You have five minutes to pull yourself together, cadet." He steps out of my way, not taking his eyes off me and I quickly retreat towards the door.

Rushing outside, I take several deep breaths and sit down on the stairs, hanging my head between my legs. I'm so mad at myself. I should be able to do this. It's an irrational fear from my past. I'm not nine years old anymore. I'm a grown woman. *Get your shit under control, Nadi!*

After a few minutes, I'm able to sit up straight, the tightness is gone, and my breathing is back to normal. I take a few more deep breaths before standing back up.

Jeff comes walking out the door and looks at me carefully. "You okay?" His voice is quiet and guarded.

"Yeah, I'm fine." I paint the best smile I can manage on my face.

"If you need more time just say the word." It's evident in his face he still doesn't think I'm okay.

"Please, I'm ready to go back in there and kick your butt." I try playing it off as I punch him in the arm.

He takes a hard look at me again and then smiles. "Actually, we have moved on to weight training. We're supposed to be working on our arms and shoulders. So, I think we should go in, because those arms of yours are looking a little skinny."

"Hey, these skinny arms managed to throw you on your ass a few minutes ago!" I grin broadly, and he gives me an exaggerated look of shock. I laugh out loud, feeling a little better and start back towards the gym door.

As we walk, I'm stopped suddenly as Aerick steps in front of me. "Not right now, but you will explain to me what just happened. Is that clear?" His face is hard and his voice low.

"Yes, Sir," I say and step around him to go workout before he can say anything else. Out of the corner of my eye, I see him shake his head and then walk over to talk to Paulo, and I'm glad he's letting it go. At least for now.

* * * *

The rest of the morning and afternoon go by quickly. Tia explains our education program. It turns out that, in addition to attending each of the six classes twice a week, we also have to complete one homework assignment per week for each subject. Failure to complete our homework will result in extra PT time. When she shows us the scheduling, I notice that she doesn't teach anything on Sundays, so I asked what happens those days. She informs the class that besides PT and a one-on-one counseling session, our Sundays are free time; although we were expected to use our time wisely. That is some good news after the shitty morning I've had, but the little bit of good news is soon overshadowed when she also informs us we will be receiving our homework for both classes today.

Lunch is uneventful, and I complete the meal cleanup with Joseph, Karen, and Mike. I stay quieter than usual during lunch, still mad at myself for freaking out earlier. I'm stronger than that. Somehow, I manage to put on a deceiving smile and pretend nothing happened at all.

Knife throwing is exciting. Trent shows us how to stand and release the blades when throwing, and specific techniques to hit the center of the target. Of course, Aerick had to put his two cents in and explained how this task was supposed to get us to focus and pay attention to detail. When we first start to practice, I can barely even get the knife near the target. Trent comes over, critiquing my stance and release, which helps a lot. By the end of class, my knives are sticking, though still not near the center. Despite not mastering it yet, I felt a sense of accomplishment.

While we are there, in between throwing and waiting for instruction, I noticed that Aerick keeps looking at me. Sometimes for a few seconds, and sometimes a fleeting glance. Usually that kind of thing doesn't bother me, but the expression that mars his features make me feel distinctly uncomfortable. It is quizzical – like he is trying to solve a puzzle. I try to shake it off and focus on the class, but it continues to nag at me.

Math class is easy. The work is mostly pre-calculus, which is all review for me. My mind drifts away as I gaze out the window, wondering how my family are doing back home. I have to admit, I miss my brother and my parents. By the end of class, I convince myself that I need to stop dwelling on it. My time here is just beginning; I make a commitment to myself to not think about them again while here – it's easier that way.

Royce and Joseph sit with me, Patrick, and Jeff for dinner. Royce is quite the looker. He appears to be of mixed heritage, with a rare set of the most beautiful soft, green eyes that stand out against his darker skin. He spends most of the dinner explaining how irritated he's getting with Leena's flirting, which is why he came over to join our group in the first place; he was trying to get away from her. I quietly laugh to myself confident that my initial assumption about her was right.

When we finally make it to evening PT, I'm already exhausted. We stretch and ran half a mile, before Brand runs us through the workout. We are all so worn out that the whole session consists of the instructors yelling at us to 'get up,' 'go faster,' and 'pay attention.' Even I am getting yelled at – by this stage I'm not feeling so fit, after all. Aerick has gotten in my face several times, and it's pissing me off, but I have nothing else left; I'm absolutely spent.

We end up getting dismissed fifteen minutes late because we 'aren't putting any effort into it.' Somehow, I manage to drag myself into the dorm and, not to bothering to change or even remove my boots, I lie down and fall fast asleep.

CHAPTER SEVEN

(Monday, June 1st)

Aerick POV

TODAY HAS BEEN an irritating day. Usually, I'm happy to be here, since my work schedule doesn't allow much of a social life. The staff here work four and a half months straight during the boot camp sessions. We are required to do a week of preparation before the cadets arrive; the cadets are here for a four-month camp, and then we have a debriefing week once the camp is over. We get two months off in between sessions, which is when I go back to my scenic apartment on the Puget Sound in Des Moines; but during my off time, I tend to get bored and restless.

The only thing there is to do for eight weeks is workout, and occasionally hang out with friends, but I only have a few people I consider friends. Quite often I fill in time teaching the kickboxing or self-defense classes at Aaron's gym while I am home, just to have something to do. I don't need to do it for the money; I make pretty decent money here. Aaron and I aren't exactly friends, but he was an instructor here when I was a cadet. I had so much anger then, and he taught me how to focus it. He helped me turn my life around. His gym is only a few blocks from my condo, so he calls me when he has someone call in sick or if there is a request for an extra class. It's a perfect arrangement; I get a free gym membership and something to occupy my time, and he gets someone on-call.

It's wonderfully quiet in our dorm right now, which is how I like it. The other guys went to hang out with the girls, and I volunteered to stay in the dorms since one of us is required to be in here during 'free time.' Hanging out with the staff isn't typically my idea of a good time. Occasionally Paulo will join me in the gym, and we'll spar together, but I rarely hang out with the rest of them, except when a few of us play poker in the cabins. Sometimes it's held here in our dorm so that everyone can play, and I play along just to keep their noise from irritating the shit out me. Plus, I usually walk away with more than I started with. Poker is based a lot on strategy, making it an ideal game for me. I was terrible at it to start with, but then after reading a bunch of books on it, I rarely lose.

It's only nine-thirty in the evening, but I've already completed my daily log. I decide to check on the cadets. Picking up the tablet, I start it up and pull up our security application. Jake's shift is up at ten, and then it becomes our duty to keep an eye on the cadets for the night; although with the tracking bracelets, we would know the minute someone tried to leave the dorms.

Once the app starts, it shows me a map of the entire property, including the outlines of all the buildings and their inner walls. The outline of the beds also appears in the dorm area. The larger furniture is attached to the floor so it can't be moved, making it possible to program it into our system.

I first check to make sure all three of the blue dots are accounted for. They represent my cadets. Each dot has the first letter of the cadet's first name on it to identify who it is. I see all of Paulo's green dots, Trent's red dots, and Brand's yellow dots. Most of them are in their assigned dorm, but a few are in the bathroom. I guess they haven't had time to get to know each other much, which is why they are all in their own dorms, and why they are so quiet. That, and I am sure they are all exhausted after today's events. The first week is usually the most exhausting. My eyes focus on the blue dot with the "N" on it. It looks like she is on her bed.

She is the source of much of my irritation today. Yesterday she came off as such a smart ass, testing my patience. Every camp there is always at least one with a smart mouth who likes to push the instructors. Typically it's a guy, and they don't dare challenge me because I am more intimidating than others, or so I have been told. But this time it's her, and she didn't seem to be intimidated by me at all. She thought she could get the best of me yesterday when she opened her smart mouth in the bathroom, but I turned out to be victorious, as usual. The difference was I felt more joy over my victory than usual, maybe because of her lack of fear toward me.

I click on the A dorm security camera and a high definition picture of the dorm pops up. After the exchange between me and Nadi, I made sure to say something about it to Ayla, knowing she would be going in there. I watched the camera as she asked Nadi if she needed anything and I saw her blush. I turned that one around on her. I smile a little at that thought. *She won't get the best of me.*

I have learned to control my emotions; that's something that she needs to learn, and I'm sure I'll be able to teach her. It's a continual struggle for me, but I manage it well these days. Although I swear, Brand tries to see how much I can handle. It's purely out of jealousy over a make out session he walked in on. Before they started dating, Tia and I were drinking together and things went a little farther than I would generally allow with a co-worker. Ever since he has made it his mission to make my life hell.

It's not like I liked her anyway; it was just something to bide my time. She is cute and all, but I don't think we would have worked out. It never does. Women don't typically respond well to my attitude. I don't show weakness, and most women want cuddly romance stuff. That's just not my style. At least this time I am lead instructor and set the schedule allowing me to be away from Brand as much as possible.

I stare at the screen and click the sound icon to turn the

volume on. Nadi appears to be passed out on her bed. I'm still confused about what happened during our self-defense class today. I was watching the cadets in front of me when I glanced over at her and Jeff. He had a worried, upset look on his face, and Nadi looked like she just saw a ghost as she stumbled to the side of the room. I went to check on what happened, thinking maybe the boy did something to her, but that the dumb ass kid shocked me when he had the nerve to try to stop me. That confused me more; if he had done something, why would he be so protective of her? I was even more stunned when she had the nerve to yell at me.

Usually, I would not take shit like that from cadets. Any slight insubordination is reason enough to make them run laps or do some other physically exhausting task. It was that look – a mix of panic and fear – that made me hesitate, though. Then she spoke in a whispered plead, "please." It was just one word, but it completely disarmed me. That has never happened to me before. *What is it about this girl?*

I let her go outside, which is something I never do either, but she had already managed to break my composure, and I was confused by my own emotional reaction. I was angry that she yelled at me, but then worried by the look on her face and her totally out-of-character plea; I felt an overwhelming need to protect her. I needed her away from me so I could compose myself. My feelings were, and are, entirely unacceptable.

When I walked back over to Paulo, he gave me a confused

look, but I explained that the situation was under control. He just raised an eyebrow and went back to watching the other cadets. I was mad at myself for losing my composure and even more furious that another instructor saw it.

I had to show her, and everyone else, that it was a one-time thing. At evening PT, I was much harder on her. It was clear she was utterly exhausted, but my stubbornness kept me pushing her harder. I've got to admire the fight in her. If it was a few other cadets, they probably would have just dropped and refused to finish. She reminds me a lot of myself.

I reread her file once back in the dorm. She's in for assaulting some guy that was almost twice her size, which initially I thought was a little funny. She most definitely has guts. My time in here was for assault, so I can't look down on her for that.

She appears to be a good student. Her transcript from school showed she has a 3.8 GPA, even taking advanced placement classes, so she is smart, too – a quality I admire in people. All her previous arrests were for assault as well, so apparently she just has a problem with anger. But that still doesn't explain what happened today. I'm still not sure why I care, but I can't seem to let it go.

The clock shows it's only ten minutes until lights out. I have been sitting here lost in thought for twenty minutes. *Crap.* As I am about to set down my tablet my eyes are drawn back to the screen. I watch as Jeff walks up to Nadi's bed and shakes her shoulder.

The voices float up through the tablet and I turn up the

volume.

"Shit, she's passed out cold. I don't think she's going to wake up," he says to the kid on the other side of her bed, the one named Patrick.

I have noticed those three hang out a lot. They seem awfully close already, especially with the way Jeff got so defensive when she freaked out earlier. Cadets rarely know each other before being here but it isn't unheard of, and I'm positive that these three do. Troubled kids tend to hang out with troubled kids.

"Okay, let's do it," Patrick says after pausing for a second.

I panic immediately and jump off my bed, but then pause for a moment to see what is going to happen, trying not to jump to conclusions. *Fuck! What are they doing?*

Then I see them removing her shoes. *Shit!*

I throw the tablet on the bed and hurry into their dorm, trying to keep my composure. I'll be damned if those boys take advantage of her while she's asleep. As I walk into the dorm, I see them pulling the blanket out from under her. I stop, confused and Patrick looks up at me. Jeff's back is to me, and he doesn't see me. He pulls the blanket up to her neck and then moves her hair out of her face before turning around and looking at me as well. He seems startled to see me standing there.

Their intentions appear to be completely innocent. I look at my clock and then look up again "Lights out in five minutes." I turn and walk out playing it off as a planned visit.

Okay, I need to get a hold of myself; my anger is exploding, and there is no reason for it. Back in my dorm, I get ready for bed. Switch the camera view to a split screen so I can see both dorms and the bathroom; I set it on its stand on my night table. *This is ridiculous.* I take off my pants and shirt and put on a tank top.

As I am lying down in my bed, the lights go off. Looking at the tablet, the cameras have switched to night vision, and everyone is getting in bed. I look at Nadi one more time. She has curled up into a ball under her covers.

A few minutes later, the other guys come into the dorm, breaking me out of my trance. Quickly I move to lie on my back and stare at the ceiling. *What the hell is it about this girl?*

✳ ✳ ✳ ✳

"Stop." I am startled awake by someone talking. I sit up and look around, but the guys are all asleep. They are much heavier sleepers than I am and rarely wake up to anything small.

"Please," the voice sounds scared. I look over to the tablet, thinking I have a dumb ass guy pulling some shit, but no one in either room is moving. I switch the screen to the map, and all dots are in their beds. I go back to cameras and I still see nothing abnormal.

Deciding to look in the dorms, I move through the bathroom to the B dorm, and I walk down to the furthest bed, checking each one as I pass, ensuring everyone is here. Once done, I go back through the bathroom to A dorm and start checking beds. As I come to the last bed, I hear it again – "Stop!" – and I freeze.

That was Nadi's voice. Moving over to her bed, it's my

intention to ask her what's wrong, but her eyes are closed. She moves around a little, restless. She must be having a nightmare.

It isn't uncommon to have cadets that talk in their sleep. Mostly it's annoying, but sometimes it can be quite entertaining. I just stand and stare at her, but even as I say it in my head, it isn't to see if she says anything else. *I'm not some psycho stalker.* I mentally kick myself shaking my head in disapproval.

As I'm about to walk away, she starts whimpering. It must be a horrible dream. I reach out and put my hand on her shoulder to wake her, but as soon as my hand touches her, she stills and becomes quiet. I'm frozen with shock. *Did my touch just calm her down?*

Without thinking, I rub her shoulder for a minute and then stand back up. She turns on her side, and her breathing evens out. Her nightmare must have finally passed. I stand there for a moment longer to be sure and then walk back to my own bed.

I'm confused about what just happened, and my emotions toward her are entirely off the wall. Yes, she is pretty, and I admire several qualities in her; but she also irritates the shit out of me, and I don't like to be challenged or disrespected. Then there is the fact that she is a cadet. This behavior needs to quit; I am becoming soft; this isn't me. It's two in the morning, and I need get some sleep.

Climbing back into bed, I glance once more at the tablet, and everything is still. I need to stop letting my emotions control me.

I know better than this. I learned to control my emotions years ago, and I am not about to let some girl get into my head.

CHAPTER EIGHT

(Tuesday, June 2nd)

I WAKE UP out of breath. Nightmares rarely haunt my nights anymore, but the events of yesterday must have rattled me more than I realize. My body feels like lead and it's only four in the morning. After falling asleep so early last night, it isn't from a lack of sleep. Goosebumps run down my arms as the remnants of my dreams hang at the edge of my mind.

I'm still in my clothes from yesterday, but my shoes are off and somehow my blanket is over me. I have a pretty good idea who is responsible, and I wish they would have woken me up; I needed a shower after yesterday. Well, now is as good a time as any. At least no one will bother me while I take a nice, long and hot shower.

I root through my chest, grabbing a fresh set of clothes. Yesterday it was chilly outside for PT, but the workout was grueling and by the end of it, sweat soaked my shirt. A tank top seems to be a better option for today and I figure I can change into a shirt afterward. Hopefully a quick shower afterward will be possible too.

The soreness from yesterday is making itself present in my aching muscles. This place is quickly living up to its name. Everyone needs to get their shit together to avoid more work than what is needed. Dragging myself, I head to the bathroom to take a shower. The lights are on, but they're still dimmed down.

The faucet turns easily, and I allow it to get as hot as possible before getting in. The almost–scalding water feels so good on my sore, tight muscles. It only takes a few short minutes before my body begins to relax and a sense of relief washes over me. I close my eyes and clear my mind, allowing myself to experience a rare moment of Zen.

The slowly cooling water alerts me a short while later that the hot water is running out. I'm so relaxed, I begin singing along with the music in my head. Normally I don't do that in front of people but everyone is asleep, so there really isn't a problem.

As I sing and wash up before the warm water is gone, my mood lifts even more. Music has always been my own personal getaway, no matter where I am or what kind of mood I'm in. It's a way to block out the world, and the best place to sing is in the shower. The acoustics of bathrooms can make anyone's voice sound amazing. *Even mine.*

It's the most satisfying shower I've had in a long time. I get dress and open the door; instantly I stop singing and freeze. *Holy Shit!* Aerick is standing at one of the sinks shaving, wearing only a tank top and a pair of boxer briefs revealing his near perfectly sculpted body. His eyes rise to find mine in the mirror in front of him, warming my face instantly to a bright shade of red – not just because he caught me singing, but from seeing him stand there like a model in an underwear commercial.

He raises an eyebrow as I continue to stare at him speechless. "See something you like?" He smirks slightly as if he's trying not to laugh. *Absolutely, not that I am willing to admit it.*

"You're up early, and so full of energy... don't stop singing on my account." His voice is thick with sarcasm. My mood instantly shifts from embarrassment to irritation. I go over to where he's standing and stare, this time giving him my best pissed off look.

"You got something to say, cadet?" His voice is suddenly serious as he stands up straight as an arrow. He turns to face me, looking straight into my eyes. I groan inwardly; this is not how I wanted to start my day. Without a word, I toss my wet towel in the basket next to his feet, turn back to the dresser to get my brush, and coolly walk back to my dorm. *Disaster averted.*

I try to calm myself as I put away my dirty clothes, make my bed, and sit down to brush my hair. *Wow!* He sure knows how to dampen my mood. How did I not hear him come in, and why does it seem like it's Aerick's mission to irritate the shit out of me? I'm sure it's partially my fault for mouthing off as I do, but I can't help it – that's just me.

Tossing the brush on my desk, I quickly braid my hair to keep it out of my way during PT. I'm tempted to go brush my teeth and put my hairbrush away, but I don't want to see Aerick again right now. Instead, I settle for putting on my shoes, he can't stay in there forever. Just as I get my feet in, all the alarm clocks go off. It's shocking to realize just how long I was in the shower. The room goes quiet after a minute, and Aerick tells us through the speaker that we have five minutes.

Patrick is still sleeping after the ruckus of the alarms and I stand shaking him until he's awake. He's going to have to start waking up on his own. The others sleepily remove themselves from their beds to get ready without my help.

"Everyone, make your own beds. I don't want extra PT today," I say, loud enough for everyone to hear me. Jeff eyes me, a little confused – my guess is that he's trying to work out how I'm already dressed and have my bed made. Patrick is dragging still, so I go over and quickly make his bed for him. "Come on dude, I'm serious. I'm already sore as hell." He picks up the pace slightly.

We manage to get out of the dorm by five after five, but barely. We shuffle to the stage to get lined up. Brand is on the stage, and the other instructors are in front of it, ready to go. Aerick is holding a tablet and Jake stands next to him, to the side of everyone else. The other dorm drags out a minute behind us and lines up as well.

Aerick looks up at Brand, shaking his head and shouts, "B

dorm, you failed to make your beds again. Your dorm will have an extra fifteen minutes out here this morning." *How the hell does he know that? He didn't even go into the dorms.*

Jake walks up to me and grabs my wrist, causing me to jerk away. Jake looks at me a curiously, then looks to Aerick, but doesn't attempt to grasp me again. Aerick's eyebrows pull together in irritation as he explains, "Jake is checking your trackers. This will be done every other morning to make sure they don't get too loose or too tight. With your healthy diet and all the physical activity, your bodies will inevitably change."

Satisfied with the explanation, I give my wrist to Jake; it takes him about a second to check it. He finishes checking them all in less than a minute and walks off without another word. The second he's done, Aerick looks at Brand. "Alright, Brand, let's get this day started."

Brand stands a little taller, obviously enjoying the little bit of power he has been given. "Cadets let's get stretched, arms to the sky." He begins taking us through the stretches. As soon he tells us to do four laps, I turn and start running before he can get in front of me. Being in the front helps me clear my mind, and I can almost believe that no one else is here. I only make it a few steps ahead when Aerick runs up beside me, but I ignore him and push on.

"What, no singing?" Aerick says as we complete our first lap. His lip is slightly turned up.

"Glad I amuse you," I say, rolling my eyes in annoyance, but before he can say anything else I fall back a little and let him take the lead. Why do I feel like he's goading me to get a rise out of me?

When we finish our run, we line up and Brand continues with the workout. Aerick, Trent, and Paulo are relentless as they walk between us, shouting at those not doing it properly. They're even more forceful this morning than they were yesterday.

Aerick stops next to me several times, critiquing my positioning, "Get your legs up higher… you're not getting up fast enough." His face is a stone wall and it's irritating, but he seems to be doing it to everyone, so maybe he just likes being a dick to us. He appears to enjoy pushing us all as hard as possible. I'm not looking for any trouble this morning, so I just try to focus on my workout.

"Alright, cadets in A dorm, you're dismissed. B dorm, we will continue." My bunk mates and I start falling out to go back to the dorm. "Not you, cadet." I turn around and see Aerick in Jeff's face. *Shit.*

"Where is your name tag, cadet?" He yells in Jeff's face.

"I left it on my desk," Jeff says, frustrated.

"All cadets are to wear their name tags any time you exit the dorm. Maybe two laps will help you remember it next time. "

Shit, really?! It's not that big of a deal. Aerick's head snaps my way, and he stalks over, coming ridiculously close to my face. He is way too close for comfort, and I fight the urge to step back. "What was that cadet?" *Dammit, did I say that out loud?*

"It's just a name tag, it's not like you use our names anyway," I say. The anger rising inside of me is making me bolder.

"Well, *Nadalynn*, since you can't follow the rule of keeping your mouth shut, you can join him," he tells me in a quiet, cold voice, drawing out my name as he speaks it.

Shit! I look at the others and see that everyone has stopped to watch our little exchange. Brand is staring at me with an apologetic face. *I don't need his pity.*

"Fine. Jeff, let's go." I turn to start running without waiting for him. Aerick is a fucking jerk. He said my full name just to piss me off more. I push myself into a fast run although I'm already tired; it helps my anger subside.

We finish our two laps and then head into the dorm. Jeff runs at my pace, to my surprise, and finishes with me. Then again, his legs are longer, making it a bit easier. "Nadi, you really need to learn to keep your mouth shut," Jeff says as we reach the door.

I pull to a stop, looking at him with a raised eyebrow. "And you need to learn to remember your name tag," I say, with just a hint of amusement. This day will go better if I stop this argument before it starts. It works; he grins, and we go to get ready for breakfast.

I grab my tee shirt, but I don't have time to take a shower now. Everyone is still in the dorm, but I don't want to stand in the shower to change. This is stupid. I have a sports bra on, it's no different than having a bikini on, although I usually don't wear those either.

Making sure no one is paying attention, I turn toward the wall and quickly change out of my tank top into my shirt. I look over at Patrick and he raises his eyebrow at me. "Oh, shut up," I snap at him and go to the bathroom to brush my teeth before anyone has a chance to say anything else.

As we walk to breakfast my stomach growls; I'm starving. The physical activity from yesterday and this morning must have drained me. My body needs more protein if I'm going to be able to keep up, so I grab some eggs and potatoes along with some much-needed coffee. I sit down at what is becoming my regular spot at the end of our group. Since our group is relatively small, it puts me right in the middle of the table. I try to ignore the instructors as they walk in, and line up to get their food.

I'm talking to Jeff when Aerick comes and sits right next to me. *What's his problem now?* Usually he sits a few seats down from me. His sudden change causes me to freeze in place for a minute, my fork halfway to my mouth. I'm hyper-aware of the closeness of his body, and my heart starts beating faster even though he isn't touching me. *Can't this asshat just leave me alone?* When I'm certain he isn't going to touch me, I resume eating and talking to Jeff. Thankfully he sticks to his own space.

After breakfast, I check my schedule. My first class of the day is Social Studies, and after that is Self Defense. In the afternoon, I get to go to Archery and Science. Archery sounds fun; I've never touched a bow and arrow before, but I think it would be cool to learn. I don't have any classes with Jeff and Patrick, which saddens me a little, and I'm nervous to go to Self Defense without them. *I can do this; I have got to do this.* Maybe if I keep repeating it to myself I will actually begin to believe it.

In Social Studies, I learn that we'll be starting by studying politics. That's an interesting choice, but I guess I see the reasoning behind it, they are trying to get us functioning in society. So far everything we're learning in class seems to be standard high school work, but is a little below my normal advance placement classes. My stomach turns a bit as we are given more homework at the end. The homework we got yesterday is still sitting untouched on my desk, since I passed out as soon as I got back last night.

I try not to frown as I head over to the gym next door. Instead of Aerick and Trent on the mat where I expected, they're over by the punching bags. The class gather over by them.

Royce comes and stands next to me. "Hey! What's up?" His grin is big enough to make me feel slightly better. That and the fact that we are obviously not fighting each other again today. If I'm lucky it will be a completely hands-off day.

"Hey, how have you been doing?" I try to make light conversation, but we're interrupted by Aerick.

"Cadets. Today you will be learning the proper ways to punch and kick. Watch Trent carefully as he demonstrates, then you will practice on these punching bags." *Does this man love to hear himself talk or what?*

I'm more relieved that he validated my thoughts that we

won't be doing anything hands on with each other and my body visibly relaxes; I hadn't realized how tense my body was. It feels like a weight has lifted off my shoulders. Trent steps up and starts showing us proper form. My eyes tune into his actions, attempting to absorb as much as possible and to ignore the pull to look at Aerick.

Trent finishes and has us line up at a punching bag, giving each of us a pair of gloves. "I want you to practicing punching on the bags," he says. Aerick goes behind us to watch. It's irritating me that my mind automatically registers where he is anytime he is in the same room. Ignoring my frustrations, I put my gloves on and begin practicing.

The bag is hard and it doesn't move much when I hit it. I try to hit it harder, but it continues to hang limply, vibrating only the slightest bit. These things must weigh a ton, but it moved so much more when Trent was showing us. I look next to me as I continue to practice. Royce, who has positioned himself next to me, punches the bag and moves a lot more then when I did, but not as much as when Trent did.

Suddenly tingling shoots up my spine bringing me to an abrupt halt as someone stands behind me. The person is so close I can feel their body heat and breath on my neck. Whoever it is, they're not touching me, but that doesn't stop my chest from starting to get tight. "I suggest you fucking back up now," I hiss through gritted teeth, without looking to see who it is.

"Careful now Nadalynn. Reel in your anger, it will do you no good when it counts. You need to stay calm and collected." Aerick's voice is low and relaxed, full of some emotion I can't place, and the tightening in my chest subsides, but my heart's still racing. "You need to learn to control your emotions." He lets what he said sink in for a moment.

When he starts talking again, his voice is different, like he's back in boss mode. "Your stance is wrong; spread your feet out a little." I don't move. *How does he change so quickly like that?* He kicks my foot lightly and I move them a little farther apart. "More... and bend your knees." His voice is even, but he's breathing harder, causing me to do the same. "Now punch and make sure you are going straight out, don't arch your swing, and make sure to breathe out as you strike." He still hasn't moved. "Punch!" He says a little louder, and I finally react to his command.

He holds his close position for a few more seconds and then takes a step back. "Good, now continue." I look back to him, but he's already walked over to another person – although he isn't standing close to him like he just did to me. I try to steady my breathing and continue practicing, keeping in mind what he told me, and the bag sways a bit; a slight improvement. I'm not quite sure what the hell that was, but hell, it was intense.

Thankfully Aerick doesn't get close to me again for the rest of class, but it doesn't keep him from stopping to watch me several times.

After lunch, I hang out with Steven until our archery class. He sat with us at lunch today, and after we found out we both have a brother named Evan, we just kept talking. He reminds me a lot of my brother, aside from his Native American dark tone; he's charming. It's odd how quickly I've been making several friends here. A thought in the back of head wonders why that is. I've never really been big on making friends. We sit on the grass outside the dorm while we wait for our next class – it's such a beautiful day.

Steven continues to tell me about himself. He used to live in Montana on the Indian reservation but was sent to live with his elderly aunt in Chicago. Like me, he's in for assault. He explains that he was drinking and got into a fight with some guy at a local hang out. The man spent a week in the hospital, and the judge wasn't impressed that he was drunk when he was arrested.

I drink every once in a while, but it isn't my thing. *Hangovers suck!* We continue talking as we walk to class, heading around the side of the gym where our schedules indicate class is today. When we round the corner, there is a wall of hay with several round wooden targets in front of it. A jolt of excitement spreads through me. Steven and I stand against the building continuing to talk as the rest of the class arrives. It's nice that I have some friends here. The smile on my face feels good, and being in this place doesn't seem so bad right now.

Aerick and Brand walk over right as the class is scheduled to begin. Aerick moves to stand at the end of the wall, leaning against it with his arms crossed, while Brand steps to the front of the loosely scattered group in front of us. "Alright cadets, quiet," he says, and everyone stops talking. "In this class, we will teach you to be good archers. Archery is good for learning control, precision, and patience."

He picks up a bow off the ground. "In this class, it doesn't matter how strong you are." I glance at Aerick and see him roll his eyes. Apparently, he has a different opinion, but to my surprise he stays quiet as Brand continues. "It only matters how good you are at remembering how to stand, breathe, and release. It takes a lot of control and precision to do this. The patience will come into play when we start using moving targets."

Brand moves in front of the target and starts explaining the types of bows, arrows, and other tools we'll use. He demonstrates how to put on a bracer to keep the string from hitting our arm. Then he shows us the correct open stance form that we should use.

Several lines are painted on the grass, spaced out in front of the targets. Brand is standing at the one furthest from the target. He pulls back his arrow, breathes in, pauses, and releases. He hits the target dead center and his lips pull into a small smile. *Wow, he's good.*

He turns to us and tells us to stand in front of the targets and practice. The bows, arrows, and bracers are all sitting at the closest line to the targets, so I assume that is where we're supposed to start. I move in front of the first target closest to the building and pick up the equipment. My bracer slides on easily and I position myself just like Brand showed us. I take a second to make sure I'm in the correct stance before I draw, take a deep breath, and release. My arrow hits the edge of the target. *Yes!*

Steven, who picked the target next to mine, smiles. "Nice shot, you're a natural." I'm flattered, but don't know what to say, so I just smile back. Aerick lets out a grunt as he walks past me down to critique their stances. *What's his problem?* I take two more shots, trying to shake off how much he bothers me. The first one misses but the second one hits the outside ring of the target, just slightly inside of my first shot.

Brand steps in beside me. "You're off just a little." He reaches up toward me; I lower my bow and step back. "I'm just trying to help." His tone is soft, almost comforting, and he gives me an apologetic smile.

I've got to stop flinching every time someone touches me. Shaking off my nerves, I get back in my stance. "Drop your shoulders a little." I do as he tells me.

He pauses and looks at me until my eyes meet his. Keeping eye contact, like he is warning me, he reaches out slowly and with a feather touch, he raises my elbow, then moves my hand closer to my mouth. "Now breathe in, hold your breath, center yourself, and release."

Following his instructions, I release, and my arrow hits the ring just outside of the center. "Nice job." He seems pleased, and I can't help but grin from ear-to-ear.

He smiles broadly in return, then goes to over to help Huck. I glance around and find myself locking eyes with Aerick, who is staring at me from behind the other cadets. He looks angry although I'm not sure what I could have possibly done to piss him off this time.

As our eyes connect, he speaks up. "Well. It like you've got it all figured out cadet. Since you are so good, why don't you move back to the last line."

Brand turns toward Aerick clearly irritated. "They're just getting started, give them a chance to practice."

"Quiet, Brand. Don't forget your place," he says in a level voice.

Brand looks at me, his lips pressed in a line, and nods for me to go. *Great.* I grab the bag of arrows and move to the back line. Once again, I get into position, trying to replicate the same stance Brand just showed me. I breathe in and release, but the arrow goes under the target. I look at Aerick; he has a slight, satisfied smile on his face.

"What Brand here failed to explain is the farther away you get, the more you need to take into account other factors such as the wind, and the natural arch an arrow will take the further you are away from the target," Aerick shouts to everyone, but still looking at me. Brand shakes his head but remains quiet. "Keep practicing – and Nadalynn, you can stay there, since you seemed to have already mastered shooting up close." He turns and goes to stand back at the wall, not giving any further instructions. *What the hell did I do?* I wasn't even mouthing off this time.

I continue practicing but the arrows can't seem to connect

with the target. By the end of class, my frustration has peaked. Some of the arrows get close to the target but nothing hits. I'm irritated that Brand doesn't bother to come back over to show me what I'm doing wrong. I'm even more pissed off at Aerick. He has managed to ruin my mood yet again.

* * * *

After evening PT I head back to the dorm, happy that I've somehow managed not to get in any more trouble this afternoon. Aerick pushed me hard again during PT, almost taunting me, but I was able to keep my mouth shut this time. I grab a tank top and shorts and head for a quick shower. I'm tired and would love nothing more than to just crawl into bed, but I need a shower and should start on the homework that's piling up on my desk.

When I get back to the dorm, only Mike and Tara are there. I lean down to put my stuff in my dirty laundry bag and as I'm standing back up, somebody behind me tries to tickle my sides. My chest starts tightening and without another thought, I turn around and punch.

"Fuck! What the hell?!" Mike gasps, rubbing his cheek.

"Never touch me without my permission, you got it!" I shout at him my chest heaving as I try to regain control.

"I was just playing around Nadi. You didn't have to fucking hit me."

I turn at Patrick's voice as he is walking in. "What happened?" He looks from me to Mike like he's going to be the next one to hit Mike.

"Nothing, I was just playing around with her and she fucking punched me." Patrick tries to hide a smile but fails miserably and he is still positioned protectively in front of me.

"It's alright Pat. He tried to tickle me, and it took me by surprise." The tightening in my chest begins to subside.

Patrick doesn't try to hide the smile anymore. "A bit of advice, don't touch her unless she asks you too." Patting Mike on the shoulder, he moves back toward his bed.

"Yeah, that would have been good to know two minutes ago."

He's still holding his cheek, which now sports an angry color of red, and a sliver of regret hits me. He was just playing around, and again, my reactions were uncalled for. "Sorry, Mike. I just don't like to be touched. Still friends?"

He looks at me for a minute and then sighs, "Yeah, we're good."

I turn back toward Patrick to talk to him, but Aerick is standing behind him with a tablet in his hand. He looks from me to Mike and back to me again. It doesn't surprise me that he seems to assume I'm involved – or maybe he heard the end of our conversation.

"Does someone want to tell me what just happened here." I'm confused by his tone and the look on his face. It were like he's mad but amused at the same time. None of us say anything, and Aerick is still looking at me. "I want an answer, or you all will be running laps; someone speaks up now!"

I was about to say something, but Mike speaks up. "It was just a misunderstanding."

"Is that so?" Aerick raises an eyebrow at him completely unconvinced. Mike and I nod our heads in unison. Aerick looks between both of us again and rolls his eyes. "You two, outside now."

Great, more laps. I slip my boots on but don't tie them because Aerick is already walking outside with Mike. Outside, Aerick turns around and faces us. He looks over to Mike first. "You, go to the infirmary and get some ice for that." Mike nods, walking off without a word but gives me an apologetic smile; a little ironic, being it was him who got hurt.

Once Mike is out of hearing distance, Aerick steps closer to me so that there's barely a foot separating us and looks at me. "Now, do you want to tell me what really happened?" His face is stern, but his voice isn't loud.

"Like he said, it was just a misunderstanding." My words break; again his invasion of my personal space causes me to hesitate, and it comes out as a stutter. As a wayward thought, I'm surprised that the tightening in my chest is absent.

"Do not lie to me *Nadalynn*. I don't like people lying to me." He stares directly into my eyes, and it's a struggle to concentrate; his eyes are deep enough to get lost in.

"I don't like to be touched, he touched me, I touched him back. Like I said misunderstanding." I mumble in a lost voice. *Why did I just admit that to him?* I don't think anyone in there would have ratted me out.

Disappointment crosses his face. "We do not condone violence here. Next time it will result in disciplinary action. Do you understand?" I look at him confused, and just shake my head 'yes'. *Is he letting me off?*

He leans in closer to me and speaks just above a whisper. "You need to learn to control your emotions. Understand?" I nod, but my face betrays me. I've been trying to control them for years.

He stares at me, his brows pulling together as he contemplates something, then he leans even closer and whispers next to my ear. "If I can do it, so can you." He stays there for a fraction of a second and then walks around me, going back to the dorm.

What the FUCK?! I let out the breath I didn't know I was holding. This man is so confusing. He thinks he knows me? He has no idea what I've been through. Why the hell does my body react to him like that? I'm so confused; I hate being confused!

I head back into the dorm once I've collected myself, and everyone is staring at me with expectant looks on their faces. "What?" They continue to look at me. The last thing I want to do is explain the last few baffling minutes. Instead forcing a smile, I play it off putting my fingers up in the air to make quotes, "We don't condone violence here."

Patrick and Jeff laugh at me as Mike walks back in with a disposable ice pack on his cheek and everyone's attention moves to him. "Word of advice fellas, she doesn't like to be touched." He grumbles as he walks to his bed. His entrance has effectively ended questioning.

Jeff laughs, "Oh we already know."

"What do you mean? You and Patrick touch her all the time." Mike almost looks like he is pouting. What's the big deal with needing to touch me anyway?

"Well, we've known her for a long time, and we know how to touch her," Jeff says with a huge grin on his face and wiggles his eyebrows.

My boots are still untied, so I kick one at him, hitting him in the leg. "Shut up, ass. It's not so much how, as it is who," I say smiling.

"Ouch! I was kidding." We are both laughing.

"So, you guys knew each other before you came here?" Huck asks.

Patrick smiles, "Yeah, we all go back to elementary school."

"Really?" Mike says, interested. He must be feeling better. Hopefully there are no hard feelings.

"Yes," I say with a smile, pushing past Patrick to get to my desk. "Now, if you don't mind, there is a ton of homework calling my name." Sitting down at my desk, I pull out the math work. It's my strong suit so it's mostly review for me. My longing for my iPod returns. It would be so much better if we could listen to music; it helps me concentrate.

By nine fifty-five, I've finally finished. It took longer than expected with all the background chatter in the room and the occasional person trying to talk to me. I'm going to have to find some time to sit in the courtyard where it's quiet.

Paulo comes into the room to inform us we have five minutes until lights out, so I put my stuff away. Just as I get comfortably into bed, the lights go out. "Good night guys," I tell Patrick and Jeff, but to my surprise, everyone answers back with "good night." A smile spreads across my face and I close my eyes, falling asleep quickly.

CHAPTER NINE

(Thursday, June 4th)

YESTERDAY WAS UNEVENTFUL. I was able to make it through my day without hitting anyone and, thankfully, without mouthing off to Aerick. Then again, there wasn't much of a chance. If I didn't know any better, I would think he was avoiding me. Other than the few times he barked orders at me, he didn't talk to me; he didn't even look at me. In self-defense class, we worked on more punching and kicking, along with some weight training, but his critiquing eyes never even glanced my way.

In my Nutritional Health and Technology classes, we only reviewed what's going to be covering for the next few weeks. Coincidentally, in our health class, we're going to be learning the effects of food while undergoing a rigorous exercise regimen. Without fail, we were given more homework including having to log our food intake for five days. Given we're fed three times a day and having to eat what's made; I don't see that as being very hard.

The afternoon consisted of a hike with Trent's group. Aerick led us all up to what they call the power lines, and he warned us that we shouldn't get more than thirty yards from him or our tracking bracelets would activate. This got everyone's curiosity going, but Joseph was the first to jump. When Joseph asked him what would happen if we did, Aerick got this ominous look on his face and told Joseph 'try it and find out.' My curiosity peaked, and I was starting to wonder what would happen, but no one decided to test the limit, much to my dismay.

We followed a trail that started back behind the dorms for about thirty minutes until we came to a "T" where it connected to another large open trail. Running parallel to the wide trail was a huge set of power lines. We only rested for five-minute rest before hiked back down the trail.

It was a nice walk, other than the hike which was all uphill and killed my legs. Royce walked with me, talking the whole way. He had asked me about what happened the night before in the dorm. When there are only twelve people, news apparently spreads quickly. I confirmed that yes, I'd hit Mike, who happened to be right in front of us. There is a small bruise as a reminder on his cheek. Royce laughed, causing Mike to look back and sneer at him, but he didn't seem to be holding it against me.

Royce let me in on the little previously unknown fact that Brayden, our maintenance guy, is Trent's brother – although it wasn't much of a shock since they look a lot alike. He also told me about the others in his dorm. Leena had finally gotten the hint that Royce didn't like her, so she has moved on to harassing Joseph who enjoyed the attention. He said that Karen and John were both quiet, so he hadn't talked to them as much. He on the other hand was easy to talk to, but my mind was only half there. The entire walk my eyes kept finding their way to Aerick, but his icy gaze never left the trail.

When I arrived back at the dorm last night, I took my homework out to the grass in front of the dorm. Within an hour, my English assignment was complete. It was a lot easier without other people bothering me. One of the girls from B Dorm, Karen, had been out there too but I figured she wanted quiet just as much as me, so I sat apart from her. Once finished, I laid back for a while as the sun began to set and watched the stars started to appear in the sky. I think tonight I'll do the same thing. Being out in the middle of nowhere does have its benefits.

Today's warmer than it has been the last few days. As we do morning PT, I feel it's just a little easier, but my body is feeling worn down from so many consecutive days of exercise. My mind is also tired. Trying to keep up with all the school work, and learning all the new physical stuff, is just taxing. We're dismissed from PT, so I go in to take a quick shower, change, and brush my teeth; a routine I hope to continue in the future.

I'm brushing my teeth when John comes over next to me to wash his hands. "So, are you the girl that the instructors have been talking about?"

I look at him confused; first that he has come out of his shell and is willingly talking to me, and two wondering what he is talking about. Spitting out the toothpaste from my mouth I turn to him. "What do you mean?"

"After PT last night, I heard Aerick and Paulo talking in the gym. They came in to lift weights, and I was already there taking my frustrations out on a punching bag." He dries his hands and leans back on the sink next to me.

"Aerick told Paulo that his girl had given one of the guys a nice bruise on his face because he invaded her personal space." John raises an eyebrow and smiles at me. "I'm assuming it was you; the other girl doesn't look like she would hurt a fly." I'm speechless.

That also explains how the other dorm found out about it. "So, you took it upon yourself to tell everyone in the dorm what you heard?" Irritation laces my voice.

"Well, hey, we have to gossip about something since there isn't nothing else to do." He shrugs his shoulders.

I take a deep breath, trying to calm myself. "What else did they say?" I attempt to play it cool, but my irritation is still showing through.

He pauses for a moment. "Aerick said she was strong most of the time, but she also had a big mouth, and he would break her down."

What. A. Fucking. Asshole. If he weren't a fucking ass to

everyone, then my mouth wouldn't be a problem. And 'most of the time,' what the hell is that supposed to mean? Mister 'all confusing' thinks he's any better. He has more mood swings than a pregnant woman in high heels, and he has the nerve to talk about me. He thinks he can break me down? *We'll see about that.*

"So, am I right?"

I'm brought back to our conversation. "Huh?"

"Are you the girl?" He asks for confirmation, although the look on his face tells me he already knows.

I rinse out my mouth and turn to him, drawing my shoulders back to show confidence. "Yes, I am."

He gives me a big smile, winks, and turns to go back to his dorm. "Good for you," he says to me over his shoulder. *That was a little weird.* I put my toothbrush and toothpaste away and go to get the boys so we can go to breakfast.

Tara has taken to hanging out with Leann and Karen. I've always preferred boys to girls, so I'm happy to hang out with the guys in my dorm, and occasionally those in the other dorm. We get into the breakfast line, but I'm not in the mood for food. I decide on an apple and some coffee.

My mind is still reeling from what John said, and my irritation toward Aerick just keeps building as each second ticks by. When the instructors come in, Aerick sits next to me again. Knowing from experience, this can only end badly, but my mind is set to be good today. I take a bite of my apple and try to pretend he isn't there.

"Is that all you are going to eat for breakfast?" He says not looking at me. I notice he has a huge plate of eggs and my stomach just churns. I'm not happy with him, but I'm sticking with my wits to not make a scene.

"Yes, Sir," I answer trying to hide my irritation and avoid an argument.

"You need to eat more than that," he says more demanding.

Breathing deeply through my nose does nothing for me; my composure begins to break. "Well, I'm not hungry," I say, a little forcefully.

"Eat cadet." His cold voice tries to intimidate me but all it does is add fuel to the growing fire of anger, and my silence beckons him to continue. "That's not a request."

My attempt to control my emotions fails miserably. "Eating is one thing you can't make me do, *so back off*."

He finally turns and looks at me. "Is that so? You will eat a sustainable diet, or I will teach you why it is important." His low growl demands my surrender, but it is one thing he is not getting; not this time.

My anger and irritation hit the peak and I explode, losing all control. Turning to meet his eyes, my shallow voice draws out each word as common sense disappears completely. "*Fuck. Off. Aerick.*" I've had enough of his fucking demanding insistence. I'm not hungry, and I'm not going to eat.

The entire staff become quiet in a nanosecond and stare at me dumbfounded, snapping me back into reality. *Shit.*

His face instantly becomes infuriated. "Get your ass up right now cadet and get outside." He says as he rises to his feet. His low cold tone concerns me, making me question if my actions may have been a tad overboard. Maybe I went too far this time. *Crap.*

Brand and Trent both have worried looks plastered on their faces, too. The other guys at my table are staring at me with stunned looks on their faces, except for Jeff, who looks pissed and is shaking his head.

"I said get up, and get outside RIGHT NOW!" He shouts harshly right into my ear when I don't move. It's not the bossy instructor shout; he's extremely pissed off. For the first time, I'm afraid for what's about to happen, but I lock my emotions down and don't let it show.

I breathe deeply, put my apple down, and follow him outside. Outside, we walk over to the path, and he turns to face me. "Run!" He demands, his face is dark with barely contained fury.

"How many laps?" It's not what I expected. I'm not sure what I expected, but this sure wasn't it.

"Until I say to stop." His lip turns up ever so slightly. So, is this how he's going to break me down? *Huh. Game on, Aerick!*

"Fine." I take a deep breath, trying to mentally prepare myself and start running. To my surprise, he starts running right behind me.

We jog in silence for the first twenty minutes, and after having done PT barely an hour ago, I'm already exhausted. "Pick it up! You are going too slow," Aerick barks. Somehow my feet respond, and some untapped source of energy kicks in to keep me going.

The last thing I want is for him to think he's got the best of me. John's words from earlier echo in my head, 'break her down.' That's what he's trying to do, but it isn't going to work. The thought is enough motivation to push myself even harder.

Another twenty minutes pass, sweat has completely soaked my shirt. Aerick is starting to work up a sweat too as he jogs next to me. Mid-stride, he peels off his shirt and tucks it into his pocket. *Holy shit.*

He is ripped but not in that completely over the top way that makes guys look inhuman. Every single muscle from his chest to his hips is rock solid outlining every perfectly shaped muscle in his upper body. It has got to be one of the hottest bodies I've ever seen and in a moment of lust, I forget that I'm pissed at him. When he notices me watching at him, he gives me a hard look. Although, I think I see his lip twitch in amusement.

"Keep moving, cadet." His voice still cold, but the anger seems to be gone.

After a moment, my mind catches up and I remember why I'm here. Focusing on the path in front of me, I trying to push away the horrible burning in my legs. I'm not sure how much longer I can keep this up. As much as I try to deny it, I'm exhausted, and without having eaten breakfast, my energy is spent. Aerick, on the other hand, looks like he could go several more hours.

My best bet is to reason with him to try to end this torture without giving in. "Shouldn't I be going to class?" I pant in between my heaving breaths.

"Discipline overrules class. Now, pick it up." He says directly. My head is starting to get a bit fuzzy, but my stubbornness doesn't want to give him the satisfaction of seeing me quit. It has got to be almost over, so I keep going, pushing through the burn and fuzziness. I start singing in my head, focusing on the words to distract myself, and it works. Music grounds me, distracts me, and has long been my best friend.

After several minutes, the lyrics pause. I close my eyes for a moment as I try pushing away the nausea and dizziness that are getting worse. *I can do this; I know I can.* I open my eyes and keep going.

Just keep singing. The words continue flowing in my head and I keep pushing, praying Aerick will give up soon.

Another minute passes; the words stream in my head, line by line, as I focus the tiny sliver of control I'm holding on to.

Two more minutes inch by but my body has had enough and black starts closing in on my vision. I involuntarily slow down and then fall to my knees as control of my actions disappears. My body feels like jello and my lungs struggle to pull in air. Aerick stops in front of me and kneels.

I barely hear his voice, but a triumphant smirk is plastered on his face, "Ready to give..." Losing all control, I fall against his bare chest and – the black closes further around me.

"Fuck!" Aerick breathes, and I feel his arms slide under my

legs as he picks me up and starts moving. The warmth of his chest against my cheek is the last thing I remember as the dark engulfs me completely.

✳ ✳ ✳ ✳

"Is she going to be okay?" Aerick's voice brings me back up, but I don't open my heavy eyes. His voice lacks any emotion.

"She was severely dehydrated. I've already put two bags of fluid in her and based on what you said, she hasn't been eating much. That is a huge factor in why she passed out and why she's taking so long to recover. You really shouldn't have pushed her so hard, knowing she was not getting the proper nutrition." A woman's voice scolds him.

"I didn't think she would push herself that hard. I was waiting for her to give up." He snaps defensively. "I have to get to my afternoon session; I already missed this morning. I will be back later this evening for an update."

Afternoon? How long have I been here?

"She'll be okay, Luther. She'll be okay to continue." *How many people are in here?*

"Aerick, be sure to get me your report before lights out." Luther's voice is spewing irritation. Aerick must be in trouble. *HA!*

"Once she wakes up, as long as her vitals are good, she can go back to the dorm, but I will be excusing her from evening PT. I'll continue to monitor her until then." The nurse's voice is full of authority. This is the first time anyone other than Luther has talked to Aerick like that. Everyone else backs down to him.

"Okay, I get it," Aerick tells her, and I hear several pairs of footsteps exiting the room.

It's quiet, and just when I think I'm alone, there is a voice. "Come on Nadalynn, wake up." Aerick's still here, and I feel him move a piece of hair off my face, "I know you can do it." If I didn't know any better, I would say he actually feels sorry. Quiet fills the room and he lets out a heavy sigh, "You fucked up this time Aerick," he says to himself.

I'm shocked by his comment. I thought it was his job to push us. He said it himself that he needed to 'break me.' I try to open my eyes, but I hear his footsteps retreat and decide to give into the darkness pulling at me.

✳ ✳ ✳ ✳

"Come on, wake up Nadi." Patrick's voice draws me awake again. I find I can easily open my eyes this time, but I squint in the bright light.

"It's about time," Jeff tells me, his voice full of relief.

"Hey, guys. What's up?" My voice barely comes out as a whisper. My throat is dry, and I'm extremely thirsty. "Can I have some water?"

Patrick gets up from his chair next to my bed. "I'll go get the nurse."

"Jesus Christ Nadi, you scared the shit out of me," Jeff says, his eyes closed as he engulfs me in a hug. "I told you about keeping your mouth shut. Why would you purposely piss him off like that? He's crazy!"

I roll my eyes, pushing him back as much as I can in my weak state. "Maybe because he was pissing me off." My voice is still quiet, but a little strength has returned to it.

"When I saw him carrying your limp body across the courtyard," he pauses, closing his eyes and shakes his head, "murderous thoughts crossed my mind." A slight smile touches my lips. "I tried to follow him, but he told me if I didn't get to class I would be next. I'm so sorry, Nadi."

"What? Why are you sorry?" My eyebrows knit together.

"I should have told him to fuck off and stayed with you." The half smirk on his face is adorable, and my lips turn up more.

"I would have loved to see his reaction to that!" Jeff laughs, and the nurse comes in.

"Hello Nadi, I'm Terrie. How are you feeling?" She has a sweet, calming voice.

"I'm okay; I'm just really thirsty."

"Yes, Patrick told me. I've brought you some ice chips. You will need to eat them slowly to avoid getting sick. I've been running fluid in through your IV most of the day, so you're no longer dehydrated, but your throat is probably dry."

She hands me a small cup of ice as she continues, "I also gave you a protein shot and a vitamin booster that should help you recover faster. You should avoid eating for the rest of the day except for the crackers. I will send you back with some juice and crackers that you can eat tonight and a protein bar that I want you to eat in the morning before PT. I've already warned Aerick that your PT for tomorrow is to be light." Her voice becomes irritated as she says the last part.

"Okay, am I free to go? I'm feeling much better." My voice is not as convincing as I'd like, but I'm exhausted and just want to get back to my bed. I go to sit up, but she pushes me back down.

"You will need to stay for just a little while longer, so I can make sure your vitals remain stable. Evening PT is about to start. Guys, if you want to go on ahead and pick her up on your way to the dorm afterward, she'll be ready." I don't want to stay, but apparently, it's not my choice.

"Alright, we'll be back," Jeff says and gets up; kisses me on the head and Patrick does the same.

I smile sweetly at them. "See you guys soon." They return my smile as they walk out.

"Well, aren't you the popular one!" Terrie remarks as she starts the machine to check my blood pressure.

"Huh?"

"Well, I've had more people in here today than I usually get in a month," she says with a small laugh. *That's weird. Wonder why?* "Yep and several people including your friends there and Aerick have been here more than once."

"Aerick? Why does he care? He worried I might die on his watch?" My voice is full of disgust.

"Hey, now." She looks at me pointedly. "Don't be too hard on him." She can't be serious. I'm lying in a hospital bed because of him and she was the one scolding him earlier, but her gaze never falters.

"You're serious?" I can't believe she's defending him.

"Aerick is a complicated person." I can't help but roll my eyes at her. "I'm serious. I know he comes off like an asshole, but... well, he can be an asshole, but that's not the point. Somewhere inside him, he has feelings even though he would probably kick my ass for saying so. He's known as a real jerk around here, but like the rest of us, he has his own past that he has had to deal with. Not to mention he's good at what he does. He was just trying to get his point across."

I look down at my fingers. "Oh, is that what Aerick was doing? Because it seems to me that he was pushing me until I literally collapsed in exhaustion."

She stops what she's doing and looks at me. "Exactly the point!" My eyes fly back up at her tone.

"Nadi, you're not eating enough. Maybe that's okay when you are anywhere else, but not when you are here, pushing your body to these limits. You need to have enough energy to sustain you. The only way to get that, is to eat a well-balanced meal at least three times a day and drink lots of water. If you had been eating well and drinking the proper amount of water, you would have never collapsed like that. Granted, he may have pushed it a little too far, but he was right."

Shit! She's right. "He's still an ass."

"Well, I never said that he wasn't." She pauses, moving close to me before continuing, "But something for you to think about; in all the years I've known him, I've never look seen him look so worried. That's not normal for him."

"Worried?" *Why would he be worried?* I heard her tell him that I would be okay.

She looks around to make sure we are alone and goes through what appears to be a silent debate in her head. "Do not repeat this – and if you do, I will deny it." She looks at me expectantly, and I nod my head.

"When I came here earlier, just before dinner, I was surprised to see him sitting next to you. He had such a worried look on his face. I think he feels sorry that he did this to you. I knew he would be mad if I saw him like that, so I left quietly. I don't think he noticed me. He stayed in here for about an hour and left just before your friends got here. Like I said, he is a complicated man."

"Well, the look on his face right before I collapsed would say otherwise," I tell her remembering the conceited look of triumph as I dropped to my knees. She finishes writing something down and starts to walk out.

"Get some rest. I will come back and check your vitals before your friends pick you up." She stops and looks at me. "And just so you know, the look I saw on his face when he walked in with you lifeless in his arms did say otherwise." She turns and walks out.

Once again, I'm thoroughly confused. *What was that supposed to mean?* I lean back on the pillow and wait for the guys to come back to get me.

* * * *

As we walk back to the dorm, Jeff has his arm around me and I'm leaning into him allowing him to hold me up. Something I usually wouldn't let even him do, but I'm still weak and grateful for the help.

I spy Aerick outside the gym standing against the wall. It looks like there is a bit of sadness on his face, but before I can really see him, he turns and goes inside the gym. Jeff lets out a puff of air beside me.

When we get back into the dorm, Jeff walks me to my bed and gets me out some shorts and a tank top. "Here, let me help you get dressed," he says, with a wicked grin.

"Funny. I think I'll take a shower and change myself." I snatch my clothes out of his hands and reach into my clothing chest to get my undergarments. I'm glad to see he still has a sense of humor. I stand slowly to make sure I'm steady on my feet before going into the bathroom to shower.

The shower feels good but I'm still weak, so I make it short and head back to the dorm. My appetite has returned a little, so I sit down on my bed and eat the crackers and juice Terrie gave me. Tara offers to French braid my hair, and after a moment of hesitation I let her. I'm amazed by her offer, and when she finishes, she sits on my bed as we all start talking. No one seems to be interested in doing homework tonight.

They tell me Aerick was a real jerk the rest of the day, apparently pissed off, and that ironically enough, after throwing judgment at me for not eating, he missed both lunch and dinner. I wonder why? Terrie said he was there at dinner, and that he had visited several times. Was he there for lunch too?

Royce and Joseph both come in to chat with us and ask me how I'm doing. I don't like this attention, but I try to be polite about it. After all, they're just concerned. The others from the B dorm follow not too long after. I look around as we talk, and it occurs to me that this is the first time we all have been in one room, by choice, talking to each other.

Leena stays close to Joseph, flaunting herself at him and trying to bring all the attention to herself. Other than John asking me how I'm doing and a few other off the top remarks, he stays quiet, just listening to the others, as does Karen. I also notice there seems to be a bit of tension between John and Jeff, but I'm not sure why. As far as I know, they've hardly talked to each other.

Aerick comes into the room to give us our five-minute warning. I look at him, but he looks everywhere except at me. There's no emotion on his face, but my eyes are drawn to his curled fists the blood on his knuckles. He turns and leaves just as fast as he comes in. The people from B dorm say their goodbyes and leave as we all get into bed.

The lights go out, and I lie there, my body exhausted but my mind refusing to switch off. It's hard to believe I'm still so tired after being out for the better part of the day. Unfortunately for me, my racing mind is preventing me from falling asleep. Today was such a weird, confusing day. Aerick's actions are throwing me for a loop, and I'm finding it hard to figure him out. I'm not sure why he's picking on me, other than the fact that he obviously doesn't like that I challenge him and deny him control over me.

"Nadi, if you don't stop moving around, I'm going to tie you down," Jeff says, irritated.

"Sorry, I'm having a hard time falling asleep."

After a moment, I hear him get up. "Sit up."

"I'm okay, Jeff – just go to bed." If I'm not mistaken, he's got a smile on his face

"I said, 'sit up.'" I give in knowing what he's doing; I want him to anyway. He sits down with his back against the headboard and with his legs crossed. He puts the pillow on his lap. I lie back down on my pillow, and he starts to run his fingers through my hair. He used to do this at camp years ago when I was upset or scared. He always managed to make me feel better.

"Are you sure you're okay?" His quiet, full of concern.

"Yeah, I'll be fine."

He leans down and kisses my hair. "Sleep."

"Can you two quiet down over there? And I really don't think she is up for anything over G-rated anyway."

"Fuck off, Mike," Jeff snaps. That would never happen. He has always been the protective older brother type, and yes, he's sweet, but we've never liked each other like that.

With a smile, I close my eyes. Focusing on his fingers stroking my hair, it doesn't take long for me to fall asleep.

CHAPTER TEN

(Sunday, June 7th)

THE CLOCK SEEMS annoyingly bright this morning. It's only four forty-five. I'm up early this morning and not by choice. I turn on my back and look up at the ceiling trying to ignore the irritation sitting on my side table. I can't believe I made it through the first week. The last few days since I nearly ran myself dead have been a little odd, especially the morning after it happened.

Flashback to Friday Morning:

This morning I'm feeling much more refreshed. Even after all that happened yesterday, all the sleeping worked wonders. Well, I'm sure everything Terrie pumped into me helped too. I dress quickly, make my bed and scarf down my protein bar. We head out to PT and Aerick is on the stage. We all fall into our designated spots.

"Nadi, you are excused from PT today. You will walk around

the path until we are finished." Aerick says without looking at me.

"I'm feeling fine; I can work out with everyone else." The last thing I want is any more special treatment, but when I don't move, Aerick's eyes snap to meet mine.

"You will do as I say!" His face is hard and cold.

Let's not start this again. Shaking my head, I start walking around the path as they start to warm up. More than likely he got into trouble yesterday, and now he's even more pissed at me. Not to mention he was ordered to go easy on me this morning, which I'm sure is just stirring the pot more. It irritates me that he's acting like this is all my fault. I didn't make him push me so hard, but now that I think about it, my legs are kind of sore this morning. I don't want to think about Aerick anymore, so I focus on my walk. My lips start humming the words to one of my favorite songs to pass the time.

By the end of PT, I've gotten over my irritation of not getting to do PT with everyone else. As much as I'm sure they would have loved to take my place, I don't like to be singled out.

Jeff, Patrick and I walk into the mess hall and Aerick steps in front of me. "Go take your seat." His expression is unreadable, but his voice is demanding and after yesterday, I decide not to argue.

I fall into my normal spot at the table and a minute later he sets a plate in front of me. My eyes widen; he has given me a mountainous plate of food, similar to what he has himself. He takes the seat next to me. "Eat."

My eyes are glued to the huge plate of food looming in front of me. There's no way all that is going into me, even if I were starving. Finishing this is impossible, but I'm doubting he can be reasoned with. *I have to try.*

"Aerick," I say in a pleading whisper, keeping my head down, but I notice his fork stops halfway to his mouth out of the corner of my eye. "There's no way I can eat this much, not even if I wanted to." I say it quiet enough that no one else can hear. I turn my head slightly and look at him, pleading with my eyes.

He closes his eyes for just a second as some kind of emotion flashes on his face so quickly I almost miss it. Then he glances sideways at me. "Fine, but you are eating at least half," he demands quietly, but there is no anger in voice. He resumes eating.

Thank goodness for that – although, I'm still going to have a hard time eating even that much. I sigh, deciding not to test my luck, and just start eating in silence as everyone else is buzzing around me.

I'm pretty pissed at being served like some misbehaving child, but it surprises me he let me reason with him. It's obvious that reasoning isn't Aerick's strong suit, so I reluctantly keep eating. I know he's going to be harder on me now that he got into trouble because of me, but I'm hoping that if I eat he will lay off for the rest of the day.

End Flashback

Aerick has continued to serve me my food for the last few days, but after breakfast on Friday, he only dishes me up half as much. At least it's a little more manageable. Unfortunately, despite the fact that he always finishes well before me, he sits there and waits for me to eat everything on my plate.

He's also been extremely quiet toward me, but only me. I'm beginning to think he is trying not to lose his temper. Anytime he talks to me it's in a hushed, cold voice, but he still pushes me to work harder whenever he gets the chance. I've noticed that he seems deep in thought most of the time for the last few days, or maybe he's distracted by something. It leaves me wondering what the hell is the deal with him.

Since Thursday morning, other than Aerick's odd behavior, and him serving all my meals, everything has returned to normal. The other instructors started treating me as if nothing had happened, which is how I prefer it. I managed to keep my mouth shut and get through the last few days without incident.

The alarm clocks go off, pulling me out of my thoughts. I get up and get ready for the morning. It will be pleasant to have a free day, since I have a lot of homework to get done. There is no doubt they like to keep us busy. We go outside for PT, but instead of the instructors on the stage, they're in front of it and Luther stands there with another woman I've never seen. There is also a screen set up behind him; my curiosity is peaked. Today's going to be different than just some free time.

"Good morning cadets. Congratulations on making it through the first week. Today will be a generally free day. All meal times will remain the same, you will be required to do both morning and evening PT, and go to your counseling session, but the rest of the day is free. I would like to introduce you all to the camp psychologist, Liz." The woman, who appears to be in her late twenties, nods her head.

"You each will be required to attend a thirty-minute counseling session today. Your individual times are listed in your daily schedule. I urge you to keep in mind that although you have free time, you may not leave the property, and all the rules still stand. You are also greatly advised to work on your homework. The gym is open. If you need supplies see Ayla, and please take up any medical complaints with our nurse, Terrie." Luther looks down to Jake, who is standing to the side of the stage, and he nods his head as something silent passes between them.

"From the moment you arrived here, you have been observed carefully. We pay attention to anything and everything you do from the time you wake up until you go to sleep. We do this for several reasons, but there is only one you need to know about, and that is to rank you. In life, hard work pays off in the form of reward. We believe in this fundamental law of society, so it only fits that it's recognized here as well. We have a system that helps reward, as well as discipline you, to push you to behave as you should. The list I am about to reveal will show you how well you did this week. The top two people will receive a reward while the bottom three will receive punishment. If you are one of the top two, Aerick will allow you to choose your reward from an approved list. If you are in the bottom three, then you will be on mess hall duty for all three meals today. You will also be cleaning the dorm bathroom, in which you will report to Brayden at nine-thirty this morning, and he will provide you the supplies and ensure it is cleaned properly." He turns back to Jake and nods his head, and the screen lights up.

1. John
2. Nadi
3. Huck
4. Karen
5. Joseph
6. Tara
7. Patrick
8. Steven
9. Royce
10. Leena
11. Mike
12. Jeff

WHAT? How the hell did I manage to get to the top of the list? Aerick glances over at me, and his lips twitch upward slightly. How can he possibly find this funny?

Luther continues. "Now, let me say a few things about this list. While your homework will factor in the future, it's not a factor on this list since you have not yet had any due. However, your participation in class does." Okay, I always participate in class. "Another factor is your overall improvement. It is one of our goals to help you improve in all areas, and we will push you to do that." *Not sure how well I did there.*

"Your attitude toward your fellow cadets, your instructors and the staff are also factored in." Well, I failed that part majorly when it came to Aerick and Mike, but everyone else I'm cool with. Granted, Mike was just a misunderstanding, but the thing with Aerick was huge.

"I want to make one thing clear; while we frown on defiance, we also greatly admire determination, because it leads to courage, and to be courageous is to be honorable. Be careful cadets; this is a fine line. I want to point out that I saw an act of determination this week so great, that I had not seen the likes of it in almost four – years when our very own Aerick, Trent, and Brand were cadets here." *Really?*

"To see someone who has so much determination that they push themselves to their physical and mental limits, without giving up. The heart and passion it takes are so immense; it's a rare find in a person. With that in mind, I want to congratulate Nadi for her noteworthy act of determination this week," he pauses as he looks into my eyes, "but I also warn you, we do not tolerate rebellious behavior."

Everyone in camp is staring at me, and I'm frozen in shock. The heat of embarrassment creeps up my neck, turning my face bright as a tomato. I'm confused as to how me pushing myself to simply not be outdone by Aerick, is tied to something involving courage. "Have a great day, cadets, and remember what I have said here today." Luther finishes and exits the stage.

Aerick's muscles visibly flex as he leaps up on the stage and starts leading us in our morning workout. My body moves in a daze, not really paying attention to our workout until Paulo shouts at me to pick it up. Snapping back, I push everything that just happened aside and focus on my workout. Focusing on my breathing as we exercise, I make a mental note that it is getting easier to make it through our workout today – or maybe I'm just getting used to the burning.

While the workout seems easier, my pants are making it more difficult as I find myself pulling them up several times. It's not easy to do jumping jacks when they slip down with each jump. My body has changed with all this exercising and the mostly healthy food. Today I'm going to have to exchange them for smaller ones.

We finish up our workout and Aerick steps forward. "Alright, John and Nadalynn stay here, the rest of you are dismissed. Leena, Mike, and Jeff, make sure you report to Brayden in the bathroom at nine-thirty and let this be a lesson to work harder and keep your mouths closed."

With that, I know exactly why Jeff was at the bottom. He spent all week sticking up for me, and he told me he mouthed off to Brand too. It makes me feel like shit. I'll have to find a way to make it up to him.

Aerick has also been irritating the crap out of me this week by refusing to call me by my nickname. He usually calls me cadet, but when he's forced to say my name, he always addresses me as 'Nadalynn.'

Everyone goes back inside except for John and me. We go over to Aerick who has jumped down from the stage and picked up his tablet that was resting on the edge. He keeps his face emotionless as he comes over to us. "You each get to pick one off this list." He hands me the tablet first but doesn't look at me.

1. No morning PT for one day
2. Pass on one instructional class
3. Pass on two homework assignments
4. No mess hall duty for three days
5. Sports Balls (Basketball/Football/Soccer)
6. PSP*
7. Ebook Reader*
8. iPod (1 gig)*
9. Lunch at The Cottage cafe
10. 30 min Skype chat (may not use until day 30+)
*Cadet may only choose 1 electronic item during the 4-month camp

"Definitely the iPod!" The excitement builds in me; I've been dying to have one the whole time I've been here. It wasn't even a debate. Of everything we've been without, that's the one thing I miss the most.

He raises one eyebrow, and my mind flashes back to our morning in the bathroom. My face heats up and his lip twitches. "Come to the instructor's dorm after lunch, and I will have your iPod. You will get one hour to download music and load it on your iPod." He hands the tablet to John who looks over the list.

"I'll take the Ebook Reader," he says without much thought.

"Okay, I will bring it by this afternoon. You may request books through me. If they're on the approved list, I will add them to the account and it should automatically sync to your reader. You may only use these devices during free time or meal times. If you do not follow the rules, you will lose it permanently."

"Are we allowed to let others use it?" I ask, without thinking. I don't want to press my luck, but I want to know so I don't *break the rules.*

Aerick's face scrunches, "It is yours to do as you wish. If you want to share, go ahead. But be warned, if they get broken they will not be replaced, and you will not be able to choose another one if you are in the top two again. You only get one electronic item during camp, no exceptions. Do you both understand?" We nod our heads 'yes' and then head into the dorm.

"So, what did you get?" Jeff asks as I get back in. My grin is too hard to contain. "An iPod – and you, my friend, may use it anytime I'm not."

He smiles widely at me. "Sweet!"

"Sorry about getting in the bottom, I know some of that had to do with me."

He rolls his eyes. "I'm my own person. I guess I need to learn to shut my mouth too."

My chest rumbles with an unguarded laugh. I pull out my hair tie and grab for the brush. I prefer my hair down, but with our schedule, it's more convenient to leave it up. It'll be nice to leave it free since we don't have much to do today. The guys wait patiently for me to finish, and we go to breakfast.

Aerick is still serving me food and sits next to me to be sure I eat it all. I wonder how long this is going to last, but I'm in a good mood and decide not to push my luck now. I eat all my eggs, potatoes, bacon, and fruit while our table talks, which seems to please Aerick as my fork falls on my empty plate. The slight twitch of his mouth is gone within a second and if my attention hadn't been on him already, I would have missed it completely.

Jeff stays to clean so Patrick, Royce, and I walk back to the dorm together. My iPod won't be ready until lunch, so my only choice is to get some homework done until then. I suggest to the guys that we should sit out in the courtyard since it's such a beautiful day. No point sitting in our stuffy cabin when there is fresh mountain air and warm sunshine outside. They agree, so we go in to grab our stuff and head outside.

❋ ❋ ❋ ❋

By lunchtime, I have finished all but one of my assignments. It took longer to do because most of us were out there chatting as we did our work, but I feel like I got a lot accomplished. My excitement about my iPod can barely be contained by lunch, and I'm anxious to see what they're going to let me download. Aerick sits down next to me and hands me a plate that has a chicken salad and fruit on it. Finally, something light and boy am I grateful because I'm not hungry.

"You can pick up the iPod any time after lunch," he says in a disinterested voice.

"Like I could forget!" Smiling like a fool, I'm trying to hold myself in my seat.

He eats quickly and leaves before I'm finish, which is different. It's normal for him to finish first, but he always stays to make sure I finish mine. Just in case he's testing me, I clear my plate and then continue to sit, talking with everyone until it's time for cleanup. When enough time has passed, I get up and leave, not waiting for anyone else.

No one is in our dorm, and I walk straight through the bathroom to the instructor's dorm. My feet pause just inside of the door. I've never been in here, and it looks a lot different from ours. The beds are in the four corners of the room, and they are doubles instead of singles. Maybe it is the small perks that count. In place of the standard bedding, each bed is covered by a unique comforter that must be personal as opposed to camp-issued.

There's a bunch of things on the walls like calendars, pictures, and message boards. There is a large desk for each one of them that is accessorized with a matching armoire and bookshelf. The furniture separates the room into four areas, one for each instructor, but each area appears to be neat and clean.

Aerick is sitting on what I presume is his bed, looking at his tablet, and glances up at me when I enter. "Come sit," he says, interrupting my roaming eyes. My feet unfreeze, moving over to his bed, but I'm not sure where he was implying I sit: his bed, his desk, the floor? My eyes give him with a questioning look when he moves his gaze back to me. He looks down on his bed next to him with a little nod, so I perch myself on the edge.

He hands me a blue iPod with comfortable-looking blue earbuds. "Here is your iPod. Those are high-quality ear buds, so they should be good for a long time if you take care of them." He shifts closer to me; I freeze and have to focus to stay calm.

He hands me his tablet. "What kind of music do you listen to?"

My breathing has slowed, and I try to relax a little. "Everything, but mostly I listen to rock and alternative music, especially during high-stress times. Music relaxes me and calms my anger." He stares at me. That was probably more information than was necessary and I'm fairly certain he doesn't care.

He touches a music app, and it pops up. "I have tons of that kind of music on here. Just tap on the two dots next to the songs you want and select 'Add to Nadalynn.' It will add it to your playlist and at the end, you can sync it to your iPod. If you want anything I don't have, you can use the MP3 app to download it. I have a lifetime membership, and it has everything. You have one hour. Here you can use these," He pauses to hand me blue wireless Beats. *Wow*, he must like listening to music to have such nice headphones. I always wished I could afford something like these. "They're already connected to my tablet."

I slide his headphones over my ears, and he shifts back a little, picking up a book that was next to him, and starts reading. I recognize the cover as a Stephen King book I've read before. It looks like he recently started reading it. Stephen King is one of my favorite authors, but not what I expected he would be reading. "That is a good book." I offer my thoughts.

He glances up at me for a moment and then continues reading. Apparently, he doesn't care for my opinion; it's not like he should. I turn back to the tablet and start scrolling through his music. There is a ton of music, and most of it is rock and alternative. My best guess is that he must like music almost as much as me. He even has a few bands I haven't heard before. My fingers start clicking away adding music to my playlist from his selection, including a bunch from my favorite band which he happens to have a whole heap of.

I'm starting to get uncomfortable perched at the edge of the bed, so I scoot back just a little, so I can cross my legs in front of me. Aerick is still sitting pretty close to me with one leg crossed in front of him, and the other one hanging off the bed as he leans up against the headboard. I don't want to seem rude by trying to get farther away. I'm surprisingly okay with his closeness, so I continue to scroll down through the bands adding a bunch of other stuff and ignoring my body's inherent need to move away.

Once I make it down to the bottom, I scroll back up to see if I've missed anything. Once I'm satisfied with the ones familiar to me, I begin previewing a few bands I've never heard of. Some of them aren't half bad and I decide to add them to the list. Thinking of the song I sang to push myself a few days ago, I wanted to make sure I had it on here too. He doesn't have it on his list, so I open up the other application he told me about, praying they have it. Sure enough, they do, and I download the song adding it to my growing list. After searching, I find two more songs that pop in my head that are good workout songs.

When I'm satisfied with the playlist, I have several hundred songs on my list, and it has been just over an hour. Aerick is usually very punctual. I'm surprised he didn't stop me, but as I look over, he seems lost in his book.

He looks different, a little younger, more comfortable, not guarded. After a minute, he looks up; I hurry and look down, blushing that I got caught staring at him yet again. He continues to look at me like he's waiting for an explanation.

"I'm finished," I say quickly.

He breathes deeply, picks up a cord that is next to his leg and plugs it into the top of his tablet, then picks up my iPod that is sitting between our legs and plugs it in the other end. "Go into your playlist and click the sync icon." I numbly do as he says, trying to ignore the strange feeling building in the pit of my stomach as he watches me. It starts syncing, displaying a message informing that it will take several minutes.

He reaches over to take his tablet and when I freeze again, so does he, his facial expression turning confused. Breathing deeply, I push through it and thrust his tablet toward him with a little more force then necessary. As I shove it toward him, he breaks out of his thoughts and grabs the tablet; he starts takes it looking through my playlist. "Only three songs... huh."

My head is buzzing, and it takes me a second to realize what he means. "What can I say? You have good taste in music." My forced casual tone is ruined by the edge in my voice.

He's quiet for a minute, in a silent debate with himself. "So, are you going to tell me why you don't like to be touched?" My body stills, and nervousness starts to build in my chest.

My eyes fall to my feet and my fingers start playing with my shoelace. "I just don't like it." I take long, deep breaths, trying to stay calm and steady, hoping this conversation doesn't go any further. Unfortunately, I'm not that lucky.

"Have you been that way for a long time?"

Is this really his business? "Since I was about nine. I don't want to talk about it." My chest tightens like there are a hundred bricks weighing it down.

"Does it have something to do with why you freaked out in class on Monday?" *Why is he pushing?* I don't want to talk about this; my breathing is getting shallow despite my attempt to keep it steady. "Are you okay?" His face suddenly changes, and I can't read his emotions anymore.

"Yes," I whisper, but I doubt he realizes it is the answer to both questions.

"You know you need to learn to face your fears. It's part of learning to control your emotions." The tightening subsides a bit, as the anger begins to rise. He has no idea, and he could never understand. Words fail me, so I stay quiet.

"I'm not saying just get over it," he offers after a moment, "you just need to learn to get past them. Start small and work your way up."

"It isn't that easy." My voice sounds so small but it's laced with anger. A look of distaste crosses his face. He probably thinks I'm weak.

"I never said it would be easy. Nothing in life is easy." My head shakes back and forth; he doesn't understand.

I take an exaggerated look at my watch. "I need to go to my counseling session," I lie, giving me a reason to leave.

His voice is suddenly stern, "I don't like it when people lie to me." My eyes fly up to his confused. *How the hell does he know that?* As if reading my mind, he answers me. "I make those schedules, and you have an hour. If you want to leave just say so."

I think he's angry, which just makes me angry. Not just at him but at myself for not thinking of that. He passes them out every morning, of course he knows; but he's the one asking me such personal questions so why is he getting angry?

"I'd like to go now," I manage to say in a level voice. He looks down at the tablet and disconnects the iPod handing it to me.

Quickly, I move to leave. "You know," he says almost amused, "distraction can work too." *What the hell does that mean?* I give him a bewildered look and leave the room.

I'm outside in under a minute and lie on the grass with my eyes closed and turn on my newly acquired iPod, which I'm extremely grateful for right now. *Why does he have to pull my emotions in fifty different directions?*

He's so hard to read and I can't tell if he's mad, sad, pissed, or whatever. It's damn frustrating. My finger finds the volume and turns it up as I try to forget everything around me before I have my visit with the shrink.

✳ ✳ ✳ ✳

Someone is shaking my shoulder; my eyes fly open. Aerick is crouching next to me. "Your counseling session is in one minute."

He stands and without another word, walks toward the gym. I'm watching him, still a little dazed. A noise from somewhere pulls me out of my trance and I look at my watch. He's right; I jump up and run toward classroom A, not wanting to be late for my first session.

I get there just in time, and John is just walking out. "Good luck," he says to me with a wink; I respond with a smile, as much as I can muster at the moment.

Liz greets me by shaking my hand. I'm a little nervous because the last thing I want to do is to talk about my issues with this woman, or with anyone for that matter. We sit down on a couch to the side of the room.

"Today is just basic informational stuff. So try to relax," she tells me. *Yeah right.* I give her a small smile, but if she thinks that is really going to work, she is more stupid than I thought.

We go over my family members, good friends, the school I go to, and friends that I have made here. Nothing that she probably couldn't find out on her own, but when we finish, I'm relieved I didn't have to say much. She walks me out and says goodbye. I've still got some free time; I decide to get my pants, so I can visit Ayla to swap out my clothes.

✻ ✻ ✻ ✻

When I finally make it to bed, I feel accomplished, even if it was a rather confusing day; an emotion that seems to be appearing more and more for me lately. This place is so physically and mentally exhausting. My mind is telling me I have to get through this, but right now I'm not sure how I'm going to do this.

Compared to this place, juvie is a cake walk. What I wouldn't give to do a few months in that place and go – but I know that can't happen now. Besides, the minute I turn eighteen, I'd be sent off to jail, and even though it's not something I'd admit out loud, I'm a little frightened of that. It changes people; I've seen it, and I don't want to go through that.

I must do this. I will do this.

CHAPTER ELEVEN

(Monday, June 8th)

I WAKE UP once again to the alarm going off. I didn't sleep well last night. My mind is so consumed with whether I can make it through this program. I just couldn't sleep, and what little bit of sleep I did get was restless.

But I'm determined to do this, and I'm not going to let anybody mess this up for me, not even Aerick. He was right about one thing; I need to learn to control my emotions. I'm still a little confused about our conversation yesterday, but I can't dwell on it anymore. It is what it is, and I'm sure I will understand, eventually.

We walk out for PT and I realize I just got ready and made my bed without even thinking about it. Things are becoming routine for me. Trent is on the stage as we line up; Aerick comes out of our dorm and stands in front of the stage with the other instructors.

"Dorm A, one of your beds is not made. That will be an extra fifteen minutes." Aerick says, managing to look at everyone but me.

Crap. This is not how I wanted to start off my morning. I look over at Patrick because I'm certain he was the culprit. Being too tired and lost in my own thoughts, I didn't watch to make sure he did it. I'm not his momma; he needs to do things without me having to tell him. The look on his face tells me that my suspicions are correct. Well hell, at least he managed to get up on his own today.

We start stretching and begin our run. It's become a habit for me to take the lead, usually with Aerick in front or beside me; he falls in beside me today. My thoughts are all over the place this morning, and it takes me a lap to realize he's running rather close to me. Ignoring it, I push on.

As we start our fourth lap, I'm starting to slow a bit because of the burn in my legs. "Don't slow down, push through it." His voice low but steady, like this is his first lap. Eying Aerick, he's still looking forward, so shaking my head at his comment and pushing harder, I pace him for the last lap.

We finish our run and resume exercising as I wonder what the hell that was all about. We lie down to do leg lifts, and he stops by my head, looking out at everyone. "Lift, hold, down." I hear Trent hammering out commands, but his voice is in the background because all I can concentrate on is how close Aerick is to me.

On the fourth rep, he looks down and his eyes lock on mine. Instead of looking away, we both just stare at each other as I continue with my leg lifts. Fifth rep, sixth rep, my heart is starting to pound, and I'm not sure if it's because of the exercise or those bluish-gray eyes locked on my own. It's odd how him merely staring at me can feel so intense. No words, no touch, no expression on his face, just the look of his beautiful eyes staring into mine.

Seventh rep, eighth rep. It's even stranger that I'm not at all uncomfortable with his closeness. Ninth rep... as soon as Trent calls "down" on our tenth rep, Aerick breaks our eye contact and continues walking between the other cadets. *Holy Shit*. I try to slow my breathing; it takes a minute to get under control, and it's not from the exercise.

What the hell is his deal now? Why did he just do that and what was the point? I swear he's the most frustrating man I've ever known. We finish up our workout including the extra time. Aerick avoids making eye contact with me the rest of our workout, and I try to focus, but my gaze keeps finding its way back over to him.

We are dismissed and head back to the dorm. As I walk past Brand, he's looking at me with a disapproving look. He must have noticed the exchange between myself and Aerick, but what was it really, and why would he care?

As we get inside, the first thing I see is Patrick's bed still a mess, earning him a well-deserved punch in the arm as I walk by him. "Seriously, you really need to get your shit together." Even though I'm frustrated with him, I'm still smiling because it's hard to be mad at him.

"Sorry." He apologizes with his signature smirk.

I change out of my tank top into a tee shirt, and we go to breakfast. I take my seat as the others go to get their food. Again, I feel like an errant child having my food served to me. My only hope is that he doesn't plan on continuing this the whole time we're here.

Looking around, Aerick isn't in here yet. For a short moment, I debate whether or not to just get my own, but using my better judgement, I decide it is a more suitable idea to to not irritate Aerick. The idea of not ending up at the bottom of the rankings is a good motivator not to piss people off this week. I'm startled when I feel John sit down next to me where Aerick usually sits.

He smiles at me, "Hey."

I try to give him a convincing smile to be polite, but the truth is I'm not comfortable with him sitting so close. "Hi. What's up?" My interactions with John so far have been limited since we got here, but he seems okay.

"Not much. It was kind of nice having a quiet day yesterday. I got to read something that was actually interesting for the first time since I got here."

"Yeah, that's how I feel about music. That was great to be able to put in my ear buds and block out the rest of the world; especially here." He looks down, and I get the impression he's nervous about something.

"So, what book are you reading?" I hurry and ask, trying to keep the conversation from turning weird. It seems to work – he perks right up.

"It's a Robert Jordan series. I'm on the fourth book. You ever heard of him?"

The name is familiar, one of my teachers has a soft spot for the author and has suggested his books a few times. "Yes, but I've never read any of his books. I tend to lean more toward horror books."

He raises his eyebrow at me. "Really? I pegged you more as a music girl."

My chest rumbles as I try not to laugh too loud. Most people probably see me that way. "I actually love to read. Living in a house with only one TV and no cable, it's a lot easier to take a book up to the roof and get lost in it, but music is my outlet. It tends to keep my emotions in check, especially when I'm mad or upset. I guess you can say it's my go-to hobby, but it depends on my mood."

"That's cool. So, who is your favorite author?"

"Definitely Stephen King. I love his books; I think I've read just about all of them." My words fall off at the end as I feel someone step up behind me.

"You're in my seat, cadet," Aerick tells John in his intimidating tone. It's overkill, but with Aerick it is no surprise. Everything he does these days is a conundrum. John looks up; his face goes from shocked to disappointed as he realizes it's Aerick.

He gets up without argument, "I'll talk to you later." He walks over to the other table since ours is pretty much full of everyone in my dorm.

Aerick sits close beside me and sets my plate in front of me. "Eat!" He sounds pissed, and I have no idea why.

What did I do now? He turns to me with annoyance on his face, and it occurs to me I must have said that out loud and apparently, it's not a good idea to question him. My eyebrows pull together; I don't understand why he's irritated this time.

He takes a deep breath and turns back to his own food. "Just eat, alright." *Breathe.* Apparently, both of us can't be happy at the same time. Then again, I don't know if Aerick is capable of being happy.

Jeff is sitting across from me and shakes his head slightly before going back to eating his food. Patrick is sitting next to me and leans in to whisper, "Apparently, I'm not the only one that likes to sit next to you."

I shove his arm. "Shut up, jerk." He laughs, and my face breaks into a wide grin.

All the sudden I feel Aerick's leg lean up against mine and my face falls. *Why is he touching me?* He doesn't move, and I get the impression his touch is no accident.

"You okay, Nadi?" Patrick asks and I look at Aerick quickly, then turn to my food.

"Yeah, I um, I'm fine," I stutter out and begin eating quickly. I see Aerick's lip twitch out of the corner of my eye, but I don't look at him. *What the hell?* He's doing this on purpose. Does he think it's funny to make me nervous? If he only knew, he would think twice about his actions; or, now that I understand him a little better, maybe not.

He doesn't move his leg for the entire meal, but the moment I finish, he gets up and leaves. If there is an explanation for what just happened, he clearly isn't going to share it.

* * * *

After I finish cleaning up from lunch, I go out to the courtyard where almost everyone is hanging out as they wait for our afternoon classes. Jeff is lying on his back listening to my iPod with his eyes closed. I walk over his stomach and flop down between him and John.

"Damn girl, you're going to kill me," he says, clutching his stomach and trying to convince everyone it actual hurt.

"Whatever, I'm not that heavy!" He smiles back, ruining his chance at really convincing anyone. "So, what are you guys doing?"

Patrick looks up me. "We were just taking bets on how long it's going to take for you to get in trouble again," he smirks, but then when I look at John, Mike, and Huck they have the same look. It's apparent they were indeed talking about me, but whether-or-not that's what they were saying is beyond me.

"Really, and who thinks I will last the longest?"

John speaks up. "Oh, that would be me. I give you two days."

Everyone starts laughing.

"Glad I amuse you guys, but you better stop talking about me behind my back before I make sure that I get in trouble for punching one of you."

They all laugh even harder. "I'm serious..." I back hand Patrick hard in the arm to prove my point, but the smile on my face says I'm still joking around.

"Okay, okay, just don't hit me again!" He rubs his arm.

Everyone looks up to something behind me, telling me someone's there. "Nadi, I need to speak to you for a moment." I'm surprised to hear that Brand is the one behind me and my head whips around.

He looks uncomfortable; I'm afraid he saw my exchange with my friends and I'm now in trouble. He's not talking, so I assume he didn't want to say it in front of everyone. I get up, a little saddened that maybe the boys weren't too far off, but I was joking. They knew that – no need to get in trouble for joking around. I follow him several yards away and he turns back around facing me.

"How are you doing here?" His question surprises me.

"Um... fine."

"I just wanted to make sure you're okay after what happened last week. Aerick tends to go a little overboard sometimes, and he seems to have taken a particular interest in making your life here harder than most." I'm not sure why he is telling me all this. "If you feel Aerick is unfair to you, compared to the others, you need to say something to Luther."

"I... um... I'm okay. It isn't anything I can't handle." My gaze falls to my feet, and my hands twist together. Aerick really isn't being unfair to me. I mean, I do have a big mouth, which tends to get me in trouble. Nothing I'm not already used to.

"Okay, but I want you to understand that it is an option. Aerick has a reputation for being cruel, and I don't want you to be on the wrong end of that; or if you feel more comfortable you can always talk to me. That's what I am here for." I'm not sure what that is supposed to mean, but it seems he's overreacting a bit. I mean, yes, Aerick can be intense sometimes, and he likes to push me, but it isn't like he picks on me more than the others... *does he*?

"Okay. Thanks for letting me know." My brows pull together as I turn around and walk back to my friends. That was super weird, but now that I'm starting to reflect, it's a little irritating that he thinks I can't handle myself. *Geez, can I ever just stay in a good mood in this place?*

"You okay?" John interrupts my thoughts.

I need to get out of here; I'm not in the mood to deal with everyone. "Yeah, I'm fine. Jeff, can I get my iPod?" He hands it to me and I turn, walking away without another word.

I hear John speaking in a whispered voice, "Is she okay?"

Jeff is quick to speak up. "She will be. She just needs some time to herself. Let her be." I'm grateful, but them talking about me behind my back irritates me more. Shoving my earbuds in, I attempt to block out the world. The song 'Buried Beneath' comes on and I just let it play.

I don't know where I'm going, but as my feet wander aimlessly for a few minutes, they lead me to the gym. No one is here. *Perfect!* I decide to go ahead and take my frustrations out on the punching bag. I don't bother with the gloves, I just walk over to the bags and start beating my frustration out on it.

It makes no sense why it upsets me so much when people doubt me. Learning to block out what people think of me has been part of my life. I like to think I'm strong and most the time people seem to get that, but when people act like I can't take care of myself, it pisses me off. I've spent years building walls trying to deal with what I've been dealt in life. I've had to learn to be strong. I don't want to be that pathetic little girl that feels sorry for herself just because bad shit happened to her. I refuse to let people treat me like a victim. *I will not break!*

As if it's a sign, a song comes on that mirror's my thoughts. I try to empty my mind as my punches fall into a rhythm, and just focus on the words in my head as they seem to have been my theme song for several years.

Listening to the words, it dawns on me that I'm more open with people here than I've been in a long time. I typically only hang out with one or two people, but here I hang out with most of the cadets. I've opened myself up which isn't a terrible thing for most people, but with the good, can come the bad.

I just need to stop letting people get to me. Who cares what they think? This is my life, and I'll live it the way I want to. *Fuck them!*

I'm startled to see something move out of the corner of my vision. I swing around to see that Aerick is standing back against the wall with look of wonder on his face. I yank my buds out of my ears and glower back at him as I realize I'm not sure how long he's been standing there. I stay frozen in place, not saying anything and really, I don't need to.

He stares at me and when he doesn't say anything, I turn back around. This is not the time for his games. My patience is thin and if he isn't going to saying anything, it's better I don't either. With one of my earbuds back in I'm about to continue but am stopped when he grabs my lead hand.

Instinct kicks in and I pull my wrist roughly out of his hand. "WHAT?" My voice comes out much angrier than I intended, and my face is full of frustration.

He stares at me for a minute with his cold, intense eyes noticeably warning me to calm myself down and in no time, I'm lost in them. Then slowly he reaches and grabs my wrist, turning my hand so my palm is down. I'm held in place by his stare and his touch feels like fire on my skin, but my mind is so cloudy, I can't comprehend the strange feeling.

He waits for a second, maybe to see if I'll pull away again and when I don't, he looks down; my eyes still frozen on his face. His eyebrows stitch together in irritation, as he looks back at me. "Is there something you need to tell me?"

Confusion hits me again. I'm not sure why would he ask me

that. He's still holding my wrist but his grip has loosened, and through the clouds the meaning of his words hit like a Mack truck. My eyes follow his down and I bring my other hand up to look at them. The relentless pounding on the bag has made my knuckles bright red; a few have started to bleed.

I was so lost in thought; I didn't occur to me that I was doing it. A dull ache in my hands begins as my sight and mind catch up to each other. The adrenaline pumping through me has left my hands a little numb until now.

I pull my wrist away gently, and he willingly lets it go. I clasp my hands behind my back to get them out of sight. "I'm fine. Just a lot on my mind." I try to sound as casual as possible, but my voice comes out much lower than I wanted.

"Well, next time I suggest you use gloves." He doesn't seem mad, as a matter of fact, he sounds almost understanding, until he speaks up again with his cold instructor voice. "Your next class starts in five minutes; you need to go." I take a deep breath, but don't want my voice to betray me again, so I just nod and walk away.

As my hand reaches for the door, he's suddenly right next to me again. "Wait." I turn my head and look at him. He pauses for a second and confusion crosses his face. "Make sure you stop by the nurse and get your hands looked at." Then he turns and walks away.

Again, he's left me bewildered. *Why does he do that, and why does he care that my hands are cut up?* I mean, I guess it's kind of his job to make sure we are all okay, but again, I don't need him and his overpowering need to treat me like a child. *I can take care of myself.*

✳ ✳ ✳ ✳

I've been questioned a lot this afternoon about my hands from everyone except Jeff and Patrick. They know me well enough to understand that sometimes I just need to let my frustrations out. I'm pretty surprised by how many people noticed to begin with, John being the first one to ask me about it. Each time, I explained that I was okay, but with a tone that said I didn't want to discuss it further. Most people got the hint.

I never did see the nurse since it isn't anything I can't handle. We still have an hour before lights out, and I decide to go for a walk. It's almost dark, but it's a warm night and there's enough light to see where I'm going. I sneak out while no one is paying attention to me.

I go to walk around the path, but I notice Aerick is out there running. *Great.* The last thing I want is to talk to him right now. I resolve to walk on the outside perimeter of the buildings instead. As long as I stick close to them, I'll be well within the borders. So, I walk back behind the buildings at the front of the property. I huff heavily as I realize I've forgotten my iPod, but right now there is no way I'm going back into the dorm to get it.

I start to think about what happened today in the gym. It seems like Aerick has been at the forefront of my thoughts quite frequently these days. He was oddly quiet during our knife throwing class this afternoon, in which he was several minutes late. Then he didn't show up for dinner; Paulo ended up getting my food for me, even though I wasn't hungry. I didn't think much of it except for someone who's so keen on making me eat, you would think he wouldn't skip meals either.

And Brand pulling me aside and warning me today. He almost made it sound like it's a possibility that Aerick would go too far. I suppose I don't know him that well, but I don't fear him as some of the others have admitted to. The feeling I get when I'm around him is more one of intense tension between us. Maybe he doesn't like that I'm not intimidated by him. Most of the others go out of their way to avoid him. That's why what Brand said to me earlier was laughable at best. Aerick is hard on everyone, not just me.

The sound of voices pulls me out of my thoughts. I've made my way to the cabin side of the camp, and one of the back windows is open. It's not my intention to eavesdrop, but I hear Aerick's name and my curiosity is peaked. I come to a stop and listen to Paulo and Terrie's banter inside.

"He is acting a little strange," Terrie laughs. "He came by earlier and told me that she should be stopping by and to let him know if she didn't, but he left before I could question him. She never did, by the way, if you want to pass that along to him."

"He has been a bit off this session. I think she's getting to him more than he likes. I haven't seen him show this much emotion in years, but I'm not sure if it's a good thing or a bad thing.

Sometimes he seems like such a robot, always cold and calculated; but lately, he's more withdrawn than normal, if that's even possible." *Who is the 'she' he's talking about?* There are only four of us girls.

"She is quite popular with the other cadets, and she's a born leader. I think her personality type clashes with Aerick because they have the same mindset. Tia told me she's smart too. Maybe that's the problem; they're *too* alike."

"Let's not forget she's also sort of hot... hey, you didn't need to hit me. I was just stating the facts. You must see how those boys look at her. Maybe he's attracted to her, although that's a stretch – he doesn't like anyone; not like that anyway. I mean, we hang out and all, but that's about it." I almost laugh hearing her punch him.

"I don't know, she seems to have some issues. Those boys may like her, but she clearly doesn't like them in that way. Unlike Leena, who's always throwing herself at them." Her voice gets louder as she near the window and I push myself tighter against the wall. Her voice is full of distaste when she mentions Leena's name. At least I'm not the only one that thinks like that. "It's like she has a barrier around her all the time. When people get too close she moves away, mentally and physically."

"Hey, you want another beer?" Paulo asks, and Terrie moves away from window.

My head is spinning. I don't want to hear anymore, so I continue my walk. *Who are they talking about?* At first, I thought maybe it was Leena, but that theory was shot down. They said someone who's a leader. Karen and Tara are quiet and never speak out, which only leaves me.

Could they be talking about me? Boys don't look at me all the time, and I don't think I'm a leader at all.

My watch indicates there is only twenty more minutes before lights out. It's dark now, but I'm not ready to go back inside just yet. As I get to the last cabin, I decide to sit against the side wall facing the main dorms.

Staring in wonder up at the stars, I'm still trying to understand what they were talking about. I don't know why they would say those things. Paulo saying Aerick may be attracted to me is just laughable at best, and I'm convinced it's unlikely, just as he said. In fact, I'm certain Aerick hates me.

I'm curious what boys they are talking about that always look at me. Patrick and Jeff are like brothers and always look at me, but that's their protective nature. I talk a lot to Mike, Huck, and Royce, especially when Patrick and Jeff aren't around but it's only as friends. John seems like he has been trying to get closer to me lately, but it's because we have shared interests. Steven and Joseph pretty much stick to Leena's side, so I'm certain they either like her, or Karen, or Tara, both of whom have also joined Leena's little click. They must be interpreting things wrong.

The whole thing about keeping space between me and others actually hits dead on; that's just me, it protects me. If people aren't close, they can't touch me. Everyone has pretty much gotten the message and they don't try to push it – well except Aerick. I swear he pushes my boundaries just to make me upset, but it's different with him. It's like he wants me to get mad or irritated. He irritates the shit out of me, but there's something about him that I can't put my finger on.

When he's close to me, I lose my train of thought and all my senses become hyper-aware of him. The usual tightening isn't there, but I do find it hard to breathe around him. He doesn't intimidate me, but I feel... I don't know, nervous or something. It's just a weird vibe I get from him, something I've never felt before. It confuses the shit out of me, and that makes me even more irritated.

I hear someone walking between the dorm and the cabin. It's barely light enough, but I can see that it's Aerick; he's shirtless and drenched in sweat. All I can do is stare as my breathing gets heavy at the sight of him. That man has the best-looking body I've ever seen.

He stops around back, next to the instructor's entrance, as he picks up a towel, and a large bottle of water. He takes a long draught, then pours the rest over his head. He puts the towel around his neck, holding both ends, and stares up into the sky. He must not know I'm here and I would rather he didn't know I was sitting here staring at him. He stands there for a few more minutes looking into the sky just like I had been doing a moment ago, then he looks at his watch and dries himself off quickly as he goes inside.

Wow. Despite Aerick's asshole nature, he sure is mighty fine to look at. I momentarily wonder if I'd ever be able to deal with such strong arms around me, loving and comforting me. The thought saddens me because I really don't think so. I shouldn't think of him like that anyway because it would never happen, not with him. My watch flashes a warning that lights out is in a few minutes, so I get up and rush into the dorm, ignoring everyone's looks of wonder. Without much thought of my actions I quickly dress for bed and lie down.

CHAPTER TWELVE

(Thursday, June 11th)

I'M STARTLED AWAKE by noise. A peek at my alarm informs me it's only three-ten in the morning. I turn to the sound that awoke me and see Mike is up, fully dressed, and tying his shoes.

He glances at me as I prop myself up on my elbows. "You okay, Mike?"

"I'm all right, go back to bed," he whispers to me as he starts toward the dorm door.

"Where are you going?"

He pauses, turning back to me for a moment. "I'm tired of this place, so I'm out. I have a friend over in Ellensburg that will come get me."

I'm not sure what to say to him, but part of me is screaming to try to stop him. "Mike, I don't think that's a good idea. They told us they have security measures."

He smiles at me, but it doesn't quite reach his eyes. "Come on; they just say that shit to scare us. Yeah, they may be able to track us, but by the time they know I'm gone, I'll be able to get out of town and I'll get this stupid bracelet off."

Something tells me it's not going to be that easy. "I don't know. I'll keep quiet, but they give us a lot of breathing room here. I don't think they would do that if they weren't a hundred percent confident we wouldn't be able to get away."

He thinks about it for a beat and shakes his head. "I'll be alright."

"Okay, well good luck," I say hesitantly. He slips out the door, making sure to close it quietly behind him. I jump up and run over to watch him through the window on the door. I have a bad feeling about this.

He gets about five feet from the front of the dorm, and my heart stops when he stops. "Ouch," I hear him say as he rubs the wrist that has the tracker.

What just happened? He recovers after thirty or forty seconds and starts to run again, but he only gets a few more steps before he slows down to a sluggish pace and starts swerving from side to side. He almost looks drunk. After stumbling a few seconds, he drops to his knees and then flops on his back.

Holy shit. What the hell just happened? Is he okay? Is he dead? I try to look closer, but it's hard to see. I'm not sure, but his chest doesn't seem to be moving. Fear spreads throughout my body and I have an overwhelming need to see if he is okay, but the fear of it happening to me keeps my feet planted behind the door.

Apparently, they weren't lying. The tracker must have something in it, and they must have been serious about the security measures. They wouldn't kill him, would they? I mean, none of our offenses are terrible or anything. I'm so freaked out right now.

Two figures run around the corner, slowing to a walk, and I duck my head lower to make sure they can't see me. Both men are wearing only shorts; it looks like Aerick and Brand. They must have been alerted somehow and jumped out of bed to respond.

"There's always one," Brand says. "Surprised it took this long though; usually it happens the first week."

"Check his pulse," Aerick demands.

Brand bends down and holds his fingers to Mike's neck. "He's good. Worked like a charm, as always."

"Let's get him to the infirmary and then you can go get Terrie," Aerick says, and they bend down to pick him up together.

"Why can't it ever be a girl? They're so much lighter," Brand huffs.

"Stop whining, you sound like a *girl*. Let's just get this done. Thanks to this little maggot, I'm going to have an early start today." I see them walk off with Mike, one holding his arms and one holding his legs.

Once they're out of sight, my body begins to tremble, and my legs finally give out. I can't believe that just happened. I'm not even sure what I saw. I look down at my bracelet and wonder what could be in it.

I try to feel under it, but it is pretty tight. I manage to get my pinky under and feel around. My stomach drops when I get to the underside of my wrist. There's a small hole there. It must have a needle inside that injects us with something—but what? *Fuck. What did I get myself into this time?*

I move slowly back to my bed and sit, leaning back against the headboard. Wrapping my arms around my legs, I lay my head on my knees. My mind is reeling. Man, I hope he's okay. Brands words could have meant anything. Mike is a good guy and doesn't deserve to die or anything like that. I'm starting to understand why they send kids here when Juvie doesn't work. This place is cruel. A single tear stains my cheek despite my best efforts to keep it in.

Aerick walks in, closing the door quietly, and I look up. I'm not sure how long I've been sitting here, staring at nothing, trying to keep my mind empty so I don't have to process what happened, but my bottom is numb and hurts so it must have been a while. He stops at the end of my bed and I look at him. Tears still threaten to spill over, but I don't want to give this cold bastard the satisfaction. It's bad enough I can't keep the fear off my face. He stares into my eyes, and it calms me the slightest bit.

He looks down for a second and whispers coldly, "He will be all right." He looks at me again quickly and then turns, walking into the bathroom. I release a breath I didn't know I was holding as relief floods into me.

155

Thank God it wasn't as bad as I feared, but I still wonder how bad it is. The clock reads four twenty-five, and I know I cannot fall back asleep. My head lays back down on my knees, this time with a sense of relief, but I'm still worried. After a few minutes, it occurs to me that he just implied I knew what was going on. *How did he know I saw it?*

My eyes are drawn to the red dot in the corner of the room. *Cameras!* They must have cameras in all the rooms. I've seen that light in the bathroom too. He must have checked to make sure no one else was going to try to escape. Funny, but that doesn't make me feel any safer. It seems like an invasion of my privacy, but it isn't like they don't do that in Juvie too. I just can't believe it took me so long to figure it out. I had seen that red dot before, but I didn't put two and two together.

Lost in thought, I barely notice when the alarms go off. I get up without really thinking about what I'm doing and throw on pants and a sweater.

I'm making my bed when Huck asks, "Where's Mike?"

I'm still not a hundred percent sure what happened or what I should say, but I'm going to have to say something. "I'll tell you after PT."

Concern covers Jeff's face as he looks me up and down. "Is he okay?" Jeff asks.

"I hope so," is all I can get out. I finish making my bed, tell Patrick to make his, and we head out the door.

When I finally get the courage to look up, I stop dead in my tracks. Mike's already standing in formation, and he looks completely okay. Whatever they did, he recovered from it quickly. I'm so shocked I don't even notice when Huck grabs and starts tugging on my wrist. "You okay?"

I shake my head 'yes' and look at his hand which he immediately withdraws from my wrist. "Sorry, you just looked a little dazed there." Following everyone else, we line up and I attempt to clear my head.

The instructors are on Mike hard today. 'We boring you cadet?' 'Get your feet up higher!' 'Get up faster!' 'Your legs seemed fine earlier.'

Understanding hits me that they all know what he did, not just Aerick and Brand, and they all seem irritated with him. The rest of us may as well be invisible because they don't even so much as look at anyone but Mike. The other guys in our dorm keep looking over to Mike and then back at me. I shake my head and it draws the attention of the other dorm too as they stare at Mike, confused. The attention must be the price you pay for breaking the rules.

When we finish, everyone is dismissed except Mike. Aerick escorts him over to the pathway, yelling at him to start jogging, and I pause a minute, watching them. Aerick notices quickly and sends me a glaring dismissal. Shaking my head, I turn and go back inside.

Everyone from both dorms is standing there, and my eyes widen. "What?"

John takes a step toward me, getting too close for comfort. "Come on; we already know you know what happened, so just tell us."

It's no use; I might as well. I walk over sitting on my bed, and everyone spreads out on the various beds, sitting to listen to my story. John follows me and sits at the end of my bed making me feel a little better that he didn't choose to sit too close. I begin to describe what happened this morning, including everything I saw and heard. I also include the bit about thinking the red light is a camera.

John gets up, and I tell him where I see it in our room. The light isn't there during the day, but he goes over to the corner of the room that sits a few feet to the left of the bathroom door. He pulls over the chair from the desk and stands on it, running his fingers along the wall, stopping when he feels something.

He looks closer, "You're right, they are pretty small, but there are two small lenses that sit flush with the wall. One is probably the camera for daytime, and the other is likely night vision." He jumps down. "Well, at least we know."

We continue to talk about what happened, and I'm glad to know everyone is as freaked out as I am. When we go to breakfast, Mike is still jogging, with Aerick pacing him and pounding out insults. It seems he doesn't get to eat, although I would be surprised by that after what happened to me.

We all eat pretty much in silence. Aerick is a piece of work, and I feel awful for Mike. I've been lucky enough not to have to deal with Aerick much since Monday, other than this morning. He's doing that 'keeping to himself' thing again, which makes it a lot easier for me not to get into trouble.

I wonder if he thinks that I had anything to do with the thing with Mike. I hope not, because the last thing I need is his attitude right now. It sucks because I want to talk to Mike, but I'm not sure if he'll be in class. He's still running when we go back to the dorm to get ready for classes.

* * * *

I couldn't talk to Mike in our first class because it was Self Defense and Aerick brought Mike in just as class started. I didn't want to push my luck, and we worked individually today, practicing hitting key pressure points on specialized body-shaped punching bags.

When we're finally dismissed, I pull Mike with me outside. "What the hell happened?"

He looks down in frustration. "I don't know. The last thing I remember is feeling a poke in my wrist under my tracker, and that was it. Next thing I knew, I was in the infirmary with an irritated nurse who apparently doesn't like to get woken up so early. Right before our morning workout, Aerick shows up looking completely pissed, telling me I'll regret it, and then he brought me out to PT."

"So, did you get to eat breakfast?" Nothing he has said really puts me at ease.

"Sort of; Aerick gave me an egg burrito and a bottle of water which he gave me sixty seconds to eat right before class."

Well, thank goodness. At least Aerick had a little sense, but I'm still irritated with him. You would think that what Mike already had to go through would've been enough. "At least it's over," I tell him, starting toward our next class.

His brows pull together and he looks down. Immediately I know it isn't. "What?" I ask, slightly exasperated.

"Well, I have to meet him in the courtyard after classes are over both this morning and this afternoon." You've got to be kidding me. Didn't Aerick get a clue when he ran me into the ground?

"Geez, I'm sorry. Just hang in there, it can't last forever." I sit down next to him and Tia starts talking about Shakespeare, so I turn to pay attention in class.

✳ ✳ ✳ ✳

We're walking to our first afternoon class, and we walk past the middle of the courtyard where Aerick is sitting and watching Mike jog slowly, yelling at him to pick it up. Aerick looks briefly up at me and then back to Mike. I feel sorry for Mike. The day's only half over and he looks burnt out while Aerick just sits there.

Before we walk through the door to the gym, Aerick calls Mike over, handing him a water bottle and some food. I walk into class and wait. Today is knife throwing with Brand's group. Brand has already got the tables set up, and Aerick walks in behind us.

Brand talks about technique a bit before he tells us to practice. I'm next to Mike, and his knives are all over the place. He must be exhausted. Looking around to make sure no one is looking, I whisper to Mike, "Come on Mike, I know you can do this. If you don't try harder, Aerick is going to notice." Mike throws another one, putting a little more energy into it, but it hits handle first on the very edge of the target and bounces halfway back, making a loud noise as it hits the ground.

Within seconds Aerick is right behind him. "That was pathetic, cadet. This is your fourth class, and you still can't get the knife to stick?!" Aerick yells at him.

Mike drops his shoulders even lower. "I'm exhausted; I don't have much strength left."

"I don't want to hear your excuses. You were so brave this morning, thinking you could sneak out of here. You don't look so brave now, you coward."

"I'm not a coward." Mike's voice is small and I'm hoping Aerick didn't hear him, but the look that's materializing on Aerick's face says he did.

"Is that so, cadet?" He looks down right pissed. "Class... knives down." We all stop throwing and lay our knives down. "Well Let's test that theory. Stand in front of your target. Brand!"

Brand steps up next to Aerick looking upset. I take it he isn't happy about this, but he doesn't look surprised by it either. Horror crosses Mike's face. "Move, cadet!" Aerick shouts even louder, and Mike resigns himself and finally moves to stand in front of the target.

"You will stand there while Brand those knives. If you flinch, you'll have another day of extra running."

I can no longer hold back my shock or disgust at the situation. "You can't be serious?" The words are out before I can stop myself and both he and Brand turn toward me. Brand has a dumbfounded look on his face, but Aerick looks more annoyed. I shouldn't be pushing him, but this is ludicrous.

"Hold your tongue, cadet." Aerick's voice is suddenly low and raspy.

I've really pissed him off now, but I can't let this happen. I should have stopped Mike this morning; this is partially my fault. "Standing in front of that target doesn't prove he isn't a coward. Cowards refuse to put themselves in dangerous situations. Just by standing there, he's proven he isn't a coward."

"Is that a fact?" He pauses and just before he speaks, Brand interrupts him.

"How about this; he doesn't flinch and his afternoon running is excused. If he does flinch he runs tomorrow." Brand is trying to give Mike something to work for, but it is in vain.

Aerick looks at him. "I outrank you, and you will do what I say."

Brand shakes his head, "Hey, I was just trying to make it interesting."

I look at Mike, and his eyes tell me everything I need to know. He isn't going to be able to stand still. "I want to take his place; he's too exhausted to make this fair."

They both turn and look at me again, but this time shock is

painted on both of their faces. Several emotions flash across Aerick's face all at once. He looks at Brand then back to me shaking his head slightly. "I have a better plan." A tight smile emerges on his face and my stomach drops. *What did I just do?*

"This is how it's going to work. You and Mike will stand in front of those targets with Brand in front of Mike and myself in front of you. We will throw three knives; the one who is more accurate wins. If Brand wins, I'll let Mike out of his afternoon run. If I win, you will both run after PT tomorrow. If you refuse, he will run all day tomorrow regardless." He looks expectantly at me.

My heart is racing, but there's no way I'm backing down now and giving Aerick the satisfaction. He wants to see if I'm as selfless as I appear to be. He thinks I will back out even if it means that Mike is now in a worse position than he was when he started. So, I turn and head for the target. "Fine."

I turn and see John's face. It's clear he's going to try to intervene, but I got myself into this mess; I don't need anyone to save me. As he takes a step toward Aerick, I give him a hard look and shake my head ever so slightly 'no'. He pauses, and Aerick looks at him looking almost as if he wants him to try something.

When John doesn't continue, he turns back toward me. "Alright, feet shoulder-width apart and hands behind your back just above your ass." We both adjust ourselves, and I whisper to Mike, "You got this."

"I will throw first. Closest to outside of right knee." Aerick stares at me with his cold eyes and I feel the cloudiness that comes with his staring eyes start to set in. I barely noticed he's thrown it until I hear the thud. I look down at the knife that's damn near touching my knee, and a smile spreads across his face. I watch Brand and then glance at Mike. He squeezes his eyes shut, and Brand throws. It hit outside of Mike's knee, but Aerick's is closer.

"Come on Brand, you're not even going to try?" Brand scowls in irritation but doesn't say anything. "Alright, second one closest to the left elbow."

He breathes deeply and focuses himself. Then his gaze finds mine again, and he holds it. I'm lost in his eyes when I hear the knife thuds close to my elbow, but not as close as the last one.

Brand smiles and Mike closes his eyes again. Brand throws his knife, and it's almost touching Mike's elbow. "Looks like we're tied." Brand smirks. Their casual banter makes me believe this is something that happens often. Recalling Brand's warning earlier this week makes my breath become shallow.

"Fine, last throw, the right side of the neck." Aerick smirks and my eyes close in fear. "Oh no, Nadalynn, eyes open and if I were you, I would hold very still." My eyes fly open and meet his. Neck, neck means arteries, which means very dangerous if he even misses his target by an inch.

He's not going to make this easy on me. His face gets very focused. He stares deep into my eyes, and I lose focus of everything in the room except him. His eyes change for just an instant, and I hear the thud, loud and close to my ear. There are barely millimeters between my neck and the knife. Shit! I think

Aerick is going to win this, and the smirk on his face indicates he believes it too.

Brand shakes his head. "Stand still, Mike." Mike closes his eyes once more. Brand throws the knife quickly, and Mike swears as his hand shoots up to his neck. I look over and see a small bit of blood on his fingers that he is now staring at.

Brand turns toward Aerick, "Well Aerick, it appears that I won." He smiles. "You never said we couldn't draw blood."

Anger crawls over Aerick's face, and for a moment it seems he might throw one of the knives at him. "Brand, finish up class," he spits, glancing at me before he goes barreling out the door. *Sore loser.*

Once he is out the door and it closes behind him, I turn to Mike. "You okay?"

Brand comes up beside us and removes Mike's hand from his neck, inspecting the damage. "It's just a little scratch you – will be all right."

"Seriously, you just cut me," Mike says, his pride obviously wounded.

"Be thankful, you little shit. I just got you out of another day of torture; all while you willingly let your friend be offered up to join you. You're a selfish prick."

He turns to me. "And what did I tell you?" I'm at a loss for words; I've never seen him this mad. Everyone else is staring at me now as well.

Ignoring the fact that I still haven't answered, he turns and walks away. "All of you get back to practicing." He stands against the wall, focusing on the knife he still has in his hand, taking deep breaths.

Several people are still looking at me like they want an explanation. "What? He warned me not to push Aerick, that he can be cruel. You would all do well to remember that too." I glance over to Brand; he has a half smile on his face now, although he's still looking down. I walk back to my spot, and everyone else mimics me. I start throwing my knives, trying to focus on the actions and not the fifty other things running through my head, like how stupid my actions really were.

After class Mike comes up and thanks me while several others tell me I was crazy. I smile at them, but my mind is on how Aerick is going to react to what happened in class.

✳ ✳ ✳ ✳

It's been an interesting and exhausting day. I lie in my bed staring at the ceiling, listening to my music as loud as it goes. Drowning out the world, I try to clear my mind before lights out. The next song comes on; I close my eyes and focus on the dark as I tap my foot to the beat of the music.

After the first half of the song, I yank my earbuds out. The damn song is making me think of the very person I'm trying to forget right now.

Jeff looks at me with a raised eye. "You realize you were humming that, right?" I roll my eyes and feel my cheeks get warm. "Hey, I don't mind, you're pretty good. I've always told you that.

Besides, that's an awesome song." I'm too distracted lately.

"He's right you know, on both counts," Huck adds his two cents, and I'm completely uncomfortable, but thankful they're the only two in the room. Well, Mike's in the room, but he's already asleep and everyone else is off somewhere else. It's almost lights out, so I hurry out of the room to brush my teeth.

I take my time brushing my teeth and splash water on my face, praying for some restful sleep after today's events. I walk back in the room, and everyone has returned since lights out is any minute now. Just as I lie in my bed, the lights go dark.

"Goodnight, our fearless and brave leader."

"Fucking shut, up Patrick," I tell him annoyed, but I can't help but smile as everyone laughs and says good night.

* * * *

I wake up covered in sweat. I knew this would happen and I detestation those dreams. This time it was a little different because all I heard was the thud of the knives next to me. In the dream, everything was dark, and I couldn't see anything. Then the thuds morphed into the sound of boots walking down the hall, and I knew what was coming.

I try to shake off the tightening in my chest. The clock shows it's just before midnight. I get up and go into the bathroom to use the toilet even though I don't need to; it's just needing get up and move. I wash my hands and lean on the sink wishing I could control this; what I wouldn't give to sleep without dreams.

I splash some water on my face and take deep breaths to wash away the remaining nausea lingering in me. I feel him before I see him. I stand up straight, and my head almost hits his face. He's so close without actually touching me.

My eyes meet Aerick's in the mirror. He has a half smile on his face, and his gaze is locked on mine. "Is the fearless and brave leader, not so brave and fearless in her dreams?" I'm frozen in place wondering what the hell he's talking about.

Suddenly I remember before bed and realize he must have seen it, not just seen it but heard it. "Can you say stalker?" My voice is not as sturdy as I intended, seeming small compared to his smooth voice.

"What? Are you saying you don't like it?" I shake my head not trusting my voice.

His lip twitches. "I think you're lying to me," he whispers.

He looks down at my shoulder and moves his fingers down my arm so lightly they're barely touching me. I breathe in deeply at the contact as I yearn for more. "Hmm... yeah, you're lying to me." I close my eyes, trying to keep my breathing steady. I feel him pull the hair back off my neck, but I can't bring myself to open my eyes. I feel him lean in close to my ear. "Better get to bed before trouble finds you."

His voice is so hot against my ear as he lingers for just a second and then I suddenly feel a cold breeze and all his warmth is gone. I open my eyes, and he's vanished. My hands grasp the sink as I try to regain my center. *How the hell did he do that?* It was the most intense feeling. Something so deep, I've never felt it before.

In a bit of a daze, I go back into the room and lie down. The red light out of the corner of my eye draws my attention, and I turn to stare at it. Something deep in me says he's watching me trying to get myself under control. He did that on purpose to try and break me, and he did just that. I'm suddenly pissed off. I know he doesn't actually have feelings for me so why work me up like that? It's truly cruel.

On the other hand, I've never been able to let a guy touch me like that and not freak out. Even Patrick and Jeff have to be careful about how and when they touch me. But what just happened… I don't even know. I was so caught up in the moment; I didn't have time to panic. It was almost liberating, and for that I'm grateful.

"Thank you," I whisper, still staring at the camera. I turn over and cry myself to sleep, not out of anger but out of equal parts of joy and sadness because it felt truly joyous to be free from my fears, even if it was only for a few moments; but it's also saddening because it isn't likely to ever happen again.

CHAPTER THIRTEEN

(Friday, June 12th)

Aerick POV

FUCKING HELL! LOOKING at her on the camera, I try to process the words she just whispered. I am thoroughly confused now.

Confusion seems to have become the norm lately. I shake my head, thinking about the last few weeks. My emotions have been all over the place, and I don't like that. It makes me weak and it all stems from her.

I have spent years building up my walls to keep my emotions under control. I have always had so much anger in me. Anger at my father for never showing me love and always pushing me to be the best, no matter the cost. At my mother for always being exactly like him. At my older brother for always being better than me at everything, gaining all the praise from my parents and throwing it in my face. I never heard the words 'sweetie' or 'love' or 'good job.' It was always, 'not good enough,' 'man up,' 'you're not trying,' 'only the best is acceptable in this house.' At one point my father made it clear that I was worthless and a mistake because my mother's birth control failed. All I ever knew was that I had to be perfect at everything I did.

That's why my job is so perfect for me. This job takes someone committed, someone who understands, someone who doesn't take any shit from little runts that got themselves in too much trouble and now must pay the price. *I did my time.*

For a while I let my anger get out of hand. Every once in a while, I would get into a fight at school, but it was never terrible and I usually let the kid beat me up because the physical pain helped numb the emotional pain; that was until the last time it happened. I ended up putting a boy from school into the hospital for teasing me.

He had been picking on me for years because I was that quiet, smart kid that other kids picked on, but that day I just snapped. It took a group of people to pull me off him, and that was before I even learned to fight. It was then I realized I had a problem holding it all inside; although, to this day I still believe the guy deserved it.

These kids are usually all the same as I was and when they leave here, I have often taught them what it means to work hard and control themselves, so they can be productive in society. But she, she is different. She is a conundrum. She is strong, a leader, smart, and a smart ass, but there is something she keeps deep inside her that I am still trying to figure out. She insists on always pushing me and I have made it a point to push her back, sometimes a little too hard. Most people only push me once and learn their lesson but not her, and what's worse is this girl has absolutely no sense of self-preservation.

When I made her run last week, I was stunned when she passed out on me. I knew she wasn't eating or drinking enough, but I never expected her to push herself that far. I hated that gut wrenching feeling that settled in my stomach as she collapsed in my arms. So many emotions passed through me.

I felt like I had failed as an instructor. I should have known her limits; it is my job. Terrie, Luther and even Brand were all sure to point that shit out to me. Part of our job is to protect the cadets and what I did was dangerous, really dangerous, but I let the need to teach her a lesson get in the way of common sense. I actually felt fear that she wasn't going to be okay.

Sitting there just watching her lie on that bed, the IV in her arm, I felt like I would break if she didn't wake up. To be responsible for hurting her, I couldn't have that shit on my conscience. I didn't like that feeling, and it took several trips to the gym that day to work off my frustration.

It isn't even just that. I feel so protective of her, and I have no idea why. Ever since that day in self-defense class, the look she gave me, it reached something deep inside me. I don't like these feelings, but I am also having a hard time bringing them to a halt. Just when I think I have them under control, she pulls some shit like she did today.

I admire her courage, but the way she puts herself in danger for others is not smart. She is truly selfless, but it's a dangerous game. I didn't think she was going to step up to that target, and once again she proved me wrong; it pissed me off. I wouldn't hurt her, but for just a moment before throwing that first knife, I thought about cutting her knee just to teach her a lesson. Then that look in her eyes, there was no way I could do it.

It took all my self-control to throw that knife on target because when she looked at me I didn't want to throw it at her at all and it started to show when that second knife was several inches from her elbow. I think Brand knew it too, egging me on like he was. We have done this same thing many times before, mostly so I could prove a point to a mouthy cadet or teach someone a lesson. Brand's skill is damn near equal to mine, but when I went to the last knife, I had begun to lose it. My composure was breaking as my protective nature for her grew, but I couldn't show Brand that she had any effect on me.

Having her look in my eyes wasn't only for her but for me as well. It didn't take long to figure out when camp first started that she freezes when she looks into my eyes, almost as if she is lost, and I needed her to be as still as possible. It also helped me focus better, too. Those cavernous green eyes seem to calm me in the oddest way. My mind cleared, and I could see the point I needed to hit. It was as if we were the only two people in the room as I released the knife and it hit exactly on point. I slowly let out a breath of relief, sure no one would notice, and I felt proud because I was confident I would win this time.

There was no way Brand was getting closer than that, but then he did. In my haste trying to get her to back down and my irritation that she didn't, I forgot to say, 'no drawing blood,' and Brand exploited my mistake. *Fucking bastard.* Not that I should have to say it. The words are more to scare the cadets then actually doing them. Luther would be outright pissed if he knew Brand had cut a cadet on purpose. It's the only reason Luther turns his head when we do things like this. He doesn't mind us using scare tactics but we are strictly forbidden from doing harm purposely. But that didn't stop Brand this time.

He won, and I hate to lose. Nadi needed to pay for making me look bad. It had to be calculated and in the right circumstances. When she got out of bed while everyone else was asleep, including the guys in my dorm, I knew it was my chance.

I put my paperwork aside and went to surprise her. I knew exactly how to rile her up, and it would also answer a question that has been burning in my head. I've been watching her, the way she looks at me. I try to stay away from her as much as possible, mostly to avoid my continual internal conflict, but I still watch. I even noticed on one of the cameras that I was reviewing earlier this week; she had seen me finish one of my runs.

She probably didn't know the camera was there, but my gut told me someone was watching, which is why I checked. I had been shirtless, and it made me smile seeing the look on her face as she stared at me. It occurred to me that she also saw me staring at the stars, something I still love to do, although I would never tell anyone that. She got a glimpse of me people rarely see and never would I show it willingly.

When I entered the bathroom, she had her face down near the faucet and the plan formed in my mind. Quietly, I snuck up behind her, but she quickly stood up straight, like she had felt I was there, and I could only stare into her eyes. It took everything in me not to turn her around and place my lips on hers. Those beautiful green eyes locked on my own, making me feel something I couldn't explain. I tried to empty my head and teased her to cover up my own emotions. After the words had exited my mouth, I had an errant afterthought that made me realize how bad those dreams are and my choice of words may not have been ideal to use as a joke, but thankfully the same thought did not seem to cross her mind.

It only took her a moment to connect the dots that I had been listening earlier. She had been humming a Linkin Park song that I know well. It confused me when she tore the buds out of her ears, looking pissed off. Then her friend had told her that she was humming, and she seemed to look embarrassed. I'd gotten the impression she doesn't like to sing in front of people the morning I saw her coming out of the shower looking embarrassed, but I don't know why, because she has a lovely voice. Apparently humming is a no-go, too.

It's funny she implied I was a stalker when she has no idea

that I had told myself the same thing that night I calmed her from her dream. I'm glad she took the joke and returned it, but her voice was off.

Observing her over the first few days, it was overly clear that she automatically reacts to people touching her. However, I've done it just a little on several occasions without her pulling away. Just like the day I pressed my leg against her in the mess hall, just to see her reaction when I was still testing my theory.

Completely to my surprise she just stayed there – not her normal reaction, but it did please me that she at least paused in surprise. Or when I went to the gym to work out my frustration, and she was there pounding away at the bag. I leaned back against the wall to watch her. Her form is getting better, but that was overshadowed by the fact that she seemed pissed about something. Then my attention was drawn to her hands; she hadn't put her gloves on. I always wear gloves unless I am furious, but for me, it is purely to feel the pain.

I found myself wondering what could have made her so angry and it only took me a second to realize it may have been me. I'd pushed her hard in PT that morning. She is strong, but I decided that she needed a little push to work through her pain. It was to help her. By getting her to look at me, she would forget the burn and push through the exercise. I suppose part of it was also the fact that I like to gaze into her eyes, those beautiful green eyes.

When she finally realized I was watching her punch away whatever frustration she had, she stopped. I hoped she would be finished or at least say something, but she just gave me an odd look and almost started again, until I ceased her movements. The pull to check to see how bad her hands were was too much. At first she jerked away, but I went with my go-to tool to gain her focus, making her look at me.

I was able to take her by the wrist and assess the damage. Her knuckles were beaten raw, to the point a few were bleeding. The confusion on her face told me she hadn't even noticed.

How could she not notice? When I do this shit, it's to feel the pain, because for me it's calming. Otherwise what's the point?

As she began to leave, I had an overwhelming urge to go clean up her hands to at least make sure that she was okay, that she didn't do too much damage, but that would be crossing a line. These feelings that keep rising in me need to be controlled.

Back in the bathroom, I wanted to push her, to irritate her but I was also curious if this control I seem to have over her is due to some misplaced feelings she has toward me. An unmentionable thought, partly because I couldn't understand how she could possibly feel anything but anger towards me. As it turned out, I was right.

I pressed her, teased her, and when she shook her head no, I was sure that she was lying; my traitorous feelings were actually happy about that. Moving my hand slowly down her arm, I could almost hear her heartbeat; her breathing had changed subtly, and she closed her eyes as if trying to calm herself, as a foreign, intense ache appeared in my own chest.

She likes me, and as much as I don't want to admit it, I want her too. I've been such a jerk to her and yet she still likes me. Something I have never seen and can't begin to understand. Without thinking, my fingers moved pulling her hair back off her neck wanting to feel her beautiful skin on my lips.

I could give her so much pleasure if she let me, and I wanted her to. To feel her naked warmth beneath me, to see what she looks like as her orgasm explodes inside her. I felt myself twitch at my wayward thoughts. *Fuck.* Just the thought is almost too much.

STOP THIS NOW! My internal voice screamed, and I stopped myself just in time. I looked up at us in the mirror; I am grateful she hadn't seen my face so full of lust. It isn't right; she's a cadet, she's still seventeen. This isn't even legal, at least not for a few more weeks until she turns eighteen.

But it isn't just that. I can't have feelings for this girl; I can't. It's not in my DNA to care for others. My feelings are pure lust and nothing more. She doesn't deserve to be hurt that way. I whispered in her ear a warning and giving her one last look, I left. I watched her get back in bed and then deliberately turn to look at the camera. She must have known I was watching. Then she whispered a saddened, 'thank you' and my gut dropped to the floor.

What the hell was that? Her words were so full of sadness and she had a sad smile on her face. I am confused as hell, and I don't get it. She turned over and after a few minutes, I heard very quiet sniffles. Watching her more closely, I'm sure she was crying.

What the hell did I just do to her? I fucked up again! The story of my life.

I sit there watching her and after a while, her breathing evens out, and her sniffles die away. She must have fallen asleep. Not knowing why, I shuffle quietly into the dorm. I'm glad to see that she is asleep, as I would be at a loss as what to say if she were awake. I just wanted to see her in person, and my emotions got the best of me.

Tears stain her cheeks and despite my cold heart, I feel ashamed. I sit on the edge of her desk and watch her. She is so strong, but at the same time, she has this fear that makes her so weak. Somehow, I just know it's the source of her pain. The pain I exploited for my own gain.

I make up my mind, determined to figure out what it is. It would be easy if I was able to access Nadi's counseling sessions, but they are confidential, and I don't have access to that. That just means I'll have to be even more clever to find out. She needs help and I will be the one to help her, but she needs to realize I am not the one for her. I don't have a heart. Love is not in my vocabulary.

I look over to the clock on her night table. I have been sitting here for almost an hour. I need some sleep or I'm going to be dragging tomorrow. I get up, but before walking away, I pull back a section of her hair that has fallen over her face. She smiles and murmurs my name.

For a moment, I think she has woken up and freeze, but her

breaths are still even, her eyes closed, and she doesn't move. When I am convinced she is just talking in her sleep again, I hurry back to my room. I can't say I'm not curious to the reason why I'm in her dream. Maybe I need to figure that out as well.

I gather up my paperwork and put it on my desk, deciding to finish it tomorrow; it's already late. It isn't like the other guys here ever get their paperwork done on time anyway. I turn off the music player that is still playing and put my headphones away. I'd been listening to her playlist that is still on my tablet; she does have good taste in music. I've gotten rather attached to the two songs she downloaded and have wondered if she relates to them as I do to the music that I listen to.

Lying down, I turn toward the tablet; I need to figure out the best way to do this. If I push her too hard, it may be too much for her, but if I'm too soft, people will notice. I try to focus on her steady breaths and clear my mind. The word 'stalker' crosses my thoughts again, and a smile spreads across my face as I fall asleep.

CHAPTER FOURTEEN

(Sunday, June 21st)

I LOOK AT the date on today's schedule and realize that my birthday is a week away. I've yet to decide if I should be happy or sad. Legally, I will finally be an adult, but on the other hand, I'm stuck here with nothing to do and no way to celebrate. *This sucks!*

At least I managed to stay out of the bottom of the rankings this week. My little stunt the week before resulted in mess hall duty and bathroom cleaning. I guess they couldn't ignore my mouth anymore. It sucks cleaning up after a bunch of guys, and I don't want to go through that again. I made it my mission to behave this week, which wasn't too hard since I didn't have Aerick pushing me so much and nothing really happened. I didn't get the top two, but that's okay with me. I was happy for Jeff though, who did get into the top two today.

I wait for the guys to finish up and we slowly walk to

breakfast. As we enter the mess hall, Aerick is already sitting down and my food is in front of my usual seat. I sit down and start eating, not waiting for the others.

This last week has been a bit weird. Since our little encounter in the bathroom, Aerick hasn't said more than two words at a time to me. Though, I do catch him looking at me more often than before. Many times, he's behind everyone, just staring at me while he pulls on his lip.

I've been processing an impressive array of emotions myself this week. Denial, anger, joy, sadness, and acceptance. I feel like I'm getting over some crazy addiction. His withdrawn attitude tells me that what he did was out of pure revenge. He knows how to hit my core, but it still doesn't explain his distant actions this last week or why he keeps staring at me like he's solving a complicated puzzle. He even went a little easier on everyone else but not by much. I wonder if he's trying to figure out another way to torture me.

I feel stupid for feeling the way I did. I would have said it was all lust, but after that night it's apparent that wasn't the case. When I went back to bed, I cried myself to sleep, and then dreamt of him. I heard the boots again, but before they could reach me, Aerick was there beside me. He pushed my hair out of my face and I felt his warmth, his calmness, almost like he was my protector. It was a stupid thought; a crazy dream. After that, I fell into a deep dreamless sleep.

I was so groggy the next morning; I had a hard time getting

out of bed. Not to mention, trying to figure out if the night before had actually happened. That was put to rest quickly when I ventured out to PT, and Aerick looked at me with a sly smile before putting on his instructor facade.

I thought about talking to him, but I could never find the guts to do it, and what would I say anyway – 'Hey, you're hot and I like you.' Seriously, he's my instructor, and there's no way he did what he did out of anything other than to mess with me.

To rub it in more, at every single meal this last week he presses his leg against my own and watches my reaction. I've learned to stop freezing every time he does it, but at first, it was like a slap in the face, bringing back all the feelings from that night. I can only hope that one day I'll find someone who I can let get this close to me. For now, I've just learned to accept it and enjoy the closeness, even if it is one-sided. I'm startled from my thoughts by Aerick's voice.

"You know I am surprised you haven't asked to download some more music on your iPod. You could probably fit another fifty or so songs on that thing." He sounds oddly casual, like it's something he's expected me to do.

I remember he told John he could get more books, but it never occurred to me to get more music. "I didn't know that was a choice," I say, mimicking his tone. In the back of my mind, I'm surprised he said a complete sentence to me for the first time in more than a week, but I don't let it show.

"You can come by after lunch if you'd like." With a sour look on my face, I wonder what his plan is this time. He doesn't do things without a motive; this much I've learned about him.

His voice suddenly gets quiet, so we are the only ones that can hear. "I promise to behave." He then gets up and leaves the mess hall, leaving me speechless yet again. My mind starts pounding through the 'yes or no' outcomes. I'm not sure whether I should go. Something tells me this is a trap, but part of me wants to go and see.

Not to mention, I really could use some more music. I've thought of some more songs I would like to download, but I don't want to think about that right now. I'll decide late; right now I just want to finish my breakfast.

I retrieve my iPod and the homework I have left and make my way to the courtyard to work on it just like everyone else. We've been pretty lucky to have good weather almost the entire time we've been here. It's rained a few nights and been cloudy for a few days, but that's it. It's also nice and warm everyday, no matter what the weather, which is how I like it. I never did like Chicago's chilly climate. I hear that it's usually nice up here during the summer, but it's unusual for the good weather to start this early in the year.

I find a pleasant spot on the soft grass and settle in, determined to get as much done as I can this morning. My date with the shrink is right before lunch, and I'm not looking forward to it. Last week she managed to touch the very surface of my anger issues, and it's only a matter of time before she starts trying to get me to say the reason behind it. Damn straight I'm going to do my best not to have to tell her. I've put it behind me and the last thing I want is to have to talk about it. Thoughts begin working their way to the front of my brain. Not wanting to think about that either, I turn up my music and lose myself in my homework.

* * * *

A shadow looms over me, and I look up to see Aerick staring at me expectantly. I pull out my earbuds and he squats down next to me, resting his elbows on his thighs, so he's almost at eye level. "I won't be at lunch today; you can dish yourself up. I'm offering you a little freedom, so don't give me a reason not to do it again."

I'm delighted, and I can't help myself. "So would you consider letting me dish up every meal?" I smile sweetly at him, hoping he will see my natural charm and give into my request.

He gets what is almost a smile on his face. "Let's try this meal for now; I can't let you get away too quickly." He gets up and leaves as I roll my eyes – at least I tried. It is only a few minutes until my counseling block, so I pack up my stuff and head to my session with the shrink.

Once there, the door is already open, so I go in and sit down. She's a nice person, but I dislike that I know her intended goal. Despite the irritation, I tell myself to play nice.

"Hi, Nadi. Great to see you again."

I give her a tight smile. "Hello."

"So how was your week?"

The question makes me think. It seems like a pretty average

week, other than the fact that I'm here. "Actually, it was okay. I didn't get into any trouble."

She jots something down before looking at me again. "I want to pick up where we left off last week. We have established that one of your triggers is touching."

I just nod my head. I don't want to go down this road. "So, can you describe exactly what happened the last time. The one that ended in you being sent to this camp. I specifically want to know your thoughts and feelings during the incident."

I roll my eyes because besides my feelings, this is in the police report. The cops weren't too keen on asking my feelings when they arrested me, but at least it will draw this out a bit to cover this session, and I can avoid getting closer to the inevitable. I start at the beginning of the school day and the gossip that had been going around.

When I finish telling my story she ponders her next question for a moment. "So what bothered you more, the gossip or the fact that he touched you?"

Shit. Here we go. I take a deep breath and look down to my knotted fingers. "Him touching me."

"And is there anyone you don't mind touching you?" My thoughts immediately picture Aerick.

I'm not going there. "A few of my close friends, and my family." I don't want to go into why I can handle Aerick touching me because really, I'm not completely sure myself.

"And that's it?" Her eyebrow is raised, suggesting she doesn't

186

believe me. *Crap.* I just nod my head, not wanting to answer out loud.

"Okay." I can tell she still doesn't believe me, but it occurs to me that she may not think I'm lying about another person – rather she's in disbelief that I only allow a few people to touch me. That can't possibly be a rare condition.

She's about to ask another question when I look at my watch. "Well, it looks like our time's up." I jump up, smiling that I made it through yet another week. I catch her rolling her eyes as I walk out and then she shakes her head, writing down a few more notes.

I hurry back to the courtyard where everyone is wrapping up their work for lunch. "How did it go?" John asks.

"It was okay. Just talking about a bunch of shit I don't care about."

He laughs. "I know how you feel."

Jeff walks out of the dorm with a red iPod. "You got it already, huh?" I ask him.

"Yep, just finished downloading the music. It was pretty easy, I just copied your playlist and added a few more bands." He has a huge smile on his face that's contagious. I smile back, grabbing his arm as we walk to lunch.

When we get into the lunchroom, I follow them to the line. Jeff gives me a curious look. "I'm on probation. Apparently, prince charming has other obligations."

The guys around me laugh, and we all get our food. We get chicken salad for lunch with fruit, one of my favorite things here.

As it turns out, the food here is pretty decent, other than the ridiculous amount of protein we eat, but it sure has done something for my figure.

My stomach has begun to show muscle tone and is much leaner than it used to be. In fact, my whole body has changed, even if it's only slightly. From my arms and shoulders all the way down to my calves, my while body is more defined. I can only imagine what I'll look like at the end of these four months.

I see now why all the instructors are so fit. Even the other staff members join our PT in the morning, minus the instructors in their faces. They just fall in behind us; often I don't notice them until we finish up. The girls seem to walk around the path a lot as well, and I'm always seeing people in and out of the gym or walking the trails. If I weren't a cadet here, I would say this isn't a bad place to be.

We're sitting around eating, and everyone's talking about playing a soccer game after dinner. Huck managed to get to the top last week and chose sports entertainment. The guys have been throwing the football around all week. I agree to play; soccer sounds fun since it's mostly a non-contact sport. I played for several years in the past and was good at it.

After lunch, we all gather back in the courtyard. The guys are still talking about the game that we're planning later, and almost everyone's playing, which gives me an idea. I excuse myself and go to Luther's office; I'm happy to find he's there.

"Luther sir, do you have a minute?" I ask him. This is a stretch, but it can't hurt to ask. I haven't really talked to Luther since I have been here and when I did it was more one-sided, but he seems reasonable.

He looks rather surprised to see me, like it isn't normal for us to just show up in his office; but he smiles, putting me a little more at ease. "Sure. Come in and please sit down." I sit in the chair in front of his desk. "What's up? Is everything alright?"

I smile, trying to build my confidence, "Yes, everything's fine." He visibly relaxes a bit. "I was just wondering. Since it's mostly a free day today, I know it probably isn't a typical thing, but are you open to changing up our PT for this evening?"

He smiles widely, and I wish I knew what was going through his head as my nerves start to tighten. "You're right, it is not something that is typical, but I'm interested to know what you're proposing."

I try to organize my thoughts before I began speaking. "Well, the thing is, we were all interested in a soccer game but we only have a limited amount of time after dinner, and it's the only time we would all be able to play. I was wondering if we could have a full-on game instead of PT."

He raises an eyebrow. "Well, that is definitely a first, but to be honest, it isn't a bad idea. I am quite surprised you could pull everyone together. I don't have a problem with that, but if you don't mind, I would like to bring Aerick in here and get his take on this. I wouldn't want to step on his toes."

Of course I mind, but I'm not going to tell him that. I give him a tight nod, and he lets out a small, uncomfortable laugh as he takes out a cell phone and calls Aerick asking him to come to his office. That's weird; I didn't even know they carried those – I haven't seen one since I've been here.

"What's up, Luther?" Aerick asks as he walks through the door a few moments later. His eyes land on me in surprise. He looks back at Luther and I think he might be worried, but it's so hard to tell what is going through his head. "Is everything alright?"

I put on a fake smile for Luther's sake, and he seems to relax slightly. *What's up with everyone getting so tense when they see me?*

"Yes, everything is fine. Nadi here had an excellent idea, and I would like to run by you."

"Is that so? What kind of idea?" His voice is almost amused.

"Well, she thinks it would be a good idea to have a soccer game tonight in place of the usual PT; I, for one, believe that it is a great idea." Luther stares at him expectantly.

Aerick seems a little thrown off but doesn't miss a beat. "Um, sure, we can do that," he says without any conviction.

"Great! I will expect all the cadets and the instructors to participate." Aerick nods his head and I can see the wheels in his head are turning, but he has just a hint of a smile.

I'm so excited and happy to the point where a ridiculous smile is etched on my face. I look back at Luther. "You know sir, a typical game has eleven players. If we all play including the instructors, that's eight on each team. If anyone else on the staff would like to play, we could make full teams, or we could play eight or nine like the youth leagues."

Aerick laughs, "Well Luther sounds like you don't need me – Nadalynn here has got it all covered."

Luther laughs with him, but I can't tell if Aerick is being sarcastic or if he really thinks it is a good idea. My face turns pink with embarrassment.

"Well, I am sure Brayden and Jake would love to join in. I will talk to them. Aerick if you want to get everything set up by PT, then I think we are all set."

We both get up. "Thank you, sir." Luther nods at Aerick and me and I walk outside.

Once we're several feet away from the office, Aerick stops and turns to me. *Shit.*

He seems pissed. "Why wouldn't you ask me first?"

I had a feeling he might say that. "Honestly?" Looking down at my feet, I stick my hands in my pockets.

He seems to calm down just a little. "Yes, be honest."

After a minute of building some courage, my eyes raise to meet his. "I didn't think you would say yes."

He stares at me for what feels like forever before he speaks. "I like routine. Things work better when there is a routine, but I am not opposed to ideas. You need to come to me next time, *first.*"

Just when I think he's done, he pauses and thinks for a moment, as if something suddenly occurred to him. "Were you afraid to ask me?"

I was afraid to ask, but it probably isn't why he's thinking; I'm not afraid of him. My lack of a response gives him his answer, and something crosses his face as his brows pull together. "You don't need to be afraid of me. You know that, right?"

Again, my instincts are right. "I'm not afraid of you. I just didn't want to ask you."

He smirks as my words come out a little more defensive than I meant them. "Okay. So, did you want to download some music still?"

My smile returns as it seems I've avoided an argument. I hadn't decided, but I make up my mind to do it. There's no way I'm going to let him think I'm afraid of him. "Sure, but do you mind if I meet you there? I want to tell everyone about the match."

"Sure." His lips turn up slightly as he holds back his own smile.

I run over to everyone and stop in front of Jeff with a huge grin on my face. Everyone's sitting around doing homework and talking. "Okay. Say 'Nadi is the most awesome person ever.'"

Jeff just looks at me confused. "Why? What did you do this time?"

"Actually, I did something for all of us, now say it."

He smiles. "Nadi is the most awesome person ever. Now, what did you do? Talk your way into trouble then back out again?"

"Hmm, if you are going to be like that maybe I should tell you..." I joke around with him. Both he and Patrick smack my legs at the same time. "Okay, okay. I managed to get us out of evening PT," I smile, completely proud of myself.

"No way! How did you do that?" John asks.

"Instead of PT, we'll be playing a soccer game."

"Right on!" Huck grins.

"So, everyone has to participate. Sorry, Leena and Karen, I know you guys didn't want to play, but it's better than PT." Leena just gives a little nod. She doesn't look too upset. "Okay, well I've got to go do something. Remember to be out here at six-thirty." I turn and walk back to the dorm, satisfied with myself.

I pick my iPod up from the dorm and then make my way into the instructor dorms. Aerick and Paulo are the only ones in there. Aerick is at his desk working on paperwork, and I quickly notice that he has changed into a tank top. I stop and look over at Paulo, who's also sitting at his desk, but he pays no attention to me.

Unsticking my feet, I walk over to Aerick, and he finally turns towards me. "The tablet is on my bed, go ahead and get started. You have an hour." He turns back around to his work. Crap, he's giving me the cold shoulder again. Maybe he's still mad at me for going behind his back. I have to say, I'm a little disappointed.

I sit cross-legged on his bed and he glares at me. "If you are going to have your feet on my bed, remove your shoes." *Okay, okay. Keep your pants on!*

He raises his eyebrow, and I hear Paulo let out a chuckle. I press my lips together tightly. Oops, I must have said that out loud. After a second he turns around and continues with his writing.

I remove my boots and scoot back on his bed until my back is against the wall; I cross my legs getting comfortable. Last time it was uncomfortable sitting perched on the edge of his bed for an hour. I pick up the tablet that is lying on his pillow, but I don't see his headphones anywhere, and didn't bring mine because I assumed he would let me use his again. I pause and wonder if I should ask him or just do it without them.

Paulo gets up. "Hey Aerick, you good for a while? I have to go see Terrie."

Aerick rolls his eyes, but Paulo can't see his face. "I'm good." Paulo grabs something from his desk and leaves.

I debate my problem again. "Did you need something?" He has that damn smirk on his face. *Cocky jerk.*

"Um, yes, could I bother you for your headphones?"

He gets a wide smile as he pulls them out of the desk drawer and takes the two steps over to me. I know that look and exactly what he's going to do and there is no way I can do anything about it. He puts his knee on the bed and leans over to me, laying the headphones very slowly on my lap. As he pulls away slightly, his hand drags across my knee, and my heart goes wild. "No bother at all."

Dammit, stop looking at me with that smirk! He's frozen rather close to me but has yet to break eye contact. "You okay, Nadalynn?" He asks, drawing out my name.

I nod my head 'yes' unable to say anything. "Good. Prince

Charming wouldn't want you to feel uncomfortable."

Of course, he was listening to that. *Crap*. Apparently, his cold attitude was a charade he put on while Paulo was here.

He gets off the bed and starts organizing his paperwork. Leaning down, he signs one more and then puts them into a folder. He pushes in his chair and goes over to his bookshelf, grabbing the same book he had been reading last time. He must still be reading it.

I expect him to come over and sit beside me, but instead, he lies down on his back on the outside edge of the bed with his head on his other pillow, essentially blocking me in. The only way for me to get off the bed would be to climb over the footboard or over him, since he spans the entire length of the bed. We fit on the bed just fine like this, but there's barely six inches that separate my knees and his lower stomach. I just stare at him until he looks at me.

Once he opens his book to the bookmark, he looks over at me with a straight face. "Is this okay with you?" I can't let him know this bothers me. Not because I'm uncomfortable, but because I'm entirely comfortable with this, and that's what bothers me.

"Sure." I sound almost convincing.

"Good." He looks back at his book and starts reading.

After pausing to slow my breathing, I put on the earphones and open the music app. I see his lip twitch out of the corner of my eye, but try to ignore him. I know Jeff downloaded some music, so I try to pull up his playlist, but when I go into the playlist area, there are only Aerick's and my own.

I look over at Aerick confused. "Where is Jeff's playlist?"

He doesn't even look up at me. "I deleted it. The music he downloaded is in there; you just have to go into the menu and click 'View all music.' The music is still on there, just not the playlist."

"Then why is mine still here?" I give him a curious look.

He finally looks over to me, giving me a little shrug. "What can I say? You have good taste in music." Great, now he's using my words against me. *Whatever.*

I turn back to the tablet, and he continues reading. I open all music and a ton more tracks show up. I find Bush, Korn, Limp Bizkit, and Full Devils Jacket. I haven't heard them in a long time so I decide to add a bunch of songs.

Suddenly something almost sharp is dragging on the edge of my knee. Looking down, I see him running his thumbnail along the outside of my knee, but he's still holding the book in his other hand while reading. It's almost as if this is something normal.

Closing my eyes, the feeling resonates all the way up my legs. I don't stop him, although I really should. It's just inviting him to torture me more. I take a deep breath and look back to the tablet and pull up the downloader.

Searching around, I find a few songs that are from the nineties era. I still like some of the older stuff I grew up on, since both of my parents like rock music. Zeppelin, Metallica and Black Sabbath are all awesome, but I only have a limited amount of space, and I'm rarely in the mood for that stuff.

I sit tapping on the side of the tablet, trying to remember some other bands. Getting a little desperate, I decide to scroll through Aerick's music. I find 'The Animal' by Disturbed and add it to my playlist. As I listen to it, my mind flits back to Aerick. I can actually imagine him singing this song. It takes everything in me not to laugh at the thought.

When it finishes, I move on and find another band I've never heard of, so I play a song. The song has a catchy beat and my head starts moving to the music; it's a good song. I add it to my playlist, but I don't keep looking because I realize Aerick's thumb has slowly moved above my knee to my thigh. I quickly put my hand over his, pinning it between my leg and my hand. He looks at me, but instead of the smirk I expect, he looks confused. *Did he think I would let him keep going?*

"Do you not like that?" His voice is curious, not mocking.

"That's not the point."

He tilts his head to the side as if he doesn't understand. "Then what is the point?"

I don't want to have this conversation with him – especially not with him. My eyes fall to my lap, and it isn't lost on me that our hands still haven't moved. "I don't want to be hurt."

A flash of irritation crosses his face. "Do you really think I would hurt you?"

Shit. Why is he making me explain this? "Not physically." I glance up from under my lashes to see his face.

I think anger flashes for a moment, but then his face turns to understanding. "Well, that is not what I expected to hear."

Huh– well, it's the truth. I suppose most people feel physically threatened by him, maybe that's what he meant. He slides his hand slowly from beneath mine, and my eyes close at the loss of contact; my hand falls onto my thigh in the wake of his absence. He shifts, but I keep my eyes closed. I'm suddenly surprised to feel his finger running across the back of my hand in a slow figure eight.

My eyes spring open to meet his. He's turned on his side towards me with one hand under his head propping himself up, while his other hand moves on mine. His face looks almost soft, but that curious look is back. Oddly, there's almost a smug look behind it. "Why do you think that I can touch you and others can't?"

That's the million-dollar question and I have no idea, but I don't want this to turn into a heavy conversation. "Patrick and Jeff can." I shrug my shoulders.

"Yes, but they are still reserved when they touch you. For instance, when Jeff sat on your bed to comfort you, he only touched your face and your hair. They also never hold their touch on anything but your arms." He really has been watching me, but why the hell does it matter? It's so hard for me to think while holding his gaze, but I don't want to look away.

"Their hands never stay on you like this..." He reaches over and runs his fingers down the side of my ribs to my hip, very slowly, as if he's testing my boundaries. I swallow hard, at a loss for words, and close my eyes, taking in the electricity I feel running down my side.

"Nadalynn," he says softly. I open my eyes and see sincerity on his face. "Did someone hurt you? In your past" I can't stop myself; I'm so lost in his touch and gaze on me. I hold my breath and nod 'yes.' He closes his eyes for just a moment.

"Does anyone know?" I nod my head again.

"Your parents?" Tears form in my eyes, blurring my vision slightly, but they don't spill over; I shake my head 'no,' ever so slightly.

He thinks for a second, "Your friends, Jeff and Patrick?" I try, but I can't hold it in any longer, and a single tear falls down my cheek as I nod 'yes' again. They were at camp with me when it happened, but I cannot materialize any words right now to tell him that.

He reaches up and wipes the tear from my cheek. "What happened? You can tell me."

I shake my head and whisper, "I can't." *I shouldn't.*

He sits up so his face is just inches from mine, his arm propped up on his one bent knee, and he cups the side of my face with his hand. He swallows deeply as if he's nervous. "You can; I swear it will never leave this room."

Staring into his eyes, all I want is to close the small distance between us and forget this conversation. "Please," he pleads with me.

My heart is racing so fast I think it might burst right out of my chest. This is a different side of Aerick, I have never seen him like this. So caring, so compassionate, so full of emotion; it's so... so disarming.

I press my face more firmly into his hand and close my eyes before speaking so quietly I'm not even sure he can hear me. "When I was nine. We used to have to go to this ten-week camp in the city during the summer because it was cheaper than a babysitter. It... it was like being at a boarding school, only we did activities all day, nothing like this place. We went every year, but that year was... different."

I swallow again as I feel another tear fall. My disconnected words are barely audible falling from my mouth like they are miles away. "We had our own small bedrooms; they barely fit our bed and a desk. That year there was a new teacher." The tightening in my chest comes on hard, and I am no longer able to speak. Aerick gives me a minute, and I can't bring myself to open my eyes or even to continue. Images begin running through my mind, images of that summer.

"Did he rape you?" His voice is so small and angry I barely hear him. I move my head, indicating no. He lets out a loud breath.

"Did he touch you?" My head falls lower; I don't know if I can tell him. "He touched you."

It was not a question. *He knows!*

His voice is still quiet. "Was it more than once?" I nod my head slowly. Tears now stream down my cheeks; I can no longer keep them at bay. More images of the dark nights flash.

"A lot?" His voice has become a mixture of anger and sadness. I nod 'yes' again. I can't breathe, my chest is heaving, and I feel dizzy. Flashes of the door knob turning and the fear it brought.

"Dammit, why didn't you tell someone?"

Fuck. I can't do this anymore. I push the tablet off me and try to jump over him, but he catches me and pulls me onto his lap, holding me tight against him as I cry into his chest.

"I... I... can't... please" I gasp, struggling to get away but he is much stronger than me.

"Calm down," he tells me with a low authoritative voice. "Calm down, you're safe now." I give up, curling into his chest as the uncontrollable sobs overtake me.

CHAPTER FIFTEEN

(Sunday, June 21st)

I'M UNAWARE OF the time as we sit there until my sobs have quieted. All the unwelcome visions of that summer come flooding back to me after being blocked out for so long. Walls that I'd built up long ago, shielding all but the smallest of memories that only appear occasionally in my dreams, knocked down by my mere admission of what happened.

Aerick is the only person since that summer that I've ever told. Patrick and Jeff only knew because they saw it first hand; it was impossible to hide it from them. They were the only ones who could offer even the tiniest bit of comfort. The feeling of his disgusting hands all over me, including my most intimate areas, and the bruises he left on me from being too rough while he got himself off, started to make me flinch at anyone's touch.

To this day I'm not sure how no one else noticed – or maybe

they saw and chose to ignore it. The guys argued with me continuously to tell someone, or to let them tell someone, but I didn't let them. It took me begging and pleading with them to keep their mouths closed.

I refused to say or do anything because of the fear that he would hurt me even more. He threatened me constantly, and when he found out the guys knew, he threatened to hurt them in front of me. He told me he would make them do things to me, horrible things, and that it would be all my fault.

I was too young, too weak and too stupid to make the right decision. I just suffered through it for eight weeks, praying every night that he would stop. Hoping that he would get tired of me and, in my darkest moments, wishing he would find someone else.

Weak and a stupid little girl was what I was then, too naive to know better. I'm sure that Aerick thinks I'm weak and stupid now too. I'm not sure why he's still holding me here. Probably doesn't want to get in trouble for upsetting me like this. He has gotten in enough trouble because of me. My feet are on the edge of the bed, and he has loosened his grip as I've slowly calmed down. His chin is resting on the top of my head as his thumb moves lightly back and forth over my shoulder.

I take the opportunity to get up quickly before he can stop me. "Wait!" He says shocked at my sudden movement. My eyes refuse to even look at him after revealing the most humiliating thing in my life. I don't know if I'll ever be able to look at him again.

My feet move quickly, nearly running out the door as he continues to call after me. Once I make it a few steps outside, the roughness on my feet makes me aware of my lack of shoes. Without stopping, I remove my socks and stick them in my back pocket, but I only make it a few more steps before I stop. Everyone is missing from the courtyard, and the smell of food lingers in the air.

Looking at my watch I see it's dinner time, but I can't eat while my stomach is still tied in knots. It would only end with me bent over a garbage can. I need to move before Aerick finds me and makes me go to dinner. I decide to walk around the back of the staff cabins and when I get to the last one, I lean against it and slide down.

Why did I tell him? I'm so fucking stupid. He's better than I thought he was. He knew exactly what he was doing, touching me like that, and holding me in his gaze to calm me so he could get the information he wanted.

Why the hell did he need to know? Is that what he's been planning all week? Trying to find a way to break me. I hit my head against the wall hard. *Why did I fall for his game?*

I've always been stronger than that; I hate being weak, it reminds me too much of that summer. I made it my mission after that summer to be stronger so that it would never happen again.

My hands wipe up and down my arms and legs like I can push away the phantom touches my thoughts have brought back. I really need my iPod, but I left it on his bed, and there's no way

I'm not going back in there. At the very least, I need a very hot shower; it feels as if I haven't taken a shower in weeks.

Getting up slowly, I walk back to my dorm. I'm grateful that everyone has headed to dinner; I don't want to see anyone right now. I gather up some clean clothes, throw my hair up in a high bun, and head to the bathroom praying Aerick isn't there.

It's empty. I let out a sigh of relief and go over to the shower, putting my clothes in their spot and hanging my towel.

"Nadalynn." His voice is quiet and guarded as I hear him walk over to me.

"I don't want to talk anymore," I say forcefully. He has gotten enough out of me. *Can't he just be satisfied?*

He lays his hand on my shoulder which I instantly drop, breaking the contact. "Don't!" I try to slow my breathing because right now, I just want to turn around and hit him for getting me to admit my darkest secret.

"Are you happy now?" I ask him, trying to hold in the tears that are building up in my eyes again. Before he can say anything, I continue, "Just... leave... me... alone!" My words are slow and drawn out, bleeding anger through every word.

He continues to stand there, but just as I'm about to tell him to leave, I hear his retreating steps. When he's across the room, he pauses. "Sorry."

Really? He's sorry. Oh good, that's just what I wanted – for him to feel sorry for me. That's not what I wanted. I don't want anyone to treat me like the pitiful little victim. That's one of the reasons I refuse tell people.

I turn on the shower as hot as it will go and get in. The pounding hot water hides a few escaped tears. I wash my body meticulously three times, until I feel somewhat clean again. My skin is red from my persistent scrubbing and almost scalding hot water, but it will be mostly hidden by my clothes.

When I get out, Aerick still hasn't returned. *Good!* I go over to the sink and stare into my own puffy red eyes in the mirror.

"I will get through this!" It feels better to say it out loud. I splash cold water on my face and dry it off, taking several deep breaths. When I finally stand up, I feel a little better, and resolve to put this behind me.

I go into my dorm; my boots are now sitting on my clothing chest, so I put them on and put my stuff away. People are starting to trickle back in from dinner, chattering in excitement about the upcoming soccer match.

Jeff comes over to me. "Why weren't you at dinner?"

I give him a fake smile, but he's not fooled. "I had to take care of some things."

"Alone?" What the hell is that supposed to mean?

Then it hits me that Aerick probably missed dinner too. "Of course, alone." My eyes are drawn to my side table where a water bottle, protein bar, and my iPod now sit. *Well wasn't that nice of him.* It's impossible to resist rolling my eyes. I grab the items and smile sweetly at Jeff.

He looks like he's debating on pushing the conversation

further, but before he can, I give him a quick peck on the cheek and start walking past him. "Thanks for always being there for me. See you at the game." He freezes in shock and confusion, clearly thrown by my unusual affection, and no doubt querying the sad note I fail to keep out of my voice. Not giving him a chance to respond, I walk out of the dorm.

To avoid people, I walk around the outsides of the buildings. I quickly down my protein bar despite my stomach's protest. I'm not giving Aerick any reasons to talk to me. I didn't eat dinner, and he will undoubtedly know if I don't. As I'm drinking the water, I go through my playlist to find what I want to listen to. Immediately I notice that he synced it with the new stuff I added. Clicking on the 'recent added' icon, I look to see if it finished syncing.

Everything is there along with two other songs. The first one is 'Sorry' by Buckcherry. I hesitate before pressing play. It's been a while since I've heard it. I tend to stay away from sad music. Focusing on the song, I begin to wonder why he added this song, *"…'Cause everything inside. It never comes out right. And when I see you cry, it makes me want to die. I'm sorry I'm bad, I'm sorry your blue, I'm sorry…"* These lyrics can't possibly be how he feels, other than maybe he is sorry – just maybe.

I look at my iPod again and scroll through to the other song because I cannot listen to this one anymore. The second one he has put there is called 'Dig' by Incubus. I've never heard this song, and I'm hoping it will make me feel a little better. After all, I did say he had good taste in music.

I listen to the words, and as the song finishes, I stop walking. *What?*

I restart the song focusing on the words, thinking I must've heard that wrong. "We all have a weakness... Dig me up from under what is covering, the better part of me. Sing this song, remind me that we'll always have each other."

He can't be serious. My head is spinning. *Why the hell would he put this song on here?* I try to rationalize. He must just like the song, and thought I would too; nothing else makes sense. I lean up against the wall of the office building and stare up at the sky with the song on repeat, memorizing the words.

The next thing I know, Trent comes up beside me. He looks at my face and cautiously asks, "You okay?"

I must look like shit. I'm sure my eyes are a still a bit puffy, and I probably look as worn down as my body feels. I try to perk up and smile. "Yep." He shrugs off whatever he was thinking.

"Aerick asked me to come get you; the game is about to start."

I struggle to keep a straight face but I can't keep the shock out of my voice. "Yeah, okay." I didn't realize I was standing there so long!

At least Aerick is giving me some space; it's the least he can do. The game was my idea and I want to enjoy it, so I push my thoughts aside and focus on going out and having a good time. Trent and I head to the field together; I swig down the last of the water and toss the empty bottle and bar wrapper in a nearby trash can.

We get over to the courtyard. Someone has run a red cord around in a square, and there's a small, white painted circle in the middle. The field is a little smaller than a standard soccer field, but not by much. On each end of the makeshift field, there are two poles on either side of the 'goal,' standing about six feet high.

I walk over to the stage where everyone else has already gathered, and when I say everyone, I mean everyone. The entire staff is here, including Luther and Ayla. Luther is wearing a plain white shirt, which is odd, and everyone else is wearing their Donnelly uniform.

Aerick gets up on the stage but doesn't look at me. He just starts talking, his eyes scanning over our crowd. "PT is going to be a little different tonight. Thanks to one of your fellow cadets, we will be playing a soccer game instead. We will be playing eleven on eleven, with two twenty-five minute halves, and a ten-minute half-time. The ball must fall into the goal below the top of the poles to be good. Luther will be our referee for this game. The game will be no contact, so keep your hands to yourself; is that understood?" Everyone nods their head in agreement.

"Okay, to make this fair and easier to tell teams apart, we will be playing Dorm A against Dorm B; that goes for instructors, too. Brand and I will be the captains since we both know the game well. Andi, Terrie, and Brayden, you're with Dorm A. Tia, Ayla and Jake will be with Dorm B."

"I will lead us through some quick stretches. Then you will

have five minutes to figure out who will be your goalie, and what positions you want to play. We have red shirts for the goalies, and my team will wear yellow bands on our arms to keep the teams straight. Alright, let's get this started."

Once we've stretched, we take our spots on each side of the field. Aerick throws a stopwatch to Luther, who catches it with ease. "You've got five minutes," Luther bellows from mid-field.

"Alright, does everyone know the basic rules?" Aerick asks as he passes out the yellow pieces of fabric; everyone nods. "Good, who has played on a team before?" Brayden, Andi, Huck, Jeff, Patrick and I all raise our hands. Aerick smiles. "Good. Tie these bands onto your right upper arm. Anyone good at goalie?"

"I'm pretty good," Brayden offers up.

Aerick throws him the red goalie shirt. "We are going to play a basic four, three, three formation. The forwards will be Nadalynn, Andi, Huck and myself. The mid-fielders will be Tara, Jeff and Terrie, and the defenders will be Patrick, Mike, and Paulo. Make sure you stay spread out and call out your passes. Everyone clear?"

I hear Tara whisper to Mike, asking him what a midfielder is, and he quickly explains. "Alright, really quick meet with the people in your position and decide who will be left, right or center." I walk over to Aerick but keep my eyes on the ground.

When Andi and Huck join, us Aerick continues, "Okay, I play left-center, Nadalynn, are you okay playing right-center?"

I look at him and try to keep my mind focused. "Actually, I'm better at left-center." I'm good at left. My coaches always liked that I could shoot and be accurate with my left foot and I played forward often because I was fast.

His lip turns up just slightly. "Okay, then I will play right-center. Andi, Huck?"

"I can play left, it's a little harder, but I'm not bad," Huck says. "Alright, Andi you can play on the right?"

"It's time. Teams on the field," Luther yells. We all get into position; some of the more experienced players help, the less experienced players while giving them a few pointers. I remind our team to stay spread out.

It looks like the other team is using the same formation. I have a feeling Aerick and Brand planned that. Brand and Royce stand in front of Aerick and me; Luther steps in between us. "Okay captains who's calling it."

"Aerick can call it." Brand speaks up.

"Okay, Aerick, call it." Luther flips the coin and Aerick calls tails. Luther removes his hand and tails it is. We get the kick off and Brand and Royce back off.

Luther puts his finger and thumb in his mouth and gives a piercing whistle. *Ouch!*

He shouts to start the game. I'll have to remember not to stand so close to him next time. I swear I just lost an eardrum.

Game on. The ball is at my feet, so I kick it forward softly to Aerick to start. I can tell pretty quick that Aerick is really good at this game.

As the game gets underway, I forget about everything that happened; I'm just enjoying myself. By halftime, the score is three to three. I've scored once, and Aerick has scored twice, in which I assisted one. We go over the sidelines, and there are towels and water bottles that someone put there before the game started. Everyone rushes over to the water. I go to grab a towel but Aerick hands one to me before I can get to it and gives me a tight smile. There is something hard wrapped inside the towel; looking inside, another protein bar sits discretely.

I probably shouldn't argue, and as much as I hate to admit it, my body needs it. The fatigue from lack of a proper meal is setting in, so I devour it and gulp down a whole bottle of water. I can only hope I don't get a cramp in my side from drinking too much, but I'm so thirsty.

When we start up the game again – I feel great. The game was such a good idea, and everyone is so happy, it's contagious. Even Aerick and I are being civil to each other, giving each other high-fives when we score. When Luther blows the final whistle, we have won seven to five. I'm elated that our team won, and that I got another goal. Aerick also headed in my corner kick, giving me the assist. We work well together.

I did have a hard time going up against Brand; he's super quick with his feet. Considering Brand and Aerick's height, it's crazy to see them move with such speed and agility. Aerick is also fancy with his feet. He's clearly played a lot growing up.

Patrick and Jeff both share a quick hug with me; I give high fives to everyone else. The other team seems a little disappointed but not too bad. We all had fun. We give them the 'good game' handshake, making sure to be good sports.

Luther whistles and jumps up on the stage, so everyone gathers around him. "Thank you again, Nadi for the excellent suggestion. We may try to do that at least one more time before this camp is done, or maybe some flag football."

I see Aerick nod his head in agreement. "I would also like to make another announcement. This coming Saturday we will be having a bonfire out at 'The Pit,' which you have probably seen in the field behind the staff cabins."

I noticed the fire pit when I was walking around the other night. There's a huge fire pit and a bunch of large logs that go around it. "Assuming you behave, we will have these bonfires every fourth Saturday, to celebrate the milestone. We will provide soda and smores. Thank you guys, for a great night. Apparently, I am getting a little old and need some more exercise." He pats his nonexistent beer belly and everyone laughs at him. "I will see you tomorrow."

We move slowly off toward the dorms, chatting about the upcoming bonfire. A smile is pasted on my faces as I take a seat on the stage, looking out at the field once everyone is out of sight. I feel Aerick sit beside me; I don't even have to look to know it's him.

Taking a deep breath, I organize my thoughts and he smartly decides to let me speak first. "I need some space, Aerick. You're very observant and must see that Jeff and Patrick back off when I need it." I manage to keep my voice strong but not angry.

He's pointed out on several occasions that he watches us three, so I know I'm right. He sits there for several minutes, presumably going over his options – not that he has many. I wait, giving him time to process my request. I don't know what else to say to him, and as much as I want to look at him to gauge his reaction, I can't look him in the face – at least not yet.

"Space…" he finally says, sounding almost defeated. "Request granted." He gets up and walks away without looking back. I watch him retreat for a moment, and then my eyes find the sky. The last thing I want is to be angry right now. My iPod is still in my pocket, so I put in my ear buds and lie back on the stage. With my legs dangling over the edge, I turn the music up loud. Loud enough to drown out my thoughts and allow me a few moments of peace in my head.

I'm happy no one bothers or questions me. I manage to keep my head empty and just enjoy the high of our win. I stare up at the sky, for once just happy watching the fading sunlight being slowly replaced with bright stars. When the sun has finally set and the sky is a glittery black velvet, I finally rouse and look at my watch – there's only half an hour until lights out back in the dorms. I get up slowly, my body stiff and sore from lying there so long.

Today has been so up and down. I don't know if it's possible, but I had both the best day and the worst day since I got here, all rolled into one.

Heading back into the dorm, I shower quickly, but this time I wash my hair and brush my teeth. I have to assure Patrick and Jeff more than once that I am okay. The extra attention irritates me, but I can't be too mad; they're just trying to look after me like they always do. Like they've done ever since that summer, but I don't want to think about that.

I try to clear my mind and not think about it. I'm sure I won't sleep well, but I got to at least try. Tomorrow is another day, with another round of PT and classes. My body drags as I crawl into bed. It's been such an emotionally and physically exhausting day; sleep finds me quickly.

CHAPTER SIXTEEN

(Saturday, June 27th)

WELL, I SOMEHOW survived another week, if you can call what I've been doing surviving. I moved like a robot, going through the daily routines in a daze. It got to the point that when I was in bed at night, I had trouble recalling what I'd done that day. Just bits and pieces stand out, but not the whole picture. I think that the biggest problem is the lack of sleep.

Sunday night was the worst. I woke up screaming and I scared the shit out of everyone. Paulo came running into our dorm in his boxers and a tank top, embarrassing the crap out of me. I was a little surprised that it wasn't Aerick and wondered why he hadn't come, especially since this whole thing was his fault. Reliving that summer was just too much for me, and the resulting dreams are more vivid than ever.

The only way I had any chance of going back to sleep was to

have Jeff sit at the top of my bed with my head in his lap while he ran his fingers through my hair. The way that he did that summer when I would gather enough courage to sneak into his room to seek comfort. He never complained, he would just sit up, place a pillow on his lap, and run his fingers through my hair until I cried myself to sleep. Sometimes he would try to convince me to let him tell, but I wouldn't dare let him, out of fear that he would be hurt because of me. He was the best friend I could ever have.

Jeff woke me up again the next night, luckily, before I could disturb anyone else. I honestly think he didn't ask me why I was having the nightmares because he figured that the shrink had gotten it out of me. Thankfully, it's slowly getting better. Last night was the first night that I was mostly okay, but it was also rather confusing. Aerick was once again in my dream. he found me and comforted me before the approaching boots could reach me.

In reality, Aerick has stayed as far away from me as possible. At first, I figured it was because he had finally gotten my secret out of me. He had been pushing the issue since the day that I freaked out in class; goading me to see how much he could do before I pushed back. However, it's become clear to me that it wasn't merely a conquest – there's something more there, I'm just not sure what is. He hasn't just gone back to his normal asshole instructor attitude; instead, he's become withdrawn.

He hasn't spoken a word to me the entire week, and he won't look at me for anything. On a couple of occasions, he's rubbed against my arm or leg, but he quickly moves away, looking pissed off. That now familiar warmth stays there long after his physical touch is gone. He also no longer sits next to me at meals. He just sets my food down and goes to the other end of the table.

It's my own doing. I told Aerick I needed space and that's exactly what he's doing. I was so angry at him at the time, I didn't know if I would ever feel comfortable with him again, but over the last several days that anger has shifted into something else.

It's turned into some kind of need. The need of his presence, need of his touch, need of a closeness – something I'm almost certain won't happen again.

At the very least, I want things to be civil between us. It's weird, but I miss his odd way of teasing me, and even his crazy mood swings. I miss his eyes looking into mine, making the world around me fall away. I don't know how I could crave the company of someone who makes me so mad and confused, but it's there. None of it is logical, just like his ability to touch me without me freaking out. Maybe I just miss that touch, or maybe I'm a glutton for punishment.

Pushing the events of the past few weeks to the back of my mind, I make up my mind to try to talk to him. The worst that could happen is that he continues to ignore me. At least then I could say I tried, and his being an asshole would be all on him.

Besides, today is my birthday – surely he can't ignore me today, of all days.

At breakfast, I seize the opportunity to talk to him when he brings my food over. Building my confidence, I smile and look up at him. His eyes meet mine for the first time since last Sunday. "Hey, Aerick."

His face contorts into a confused look, and he hesitates for the briefest of moments before he sits down next to me. I let out a sigh of relief, which I can only hope he doesn't hear. Maybe he'll talk to me, and we can get back to having civilized interactions with each other.

"Hi," he says back quietly. I start eating and debate my next words, excited that he chose to join me for breakfast.

His leg brushes against me by mistake and he quickly moves it away. An idea strikes me, and I move mine back against him. He'd played this game with me all last week and I intend on repaying him the favor; maybe he'll find humor in it.

I almost spit out the food in my mouth trying to hold in the laughter as his fork pauses halfway to his mouth and his eyes widen. I see his lip lift ever so slightly, and he whispers so quietly that only I can hear him, "Careful."

Confused, I think about that for a moment. *Of what?* He switches his fork to the other hand to eat and slyly reaches under the table with his other hand.

He runs his thumbnail from my knee up to the middle of my thigh. He almost smiles as my breath hitches. Obviously getting the reaction he wanted out of me, he turns back to his food, finishing it quickly, and gets up to leave before I can fully collect my thoughts. "Happy birthday Nadalynn," he tells me in a seductively low voice. My eyes fly around me to see if anyone heard it, but they are all engrossed in their own conversations.

And the normal Aerick is back! Well, that didn't take much, or so I hope anyway. It puts me in a better mood.

Everyone has told me happy birthday this morning. Apparently, someone spread the word. It didn't help that both Jeff and Patrick were loud about it this morning, giving me birthday punches as I ran around the room trying to escape them. My arm still hurts a little. Mike had thought about joining in the birthday punches, but when I raised an eyebrow, he thought better of it. I'm not big on celebrating my birthday, but I just want to have a good day and not let anything bother me!

✳ ✳ ✳ ✳

My day has been rather good. Aerick has been finding ways to touch me all day. In self-defense class, he felt it necessary to put his hand on me to correct my position, leaving it lingering on my side while he made a slight adjustment to my stance. My whole body exploded with fire at his touch, and I had to remind myself to keep breathing. Naturally, he chuckled as he walked away, knowing exactly what he was doing. The old Aerick is definitely back.

During our hike this afternoon, he kept brushing his arm along my shoulder and every time I looked up at him he would have an entirely focused look on his face like he wasn't doing anything at all. Normally it would be irritating, but this time I found it funny knowing he was doing it on purpose.

By dinner time, I can't take the smile off my face. Today has been so average but so good. That is until Luther walks out of the kitchen with a huge piece of cake and starts singing 'Happy Birthday.' Everyone joins in and I feel my face turning a deep shade of red. Luther explains that it is a Donnelly Bootcamp specialty cake, and everyone else was dished up a smaller piece. It is by far the most delicious cake I have ever had, each bite melting away in my mouth.

After dinner, we all go to get ready for the bonfire; I grab my sweatshirt, knowing it will get cold. There is no evening PT which means we get three and a half hours out at the fire. At least my birthday won't be completely boring, and even though it was completely unrelated, we got out of PT for the night. *Sweet!*

As we're walking out of the dorm, John finds me and gives me a quick hug, causing me to freeze the moment he makes contact. *Don't hit him, don't hit him...* I take a deep breath; I don't want to ruin this day. He tries to grab my hand, but I smoothly slip it in my pocket. He doesn't seem to notice it was intentional. Ignoring my reaction to the hug, he leans close to my side and whispers to me, "Hey I have something for some of us. Find me at the bonfire."

"Okay." I try to sound casual and just give him a smile. You would think after the last few weeks people would have learned to give me my personal space.

Jeff comes up beside me and grabs my arm, dragging me past John. "You good?" He asks when we have gotten out of earshot.

I'm grateful for his intervention. "Yep, let's go." We walk to the pit; it is dug into the ground a little so the massive bonfire looks like it's blazing straight up from the dirt. I'd only seen it from far away and had no idea it was so big. The field back behind the cabins is twice as large as the courtyard, with the pit almost half way across. The logs are the perfect size to sit on and are arranged just far enough away from the fire. There are also two open coolers with soda in them.

We sit down and start talking. The only instructor that's here is Brand, and he's sitting across from me talking to Tia. I can barely see them because of the massive fire. My stomach tightens for a moment in disappointment that Aerick isn't here, but I'm focused on just relaxing tonight and enjoying everyone's company. Jeff brings me over a coke that's already open. "Here, it's my favorite."

I look at him confused, knowing full well this is not his favorite soda, so I cautiously take a quick sip. *Holy shit!* "You sly dog! Where the hell did you get alcohol?"

He smiles, "Well I can't take all the credit, but we needed to do something for your birthday."

I raise an eyebrow, "We?"

He laughs a little. "Actually, John got the rum." He looks almost embarrassed. I look over at John, and he has a big smile on his face as he lifts his can to me. I give him a smile in thanks and raise mine back.

"So, how many people are drinking?" This will suck if

someone gets too drunk and fucks this up for us.

"Just Patrick, me, you, John, Royce, and Huck." *Just? That's half of us.*

"We've made it clear that no one can have a lot; besides, it's a limited supply." I feel a little better, and excited at the same time.

"Here's to you, on your birthday." I raise my drink as he lifts his toward me and we click cans. I'm all smiles as I take another big drink. It's been a while since the last time I drank; drinking for me is a rare occasion, but when I do, it's usually rum and coke. The taste of beer just doesn't sit well with me unless it is something like Corona.

We sit and talk about party stories that we have missed in each other's lives. It seems like every time I finish my drink, one of our private drinking group brings me a new one as they sit to talk to me. That is, except for John, which is a little weird, but I push the feeling away. Although we're stuck in this place, I feel so happy and free, it's wonderful.

As soon as the sun sets, Aerick and Paulo join us, with several bags in their hands and a small folding table. They set up the table and lay out the smores supplies. I look around and notice that Jake, Andi, Terrie, Trent, and Brayden joined us some time ago; I didn't see when.

"Here you guys go, do not make a mess and don't burn yourselves," Aerick says, giving me a quick smile before walking over to talk to Terrie and Jake. Paulo walks past me and the air around him reeks of alcohol. Apparently, we aren't the only ones drinking.

"Let's get some," I say and stand up with Jeff and Huck, who are sitting on either side of me. I get a little dizzy and grab both their arms to steady myself.

Jeff bites his cheek trying not to laugh. "I guess we made yours just a little stronger. That, or maybe you're a light-weight."

I slap his arm. "Jerk! Trying to get me drunk, are you?"

"Me? I would never!" He says, with his signature goofy smile. How could I be mad at him? He's so freaking adorable.

"Sit down! I'll make you one; we don't need you falling into the fire," he jokes.

Conceding, I sit down, dragging Huck down with me for support. "I still have to walk back to the cabin – unless you were planning on carrying me," I say to Jeff.

"Oh, I'm sure there are plenty of men here willing to carry you off to bed," he laughs and walks away before I can reply, but I flip him off anyway.

Huck smiles and moves his hand to my back, making me freeze. I'm sure it's a friendly gesture to keep me from falling back, so I try to stay calm and take a deep breath. Even with the alcohol in me, I'm not immune to my fears.

Playfully I push his hand off. "Go get one for yourself, Huck, because I'm sure not sharing mine." I try to keep my voice happy, hoping he'll go.

He smiles and stands. "Will do, be right back." He walks away, and I let out a breath of relief. I sit there for a minute just enjoying the warmth of the fire and down the last of my drink. John must have noticed and comes over with a cute smile, sitting at a comfortable distance beside me, handing me another can.

"I don't know if I really should," I tell him honestly. I'm pretty buzzed; even if tomorrow is an easy day, we still have PT in the morning.

"Don't worry; I just put the last of it in your drink. It's only right that you get the last of it, being your birthday and all. Please, enjoy."

I take the can, "Thanks!" I'll just sip it slowly, I tell myself. I'm grateful that this wasn't another boring birthday. Many times, I end up spending the evening of my birthday alone on the roof of our building back home.

"So where did you get the alcohol?" I ask, honestly curious as to how he could possibly get it way out here.

He grins mischievously, "I took it from Brayden. He left his bag in the gym bathroom this morning and when I peeked inside, I found it. I figure he isn't supposed to have it either being he's only eighteen, so he would be less likely to report it." That explains Brayden's sullen attitude most of the afternoon.

"But don't feel sorry for him. If you haven't noticed yet, several of the staff and even our instructors have been drinking, so I'm sure he got some more. Otherwise, he wouldn't be so happy right now. That's why all the staff was gone earlier. I overheard them talking about it at dinner, that they were having a pre-party."

I laugh at the situation; he is right, and I don't feel bad for drinking now. My eyes flit over to Aerick who is looking at me from a few logs away where he is talking to Paulo. I wonder if he's been drinking too. He seems a little more relaxed, just like everyone else.

Jeff brings me a smore and then goes off to get another one for himself. I start to eat it, and of course, it gets all over my fingers. As I suck the chocolate off my thumb, without thinking, my eyes find Aerick's. His eyes are glued to my mouth. His clenched jaw loosens slightly as he bites on his lower lip. As if realizing what he's doing, he looks away quickly and I do the same, because the look on his face damn near drives me crazy. Damn, he looked so hot just now.

Stop, I need to stop... I try to tell myself.

I look around, trying to distract my thoughts. Huck is talking to Karen; I've had a hunch that he liked her. My thoughts are interrupted as I suddenly realize that John has inched closer to me without my noticing, and is now right next to me.

"So, read anything interesting lately?" I say, trying to keep as casual as possible and hope for Jeff to make his way back to me. He is currently hysterically laughing as he talks to Royce and Patrick. I smile at him in reaction; he really is a good friend.

Faintly I notice John is answering me; I try to listen to him. "...so have you been able to get more music?"

Stay calm, just talk to him. "Um yeah, Aerick let me add some more. I ended up getting some older stuff that I grew up with..."

His hand moves to my knee, and the tightening sets in. I have to stop this; I take a long drink of my soda. *Shit, that's strong.* I turn toward him and swallow, with the intention of making it clear his actions are unwanted. "John..." My voice breaks horribly, and I pause trying to breathe through the pain in my chest.

All the sudden, his hand is on my cheek and his lips are on my own. I try to pull back, pushing at his chest, but he moves his other hand to the back of my neck, holding me in place. Before a coherent thought can be made, my fist moves, punching him hard in his face. I quickly stand up as he falls back. "Don't you ever do that again. EVER!" My voice is low and laced with anger. Only half the people saw what happened and they're all staring at me as I stand there, my chest heaving because of my panic attack and the adrenaline that's pumping through me.

"Nadi, you need to come with me now." *Shit.* Aerick is right behind me, and he grabs my arm firmly, but I don't bother to shake it off as he starts leading me back toward the dorms. He sounds furious; he even used my nickname. I don't think he's ever done that. *Damn it!*

Fucking John, why did he have to pull that shit? Now I'm in trouble, and I'd been having such a good time before he decided to get some action. I walk with Aerick not struggling because honestly, if his hand wasn't firmly gripping my arm, I probably wouldn't be able to walk straight.

"Fucking asshole! Why would you do that to her?" I hear Jeff yelling at John as we walk away.

"Dude – she's a big girl and can take care of herself. Did you see what the hell she did?" He yells back and I hear shuffling, but I don't look back.

"Hey guys, guys, knock it off. This is over, go back to your own business." Brand stops the argument before it can progress and everything quiets down behind me as we get farther away.

At first, I'm thinking we are going to the instructor's dorm, but he leads me around the other side so we are between it and dorm B. He leans me against the wall, looking up at a red light on the corner of the building. He's clearly angry. My best bet is to try to make this as painless as possible.

I look down at my hands. "I'm sorry Aerick." I chance glancing up at him through my lashes; the need to see his face is too great.

His face goes from angry, to shocked, to confused. "What exactly are you sorry for?" *Great, he's going to make me spell it out?*

My eyes fall back at my hands. "I hit him, unacceptable behavior I know, but I'm just… sorry." I breathe in deeply.

His hand comes up and pushes my chin upward making me look into his eyes. "That asshole got what he deserved, and he is lucky you hit him first. Are *YOU* okay?" Confusion spreads through me. His hand is still on my chin and once again, I'm lost in his beautiful eyes.

Need explodes within me. I inch my mouth closer to his and then stop. *I can't do this.* If he rejects me I won't be able to deal with it, not from him. Changing directions, I begin to lean back against the wall.

Something in his eyes changes and before I can comprehend what's happening his lips crush to mine hard. I'm pushed back against the wall, his body pinning me. My eyes close and my hands wrap around his neck. His lips on mine are everything I hoped they would be.

We move together, enjoying each other's touch. My hands move into his hair, and I pull him closer; he rewards me with a deep growl that causes an ache between my legs. Running his tongue along my bottom lip, I willingly open my mouth and he deepens his motions. I'm entranced in overwhelming fire from his body. He bites my lip, and I moan at the intense feeling burning through me straight down to my core. I feel him hardening against me.

It shocks me for just a moment that he's so turned on by me, and it makes me want him even more. He moves his hands down to the back of my thighs and pulls me up. Instinctively, I wrap my legs around his waist and his fingers move, digging into my side, trying to pull me even closer.

We finally have to break for air, and he rests his forehead against mine. Both of us are breathing heavily and I'm in the clouds. "As much as I fucking hate to say this, we can't do this tonight." *Seriously!*

"Why the hell not?" I say forcefully, without thinking, and he laughs at my audacity as he pulls his head away slightly so he can look in my eyes.

"For one, you've been drinking."

Now it's my turn to laugh since his aroma is bathed in it; even his kiss tasted of it. I raise my eyebrow, "And you haven't?"

He smiles. "Well, when we do this I would prefer you were sober, at least the first time. Second, I do not have any protection on me since this is not exactly how I pictured us... hooking up." *So, he has been thinking about me.*

Then his words start sinking in. He just said, 'when we do this,' so he plans on it in the future. I'm elated at the thought, but I'm at a loss since I have no idea what he would see in me after he found out my little secret. I slowly unwrap my legs and he sets me down, then adjusts his pants, which are still bulging, without letting me go completely. As much as I hate to say it, he's right; well, not about the drunk part – I'm braver when I'm drunk. But the last thing I need is to get pregnant by a man I barely know and who I'm likely never to see again after I leave here.

Suddenly we hear people approaching, probably returning to the dorms, but we're in a dark spot and no one has to walk around this side. I wonder if he brought me here for that purpose. He takes my hand, leading me into the darkest spot where we are as he watches the red light. It must be a camera that he's understandingly trying to avoid. He could probably get into trouble if someone found out.

He leans his back against the wall and turns me so my back is against his chest and then suddenly slides down the wall pulling me with him. I have to cover my mouth so that I don't scream. He's sitting cross-legged, and I'm sitting in his lap. I lean my head back against his shoulder and relax. We just sit there for a few minutes. He runs his fingers up and down my arms and I close my eyes, enjoying his touch.

The lights in the dorm go out, and I automatically think of what happens if you go out of the dorm during lights out. Sitting up, I look back at Aerick," Am I going to be in trouble for being out here after lights out?"

He raises an eyebrow. "You think I would let that happen?" He frowns. I don't take my eyes off him and he rolls his eyes. "If you are within five feet of an instructor, your tracker will not activate. We have the ability to change the distance setting, which is what we do when we are on hikes, but only Luther or Jake can do that."

He shifts me a little to the side and pulls out a cell phone from his pocket, then pulls me back against his chest. I watch as he pulls up Paulo on messenger and sends a text, 'I have Nadi. She's a bit freaked out and I'm trying to calm her down, will be back in a bit.'

A muffled laugh rises from my chest. "Wow, is this how you calm down all your cadets?" I joke as I take his other hand, running my fingers along the back of it.

He takes several deep breaths like he's hesitating to say something. "Just say it Aerick."

He murmurs, almost saddened, "Are you really okay? Even if it were someone else, what he did would be enough to upset anyone."

I take a deep breath and turn so that I'm straddling him and lace my fingers behind his neck. His eyes get big at my bold move. The alcohol is making me a little brave tonight. "Please don't ask me that again," I tell him seriously. "I don't like people looking down at me like I'm weak." That was enough to get a laugh out of him.

He grabs both sides of my face and pulls me down to his face so we are an inch apart; suddenly he's serious. "You… are far from weak." With that, he closes the space between us, kissing me much slower, and softly, as I get lost in his touch. His hands start running down my back and he hardens below me again.

"Aerick," I moan and press into him, trying to relieve the ache between my legs.

He freezes, and I think I have done something wrong. Keeping his eyes closed, he swallows hard. "You say my name like that again, and I will not be able to stop myself."

He gives me another quick kiss, and I sigh, knowing I should be good and stop. I go to turn back around, but he only lets me go halfway, so I'm sitting sideways on his lap. I sit, cradled in his arms, and settle like that, lying my head on his chest.

We sit in a comfortable silence for a while, and I wonder what this actually is. *Does he want to be with me or is this just a drunken almost hook-up?* I want to ask him, but I don't know how.

When I peek up at him, he's looking at the stars. He seems so relaxed and content, nothing like he normally is. I decide it's now or never. "Aerick... What is this?"

He looks at me, suddenly serious and tense again. "What do

you mean?"

I'm so nervous, and my words come out fast, almost garbled. "I mean do you want to be with me... or is this just a hookup... or are you just playing with me? Because I really don't think I could handle that and..." He stops me by putting his finger on my lips. I feel tears threatening to fall because I'm so nervous about his answer. I swallow hard and fight back the tears.

"Stop!" He says with an authoritative voice, looking extremely serious.

"First of all, if this were just a 'hook-up,' I sure as hell wouldn't have stopped myself earlier. I would have just taken you against that wall without a second thought."

I'm shocked by his bluntness. "Although it did take every ounce of my self-control to stop." He swallows loudly and takes a breath before continuing,

"Second, I don't think you would be able to handle me playing with you, either. I already apologized for the way I got you to talk the other day. That wasn't fair to you, and, for maybe the fifth time in my life, I felt bad for my actions."

He pauses again, as if he's trying to organize his thoughts. "Finally, I have to tell you that I've had an unexplainable attraction to you for quite some time. You are extremely attractive, but it is not just physical. The way you seem not to be intimidated by me, the way you challenge me, it pisses me off, but at the same time, I want you to keep doing it. I crave you in the craziest ways. I also struggle to maintain my self-control around you, which is not something I have had to deal with in a long time; it is... frustrating.

"Let me tell you, if you hadn't punched John tonight, I would have. Although, if it was me, I probably would get fired for my actions. I just couldn't help myself. When I saw him with his lips on you, it made me so angry. I was out of my seat before you even reacted. Thankfully, you have amazing reflexes, even in your drunken state, and you hit him before I could get to him."

He laughs, and I smack his chest. "But there is something else you really need to know." He has to take several more breaths and puts his head back against the wall, looking to the sky before he continues. Confused by his sudden confession, I just sit quietly and wait.

"Nadalynn, I am not a normal kind of guy. I did not grow up knowing love, and I don't even know if I am capable of it. Yet, for some reason, my body and mind are pulled to you and by some miracle, something deep inside you must feel it too. I don't know how else to explain why I can touch you while others can't, or why you still want to be around me after I have been such a jerk to you. As much as I hate to say it, there is a good chance I will hurt you because I tend to screw up anything good in my life. I know I already hurt you when I forced you to confess your secret to me. I knew exactly what I was doing, and I know I'm an ass for that. Anyone here will tell you that it is just me, I love control and that need gives me an asshole persona.

"I have tried to stay away from you because it is not fair to you, but I have found it harder and harder. I guess tonight I've finally stopped trying to fight it, but we also still need to deal with the fact that we are here and I am your instructor. Technically there is no rule against it, but it is frowned upon. Others cannot know about this."

I bite my lip, repeating the words he just said in my head. He wants to be with me. His eyes find mine with a questioning look. He wants this and so do I; although he didn't exactly say it that way, it was good enough for me. His words explain so much over the past several weeks.

I pull him down to me and kiss him lightly on his lips. "Works for me."

His smile mirrors mine, and he lets out a breath of relief. I lay my head against his chest, listening to his heartbeat and staring at the stars. He begins rubbing his fingers lightly up and down my thigh as he tilts his head back and together we stare into the night sky.

❋ ❋ ❋ ❋

I feel weightless; someone is carrying me. I'm vaguely aware, but I feel Aerick's strong arms under me, holding me close.

Jeff's voice rings out in an angry whisper, but it seems far away. "You crazy prick – what did you do to her?" Aerick puts me down on my bed, pulling the blanket down as he slides his arms out from under me. I'm suddenly saddened by the loss of his touch, but my eyes are too heavy to open. My sweater is quickly swept over my head.

"I suggest you change your fucking tone with me cadet. Apparently, some of you were getting drunk. She fell asleep when I was questioning her, and now I am putting to her bed, since she is less than coherent. I will deal with her in the morning," he says forcefully in a whisper as he removes my shoes. "You wouldn't happen to know where she got the booze from, would you?"

Crap. "No, sir. I don't." Jeff calms down, and I hear him sit down on his bed.

"Hmm. I didn't think so. Get your ass to sleep, cadet, before you get yourself into any more trouble." He pulls my blanket up to my chin, his hand lingering on the blanket as he runs his finger down my cheek. I know it's his way of saying goodnight. Then he's gone and I let the darkness take me.

CHAPTER SEVENTEEN

(Sunday, June 29th)

MY HEAD IS pounding as I hit my alarm clock in an attempt to shut it off. *I need more sleep.* I feel Jeff push me and I finally sit up. *Shit. What the hell was I thinking, getting drunk last night?*

My eyes fly open as yesterday evening comes flooding back to me. I drank last night. I didn't mean to get drunk; they just kept handing me drinks. John and Aerick both kissed me, although the kiss with Aerick was much better, and consensual. *Fuck, he's a good kisser!*

Aerick and I were both drunk. I can't help but wonder if what he said last night was true; it must be, right?

I just don't get it; what does he see in me? Thinking about all his little comments the last few weeks, and the songs he put on my iPod, the way he withdrew from me when I told him to stay away. I knew something was up with him, but never in a thousand years would I have guessed it was because he might like me.

I also don't even know how to feel about what he said about love. I guess that's what he meant by his 'weakness,' but how am I supposed to process that? If he does like me, could I possibly be with someone who couldn't love me? This is all so confusing.

Jeff pushes me off the bed and throws me a sweater. In an ironic twist, Patrick makes my bed quickly while Jeff sets me on my chest to tie my shoes. I love these guys; they're the best.

We all rush outside and I realize I'm not cold. Looking down, I remember I was 'put to bed' last night by Aerick, and a smile plasters itself across my face as Jeff drags me into formation. I try to stand up straighter and my eyes find Aerick's. He raises an amused eyebrow at me as I pull myself into position, then faces forward just as Luther begins our weekly rankings speech.

Paulo leads us in this morning's workout, and Aerick and Brand are laying into John today. He's sluggish and unfocused, presumably due to his hangover. Something tells me he was giving himself a little more than he was giving others. Well, other than me, but it's giving Aerick and Brand the perfect fuel to yell at him. He has a nice-sized bruise on his jaw, and I can't help but be proud of myself.

Working out this morning is making me extremely nauseated. Trent's told me to pick it up a few times, but Aerick seems to be staying away from me. I push through it, not wanting to draw attention to myself, but when we're finally dismissed, I run back into the dorm and barely make it to the toilet.

"You okay Nadi?" I hear Jeff shout as he comes into the bathroom.

"Yeah, just please, no loud noises," I plead with him. He chuckles and walks away. *Jerk.*

As soon as I'm sure there is nothing left in my stomach, I go over to my drawer to retrieve my toothbrush. When I open it, there's a water bottle in it with a packet of Advil taped to it and a note. I flip open the note. 'Take these and drink the WHOLE bottle of water!' Wow, he can be pushy, even in a note.

He didn't sign it but I know it's from Aerick. I roll my eyes but gladly take the Advil and drink a few sips of water. I wait a minute to be certain my stomach is okay before I finish the bottle of water and brush my teeth.

I am positive I'm not going to be able to eat right now, but I don't want to get in trouble for missing breakfast, either. My little incident last night probably put a spotlight on me already. A quick shower and some clean clothes seem like a good solution to help improve how I feel right now. I hurry and grab some clothes; I throw my hair up in a messy bun, since I don't have time to wash it.

The hot water feels amazing on my drained body, but there are only a few minutes to enjoy it. I wash up and dress quickly wanting to get to the mess hall to see Aerick. I feel a little better now that I'm clean but, I'm still tired and the Advil must not have kicked in yet, because my head is still killing me. I look at my schedule and see that my counseling session is right before dinner; hopefully, I can take a nap today.

Jeff and Patrick walk with me to breakfast. When I walk into the mess hall I expect to see Aerick, but he isn't there even though we're running a few minutes late. Trent walks up behind me, making me jump when he speaks. "Nadi, Aerick won't be in for breakfast. He says you can dish up your own food."

I'm so overwhelmed with disappointment that I don't know what say and when I stay quiet Trent walks away. *That bites.* I wanted to see him; then again, I really need to chill out. I was just with him less than twelve hours ago, and I'm not that clingy type.

Besides, being here, I need to get used to it since no one can know about us. Not that I can do anything about it, but something about that really bothers me. I tell myself it isn't because Aerick doesn't want to be seen with me – rather, that he can't be seen with me.

Jeff gives me a little shove towards the line and I comply. Ugh, smelling the food is making the bile rise in my throat. At least I don't have to eat much, since Aerick isn't dishing up my food up. I grab a few pieces of toast, fruit and some coffee. We sit down, and I start to nibble on my toast, debating if I should just not eat at all.

"You better eat or Aerick might just start hand-feeding you." I laugh a little as I think how much I might like that in a certain private setting.

I pull away from my inappropriate thoughts. "Shut up,

Patrick. This is all your fault."

He smiles. "Hey, we were just having some fun. We didn't know you were going to go all Rhonda Rousey on John." Everyone at my table laughs, including Trent and Paulo. Apparently, everyone thinks my actions were justified.

I wonder if the other instructors knew we were drinking. I look over at the other table at John and his head is hung low. He eats quietly, not talking to anyone. I sort of feel bad for him. I mean, being knocked down is one thing, but when it's by a girl, it's pretty demeaning. Not to mention, the extra attention during PT was no doubt due to what happened.

I should probably still be mad at him, but I'm not. He was just acting like a drunk idiot who thought that he would be able to take advantage of a drunk girl. Unfortunately for him, he chose the wrong one; or maybe he just liked me and thought that was the best way to go about showing me. Either way, not the best idea.

Although, it worked damn well for Aerick and I. It was that little incident that gave Aerick and I an excuse to leave and go somewhere private. I suppose I am a little grateful.

Somehow, I manage to get down two pieces of toast, but I just can't eat the fruit. Jeff keeps sneaking pieces off my plate when no one is looking, and by the end of breakfast it's gone despite me not eating any of it. He gives me a sly smile. I swear he can read my thoughts sometimes.

Today is cloudy and a little chilly, so we go back to the dorm to work on our homework. I move the books and papers to my bed and get my iPod out of my desk. I want to get my work done as soon as possible because my body is begging me for more sleep.

Luckily, I only have two assignments left to finish. I completed my other homework during the week since it was very uneventful – excluding last night, of course. It helps that I'm getting used to the exercise and it doesn't seem to make me as tired in the evening, which gives me some more time.

I turn on my music softly since my head is still pounding even though it has dulled out thanks to the Advil. Math is the easiest, so I start there. Looking around at the guys, most of them look just a bit worn down. Energy levels the day after drinking don't tend to run high. I smile a little at the thought.

Tara still hasn't come back from mess hall duty. She, John, and Joseph ended up in the bottom three this week. I still didn't get the top two; I'm assuming it was because of last night. Jeff was fourth from the bottom and him mouthing off to Aerick pops into my head. He should stop sticking up for me all the time; it just gets him into trouble.

It's surprising I remember Aerick putting me to bed last night, despite me being less than coherent. I close my eyes, focusing on how it felt; I'd enjoyed the feeling of his arms around me, and I can just imagine how they would feel around me as I slept. My brain is still trying to believe that last night even happened and I'm kind of worried because it's almost as if Aerick is avoiding me. I wonder if he's having second thoughts about it. I hope not;

the way he kissed me last night was incredible.

There's only one other boy that I was ever able to get a little close too. About a year ago, I dated a guy named Alex. He was super sweet and cute, but he was kind of a weak, always getting picked on for being the smart, quiet kid.

I think I felt less threatened by him, but he was only able to touch my face and hair. Several times when we were kissing, he put his hands on my sides or around my back and I would freeze. It would take a few minutes before I was okay again.

He was patient with me, but I just couldn't get past it. After several months, I told him I couldn't do it anymore. It wasn't fair to him to be with someone as fucked up as me.

"Nadi!" Patrick shouts and throws his eraser at me, bringing me out of my little daydream.

"What?" I glare at him.

"You're falling asleep; lie down before you fall over." Laughter bubbles in me because I really was daydreaming, which isn't too far off from sleep, but I manage to keep it inside.

Instead, I turn my iPod to a little heavier music to keep me awake, and focus on my work. It doesn't take long to finish the assignment. I put it on my desk and then lie on my stomach to start reading my technology book, so I can write a paper on the advancement of technology over the last forty years. The material is unbelievably boring.

✳ ✳ ✳ ✳

"Hey," I hear Aerick whisper in my ear. My eyes open slowly, and Aerick is sitting next to me on my bed. I must have fallen asleep while I was reading.

He moves my hair out of my face. "You okay?" He asks, trying to hide a smile.

"Yes, I'm fine." A smile spreads across my face until I sit up quickly realizing that someone might see us. Aerick raises a questioning eyebrow. "Where is everyone?" I ask.

"They are at lunch, which is where you really should be since you only ate two pieces of toast for breakfast after a night of drinking." I roll my eyes at him. It doesn't surprise me that he knows that.

"Jeff came into my dorm saying you were sleeping and weren't feeling well. He asked if he could just pick you up something." He pauses and looks into my eyes. "I told him to let you sleep and that since you are *my* cadet, I would check on you to make sure that you ate. Funny enough, he didn't seem to like my answer." His lips press into a line.

"Here." He hands me two more Advil and another bottle of water. My headache is back, full force, but his presence is keeping it at bay for the moment. I take it graciously and drink a small bit of water. "The whole bottle." *So pushy.*

"Yes, sir." I roll my eyes and laugh as I remember what he said last night about having control. I drink the rest of it, not because he asked but because I'm badly dehydrated anyway; my mouth feels like sandpaper. He smiles as I comply.

"So, where were you for breakfast?" I ask curiously.

"I figured you might want to pick out your breakfast this morning after your stomach got the best of you. If I were there, everyone would expect me to give you the usual portions and watch you until you finished it. I don't think you would have been able to finish it." He laughs a little.

"It isn't funny!" I pout, pushing at his arm.

"Besides, I had a report I had to write to explain our 'little quiet' time last night. I'm not the most creative person, so it took me a second to come up with a believable story." He bites the inside of his lip as he seems to get lost in thought for a moment and it makes me remember something from last night. I couldn't be sure; I was a little drunk and everything about last night was a bit shocking. I look up at him, curious again.

"What?" He asks me, looking a little worried when he sees my expression. I'm almost embarrassed to ask. "What?" He says, a little more forceful, and even though I'm trying to see, I can't tell.

I look down trying to hide my smile, "Is your tongue pierced?" He doesn't answer and after a minute, I look back up. He's grinning at me.

"Here," he pulls me over to him, "let me answer your question." His lips press softly against mine; then something hard runs across my top lip. *I knew that's what I felt.* He's still smiling when he pulls back.

"After all the times I've stared at your mouth, how did I never see that?" *Dammitt.* Why doesn't my filter ever work when I need it to. My cheeks get hot, and I bite my bottom lip trying to reel in my emotions.

His eyes darken a little and he grabs my chin, kissing me again a little more forceful, but he doesn't stop this time. I grab his neck with my hand, not wanting him to stop. He deepens the kiss and desire explodes through my body again.

My other hand finds his hair, and I pull hard, lost in the pleasure of his hand running down my back. "Fuck!" He whispers in a low sexy voice that hits me right to the core.

I move to my knees, intending to make my way to his lap, but somehow, he slides me under him and pins me to my bed with his body. I press my pelvis up, needing relief as he hardens against me. His lips leave mine and he moves down my neck as his hand wanders under my shirt.

My whole body freezes for a moment in worry. I don't have a big chest like many girls, and without the advantage of alcohol in my system, I immediately feel self-conscious. He stops and looks up at me, a worried look crosses his features. "Too fast?" He questions between heavy breaths, and it occurs to me what he's talking about.

"No... um, I just... I just... have never really been comfortable with guys seeing my body," I say completely embarrassed looking away from his eyes.

"Hey," he turns my face back to meet his eyes. "You have no reason to be embarrassed. You are fucking beautiful." I roll my eyes knowing he's just being nice.

"Hey," he says, more sternly, "I'm serious." He looks me up

and down and smiles slightly. "Trust me; I would be a very happy man if I could just kiss every part of you right now," he says with lust in his voice as he starts kissing my neck again.

"Just relax princess," he whispers in my ear, and I can feel his smile on my neck. His words put me at ease and I relax.

Closing my eyes, I let his expert lips kiss away all my thoughts and fears. His hand goes under my shirt, and this time I stay relaxed. His hand moves over my breast and he groans against my neck. The ache between my legs begins to throb as he moves his mouth next to my ear.

"I fucking want you so bad right now." I think I'm going to die right here and now from desire. The feeling is definitely mutual.

Before I can respond, he suddenly jumps up. "Shit!" I look at him confused as he adjusts his pants, looking pissed. Then I hear voices getting closer. He gives me a quick kiss, holding my chin for just a second, then winks at me as he walks towards the bathroom quickly.

Fuck! I swear this man is going to kill me by driving me crazy. I sit up quickly, trying to gain my composure, as Mike and Huck walk into the dorm. I just glare at them; I don't mean to, but I can't help it. I grab my book that's still lying on my bed and start reading. Patrick and Jeff come in shortly after and I'm glad I had time to calm down because they would know that something was up immediately.

"Good, he brought you something." I follow Jeff's eyes and see there's a chicken wrap along with a bottle of apple juice.

"I was going to get you something, but he said he would 'fucking deal with it,' so I didn't push it." He puts his fingers up to quote Aerick. I'm trying to hold back a smile because that sounds a lot more like him than the story he told me.

"I know he's so hell bent on making sure you eat now, so I figured he would bring you something. So, do you feel better?"

I smile.

"Yep," is all I manage to get out as my mind, against my will, tries to rehash what happened a few minutes ago. To be honest, it did make me feel better.

Although, I imagine he's feeling less than comfortable right now. Getting that excited twice in the last twenty-four hours without a release can't feel too good. I may have never been with a guy, but I hang out with them a lot, and they never did hold their tongues just because I was around. As a matter of fact, I've learned a great deal about guys and the way their minds work.

I get up quickly, needing to use the bathroom and try to get my mind off Aerick. As I walk, my eyes skim over the wall and stop where the camera is. *Shit.* I never thought about the camera. I wonder if someone watches that all the time. Is he able interrupt the feed, block it, erase it, or something? I try to act normal even though I'm freaking out on the inside. I walk into the bathroom and freeze. Aerick is coming out of the shower in only shorts and has goose bumps on his arms. I look him up and down with a big smile on my face, knowing exactly why he's taking a shower in the middle of the day.

I bite my lip, trying to hold in the laughter. "Cold shower?" I can't help it; a laugh bubbles to the surface.

He gets a cute smirk on his face. "Funny, is it?" I can't say anything because I'm trying hard not to laugh again. His face turns more serious as he sucks his lower lip into his mouth, his eyes darkening as he walks toward me. *He wouldn't, not in here where people can come walking in.*

Before I can even finish the thought, Royce comes in, going to one of the bathroom stalls. Aerick immediately stands up straighter, completely composed, and he walks past me with a wink and whispers, "Careful now," by way of a threat. As soon as Aerick is out of the room, I hurry into the stall to calm myself down. *Damn, he's good.*

Once I calm down, I go back to our dorm and sit down to finish my homework. I pick up my chicken and cheese wrap – I'm hungry now that the nausea is gone. I scan over the fifty-page chapter and start writing my essay.

I know a lot of what's in the chapter, and I want to finish it before my session with the shrink, so I tell myself I'll read it properly this coming week. Aerick usually works out in the gym after dinner, and I plan on 'running into him.'

Geez! Internally I roll my eyes at myself. Who's the stalker now? I turn my music up and focus on the paper.

I finish it with ten minutes to spare. Once I've organized everything in my binder and clean up my desk, I grab my iPod. I make my way over to the classrooms but take my time, walking around the path instead of through the grass. When I reach the building, I'm still a few minutes early, so I sit on the outside step and wait for whoever is in there to come out. I pull out my iPod and turn it on. Leaning back against the side rail, I stare into the sky, trying to clear my mind before the inevitable talk.

Unfortunately, the song that comes on is a little depressing. Half way through, I yank my earbuds out and just stare at the sky. I don't know why, but I just don't want to hear that right now.

After a minute John opens the door, and I stand to let him by. He doesn't look at me; he just walks out into the courtyard. His mood seems pretty irritated, but then again, he was just talking to a shrink. Taking a deep breath, I let my feet carry me inside as I watch him retreat.

"Good afternoon Nadi," she greets me as I walk in. I give her a tight smile and shake her hand.

"Hello, Liz."

We go sit down. "So, I hear you had an interesting night last night." Of course, John would have explained why he had a bruise on his face.

"Um, yeah. Well what can I say that he hasn't?"

She gives me a tight smile. "All the same, I would like to hear your side."

I sigh. I guess it's better than talking about the alternative. I'm about to start when I glance up to the corner as the realization hits me. "Are there cameras in here too?"

She looks at me, confused; Maybe I'm not supposed to know about them. "Why would you ask me that?" She asks now curious.

The truth is, I don't want people sitting there watching what I say about my life, especially once these conversations get a little deeper and at some point, I may accidentally say something about Aerick. She's still looking at me, expecting an answer. "Well, I just know that they have cameras in some of the buildings, and I don't feel comfortable talking about this if someone is listening. I don't want to get in trouble or anything." I hope it comes out convincing enough.

She nods her head. "There is a camera in here, but they are required to be off when we have our sessions. Patient confidentiality applies here just as anywhere else. What you say to me will not leave this room without your permission, okay?"

I nod my head, feeling a lot better. I continue to tell her exactly what had happened with us drinking. I leave out who was specifically drinking, besides John and I since I feel it isn't an important part of the issue. I also stop after telling her, 'Aerick escorted me back to the dorm.' I didn't tell her that we didn't go into the dorm, or that we had a bit of a hot make-out session. I'm not ready to talk about that either. It's none of her business anyway; it doesn't have anything to do with why I'm here.

"So really, this time it wasn't as much as he touched you, as it was that he kissed you and it was unwelcome?"

I nod my head. "Yeah, pretty much. I guess he picked the wrong girl to take advantage of." I smile, again proud of sticking up for myself.

"And that is why you think he did it?" She raises an eyebrow. *Shit.*

I know right away by her reaction that it isn't true. "Damn, it wasn't that, was it? He actually likes me."

She looks at me slyly. "I can't reveal my conversation with him, but if you have something on your conscience, it may be good for you to talk to him about it."

Great. Now I feel bad because she just basically confirmed my thoughts. "Well, either way, it's not how he should've gone about it."

She chuckles. "Well, that's something we can agree on. It looks like our time is up. Did you have any last questions?" I shake my head and get up to leave, shaking her hand.

My smile reappears as I exit the room. I managed to get through another session fairly easily. Patrick, Jeff, and Huck are out in the courtyard throwing the football around, and I decide to join them. I yell to Jeff to throw me the ball. He does as everyone slowly starts changing positions, so we're standing in a square.

The weather has turned partly sunny, and this is a relaxing distraction while we wait for dinner. I've always been good at throwing and kicking a football. Huck seems impressed. "Nice arm, and not just for a girl."

"Thanks," I say trying to push away the embarrassment.

As if showing me off Jeff jumps in. "Yeah, she's amazing with a ball, watch this," he says as he runs over to me with the ball.

"Come on, just like the old days," he tells me as he hands me the ball and gets ready to run. I used to help the boys practice when they played youth football.

It's hard to say 'nom to that face. "Fine." Taking the ball from him, I pretend to be annoyed, but inside I can't help the joy pushing its way through. It's these carefree moments that I miss so much.

I nod and hold the ball with both hands, "Ready, go!" I take several steps back. He sprints far down field then cuts right, and I throw the ball hard in a perfect spiral. He catches it easily. Another errant thought enters my head, wondering why he never continued playing. He's fast on his feet and has good hands.

Jeff throws his hands in the air and Huck applauds our little demonstration. I laugh out of pure joy, and my eyes scan over the side of the field where I hear shouts of 'nice' and 'wow.' I realized several other people watched it as well, including Aerick. My eyes find his. He looks impressed, and my face heats up with embarrassment.

Jeff has since run back over to me. "Again?"

"Um, I think we have shown off my impressive skills to enough people. Let's eat dinner." I'm not doing that again with everyone watching.

He throws the ball back to Huck. "Sounds good." We walk into the mess hall, and he goes to get food.

Before I can sit, Aerick stops me. "Well, aren't you the talented one." A smile is tugging at the corner of his mouth and my face heats up again. "I think you can start serving up yourself again, if you can promise me, you will eat." His gesture surprises me, making me curious why he is giving up control, but I'm not going to question it.

It's impossible not to get excited. "I promise I'll eat," I say to him, almost too happily. We both walk over to our get food. I end up getting more than he would typically serve because I haven't eaten much today. Not to mention, I completely emptied my stomach this morning; I'm starving. As we walk toward the table, a slight smile plays across his features when he looks at my tray.

I sit down next to Jeff in my normal, spot as Aerick sits on the other side of me. Once we've settled in our seats, Aerick presses his leg against mine, and I attempt to hold in a grin. Royce sits across from us, complimenting me on my throwing skills. Talk of football erupts at our table, taking the attention off me, which is how I like it.

As always, Aerick finishes quickly and gets up to leave quietly. My excitement grows as my planned visit gets closer, but I need to be patient. I finish up my food, trying to keep up with the guys' conversation. We get up to put our trays away; the guys are going to back to the dorm, and I tell Jeff I'm going to go to the gym for a while to blow off some steam, to keep his curiosity at bay. The last thing I need is him getting suspicious.

"You okay? Is the shrink getting to you?" I nod. It's not really a lie; I don't like talking to her.

"Alright. I'll see you in a bit, and this time wear gloves," he says in an almost scolding manner. I shake my head. You would think I was a doll, the way these guys treat me sometimes.

I head into the gym, hoping to talk to Aerick. Speaking to Liz about the cameras also made me think of our little make-out session in the dorm. When I walk in, I see him already punching at a bag in his tank top. His arms and chest are so freaking hot. Unfortunately, Paulo's in here lifting weights.

Disappointed, I walk over to the equipment cage and grab a pair of gloves, then go over to the bags. "You okay?" Aerick asks.

"Um, yeah, I just wanted to work out some frustrations." He fights a smile, "So you didn't just come in to see me?" Sarcasm drips from his words.

I give him a pointed look. "Hey, my world doesn't revolve around you."

He smirks, waving his hand toward the bag. "Okay, please continue." I turn to the bag and start punching. "So, what's wrong? Liz hit a sore spot?"

I glance at him and then at Paulo before I start hitting the bag again. He's far enough away that he probably can't hear us. "In a way, yes."

He pauses for a moment. "Really?" He's curious now.

"Well, I obviously didn't say it to her, but I'm wondering about the camera in the dorm and what happened earlier."

He laughs as he goes back to punching. "Oh, don't worry about that, I saved that for my own personal viewing. You know, like when I need to see you and can't. It's a better alternative to a cold shower."

I stop, and my mouth falls open. Aerick stares at me with a straight face. "You're serious?" I can't believe he would do that, much less tell me about it! *Holy Shit.*

Finally, he breaks and starts laughing – like, full on laughing. I just look at him. "You don't really think I would do that, do you?"

"You're such an ass," I tell him and go back to punching the bag, but with more conviction this time. I notice Paulo looking over at us. Aerick goes back to hitting his bag too, and Paulo focuses on what he's doing.

"Don't worry, he has headphones in, and for the record, I prefer the real thing," Aerick informs me. "I was just kidding about the camera feed. I can't change the video feeds without someone knowing it was me. I do however know how to loosen the wire in the utility closet in the dorm to mess up the feed. It didn't take Jake long to figure out it was a loose wire and he fixed it. Thankfully, that also covered our conversation in the bathroom."

He takes a deep breath before continuing. "Unfortunately, that is not something I will be able to do often."

I relax a bit, knowing it wasn't on some camera recording somewhere. "That brings up another point though. There are cameras in every building, including this one. The camera is kitty-corner from us, up pretty high, so it can see us but would not pick up quiet talking across the room. We are too far away, but be careful what you say in the buildings, okay?"

I nod my head and keep punching. "There are also cameras on the buildings outside, although those don't have microphones on them. During the day, if you look closely, you can see the sun on the lenses, and at night they have red lights." I nod my head again.

Then I slow down my punches. "The cameras don't show us in the showers, do they?"

He chuckles. "Of course not, that is why they have high walls and why the toilets have normal doors instead of those flimsy swinging doors that you can see through anyway."

Wow, he sure is being informative today. Aerick suddenly moves over to me, and I freeze because Paulo is still in here. He smiles, gazing into my eyes. He pushes my elbow up a bit, so it's closer to my cheek, "You need to make sure to cover your face. Punch."

I look back at the bag and punch. "Again." I do, and he moves his large hand to my abs. Fire breaks out as his hand connects with my stomach. "I told you to tighten these muscles. It is important for you to build your core. Again." If anyone didn't know better, they would think he was in full instructor mode, but I do know better. I punch, but I don't stop; I keep going because I need to release this pent-up tension building inside of me. When he seems satisfied, he releases me and goes back to his own bag.

After a while I get tired, and it's clear Paulo isn't giving up so soon, so I decide to go back to the dorm. "See you at PT," I tell him with a smile. He nods his head and smiles as I leave.

✻ ✻ ✻ ✻

It was impossible to talk to Aerick after our workout without making it look obvious. I'm a little saddened that I can't say goodnight. On a good note, the very hot relaxing shower I just got out of has me feeling fantastic. I get my toothbrush out of my drawer, and there is a little sticky note on it. *'Night Princess.'* My mouth turns into a full smile for the hundredth time today, but then I remember the camera and ball the note in my hand. I brush my teeth; when I rinse my mouth, I grab a paper towel to dry my hands and slyly put the sticky note in the paper towel before throwing it away.

I go in and lie down, thinking about our little nicknames, and it's funny because we're just the opposite. I'm definitely no princess, and he's by far no prince charming!

CHAPTER EIGHTEEN

(Wednesday, July 1st)

Aerick POV

SHIT. "TRENT, CAN'T you keep tabs on your dumbass cadets?" I shout as I jog over to Leena. She collapsed just inside the tree line after her tracker activated. Joseph is standing a few feet away, afraid to move any further.

"What the hell were you doing?" Not sure why I bother asking, because I am certain I know. Trent was too busy talking to Huck to notice that Leena and Joseph were trying to sneak off together. Although, I don't have much room to talk; my attention was on Nadalynn who was talking to Royce, getting a little irritated that I couldn't be the reason for that megawatt smile on her face. I shake off the thought at once; it's not a good time to be distracted.

I have warned the cadets every time we leave not to get too

far away from us. I don't understand why they insist on pressing the limits. Joseph is at my side, his words all spilling out in a rush. "I didn't do anything, I swear. She told me to follow her, but I swear we weren't trying to run. We just wanted, you know, some privacy, and then she collapsed after her tracker poked her."

"Fucking idiots!" I say to myself, but loud enough so that he can hear me. I roll her from her side to her back and check her pulse.

Trent makes his way over with the rest of the cadets, in no hurry since we know there isn't much danger in it. "She alright?"

I turn to Trent but before I can answer, Joseph opens his big mouth. "What do you mean 'alright?' She just fainted, you asshole! What the hell do these bracelets do to us?" His tone and attitude, combined with my climbing irritation, are enough to make me snap.

I'm up and in his face in the blink of an eye. "That tracker is the only thing that gives you the little bit of freedom you get. So, I suggest you act a bit more appreciative, you fucking piss-ant. It did exactly what it was supposed to do, which is to keep idiots like you in line when they can't follow the simplest instructions. Now, go sit your ass down and shut up before I lose my temper."

Honestly, I think this kid is going to piss himself, but it serves him right. *Shit, I wasn't even yelling.* Maybe I raised my voice a little, but I've done worse. Trent rolls his eyes at my actions as if proof of my thoughts. I'm famous for being the asshole instructor of the group. I wasn't lying when I told Nadi that.

Leena begins to stir. I let out a deep sigh of frustration, realizing she needs to be moved to level ground. Putting my arm under her shoulder, and the other under her legs, I easily carry her over to a large rock on the patch of grass next to the John Wayne trail.

She is a little lighter than Nadi, but Nadi is much more athletic. Her time here has only continued to define her muscles, that now are much more visible in her stomach; some of the other guys have noticed too. *Concentrate!*

Internally shaking the thoughts away, I set Leena upright against the rock; It's going to take her a few more minutes to wake up fully. Holding back another sigh, I look down the seemingly endless trail; it goes on for two hundred and fifty-three miles. I've always wanted to hike the entire trail, but haven't gotten around to it yet.

As I'm looking around, my eyes are drawn to Nadi's. Curiosity has me wondering if she would ever want to do that with me. I look away quickly to reign myself in; this is not the time or place for daydreaming. Out of the corner of my eye, I can see the look of disappointment on her face.

The trail that splits off going down to the camp is in front of me, and I want this girl to wake up because I am not in the mood to carry her back. "Trent, text Luther that there has been an incident, but everything is under control and that we will be a few minutes late. Keep it short; we don't need him freaking out." I'm sure Jake is in the process of informing him since he should be monitoring the system right now, but it is better for Luther to hear it from us. He prefers it that way. I look back at Leena, and she is starting to become more coherent.

The Methohexital doesn't last long and doesn't have any long-term effects, but it is very efficient. It only takes about a minute to work, and then the person is put into a sort of trance, losing all control of their limbs. After about five minutes they wake up, and are fully recovered after thirty minutes. We tend to monitor them a bit longer just to be sure. It's the same stuff they use on people in the ER to reset bones without having to put them under general anesthesia. It works perfectly for us because it puts the cadets down safely, giving us time to get to them.

"Leena, can you hear me?" I ask, and she looks at me, a little confused. "I need you to focus." I wave my hand in front of her eyes, trying to get her to concentrate on my face.

"Is she going to be okay?" Joseph asks, and I give him a dirty look before turning back toward her.

"Can you tell me what day it is?"

She blinks at me for a minutes and smiles. "Yep, it's hiking day with our hot instructor, but he's sort of a jerk."

The annoyance is almost impossible to bite back. "Really. And who might that be?" I ask with a raised eyebrow.

She looks at me as the realization of what she just said kicks in. "Um, I mean today is Wednesday. What just happened?"

"You just broke the rules, cadet. You have been told not to stray from the group. Next time, listen." I stand up and turn towards Trent.

"She's fine. We will give her about ten minutes and then we will start back slowly. You need to make sure you watch her this time." I walk several feet to another large rock and lean against it, looking down the long trail.

"What-the-fuck-ever, Mister Perfect," Trent mumbles under his breath as I walk away.

My lips turn up slightly, since no one can see my face, but pretend I didn't hear it. I usually don't mind that people think I'm an asshole; except Nadalynn, of course.

I'm going against my better judgment with her, but I can't help it. Just looking at her does all kinds of crazy things to me these days. I had managed to stay away for a while, but that night at the bonfire, I lost all the control I thought I had.

Things were going fine, but then I saw another guy kissing her and my rage exploded into flames. I had every intention of beating the shit out of him, but the fiery girl beat me to it. It turned me on that she had just knocked a guy much larger than her down on his ass. I moved without thinking. When I fully realized what was happening, I was already behind her, and it became apparent we both needed to get out of there. Not just because I knew she needed to calm down, but also because I needed to compose myself, as well.

As we walked back to the dorms, all I could think about was that I needed to talk to her, but the cameras posed a problem. After quickly going over the limited options in my head, I opted to take her to the spot where I go when I can't sleep. It's hidden from all the cameras, and no one ever walks back there. Usually, I sit back there and stare at the stars. It helps clear my head and forget about all the stupid ass-shit around me.

When we got there, she instantly threw me off by apologizing. At first, I was confused. *Why the hell would she apologize when she was the one being sexually harassed?* Because I know her secret, I knew what John did must have been extremely difficult for her. She told me she thought she was in the wrong for hitting him, and hearing her say it pissed me off. All I wanted to know was how she was; I didn't give a fuck about him.

With my hand on her chin, she had looked deep into my eyes, and that aching desire started to build inside of me. An internal struggle raged inside my head. Yes, she is eighteen now, but she is still a cadet and I'm an asshole. She deserves better than someone like that after everything she's been through.

She leaned into me with so much need in her eyes. I thought maybe she would kiss me first and even though I was debating, I wanted her to. Then she stopped at the realization of what she was doing and started to lean back. The action killed me inside. I wanted her to kiss me; I wanted to know what her lips felt like on mine. Everything that I had wished for over the last few weeks came flooding out of me all at once, and the control disappeared.

I closed the distance between us and as she kissed me back – I lost my mind. I couldn't help but think how the hell such a pretty little thing could still like me after everything I had done to her. It felt so good to have her arms wrapped around me, and when her small hands pulled at my hair, all I could think about was how much I wanted her right then and there. My mind was fixated on the moment; I almost didn't realize my hands had picked her up and her legs were around me until I started becoming extremely uncomfortable from my restricting pants.

The pain brought me back long enough to think about what was happening. I couldn't be with her that night, not like that; even if her smart mouth did make it clear that she wanted it. A condom isn't something I would generally need at camp, but boy did I regret it at that moment. Looking back, I'm sure it was probably a good thing I didn't; I'm a jerk, but not completely insensitive.

She didn't make it easy for me to hold back. The moment she turned around to straddle me I was completely taken aback by her boldness, and her demanding demeanor was such a turn on. Then she fucking moaned my name like she was mid-orgasm and I thought I was going to explode before even getting to feel her warmth. I warned her for both our sakes.

Extreme discomfort brings me out of my thoughts. Discreetly I look down to the hard mound in my pants; replaying it in my head is making me hard again. Thankfully I'm facing away from everyone. I adjust my pants just as Trent speaks up. "We about ready?"

I need a few more minutes. *Shit.*

I look over at Leena then back at Trent. "She seems like she needs a few more minutes," I say coolly. She looks okay, but it's a perfect cover. He looks at her and then shrugs his shoulders. He can be such an idiot sometimes.

I chance looking at Nadi again. She is sitting next to Royce, staring at the sky. He seems to be talking to her, but she looks utterly lost in thought. I wish that idiot would get away from her. He doesn't seem to like her like that, but I still don't like it.

A smile flits across her features, and what I wouldn't give to know what was going on in that lovely mind of hers. She looks over at me; I'm caught. I give her a half smile and quickly look away before anyone sees. I must be more careful, before others begin figuring it out. I've already forgot myself a few times.

When Jeff came to me the day after the bonfire, I was more than a little worried about her. She had gotten sick after PT, and it was surprising that she even made it through it with how pale she had been beforehand. Nadi's far from weak. I despise the fact that she has to try to convince herself of that which, usually ends up with her pushing herself harder to prove it.

All I wanted was to tell her was that she could skip breakfast, but it would have been way too obvious. Everyone has seen my extreme mood swings lately, and that would have given it away. I skipped breakfast instead so she could get her own food. It pleased me to see her eat something, even if it was only a couple of pieces of toast.

That cocky little friend of hers that sat there eating her fruit has been getting on my nerves, too. Unlike Royce, his actions are not at all innocent. Even if he doesn't admit it to himself, or to her, he likes her a lot. It confounds me that she doesn't see it.

The couple of nights I watched him lie at the top of her bed to comfort her, hit me right in the gut. Once she falls asleep, he always kisses her head and looks at her with such longing in his eyes. Why he hasn't told her how he feels is beyond me. How is she oblivious to all of it? I swear that boy would jump off a building if she asked him to. I thought that since we are mostly together now, she would distance herself from his overprotective ways, but she hasn't. I'm starting to believe she has no idea at all.

He seriously irritated me that day when he came in before lunch, too. If it weren't for my concern for her, I would have run him into the ground for talking to me the way he did. Demanding that I needed to let her sleep and that he would make sure that she ate.

It didn't help my cause that I got extremely defensive, telling him that she was 'my cadet.' Of course, the implication was that she was 'all mine' in my head. Questioning marred Paulo's face, and I reeled in my temper, playing it off that I didn't like his tone.

Thankfully, I was smart enough to disable the cameras before I went in. It probably wasn't a good idea, because it wasn't long before Jake came in to investigate. Not only did I want to make sure that she was okay but I'd also been yearning to touch her again. To be able to kiss her hair like I had seen Jeff do and not worry that someone would see. I probably sat there on her bed for a good ten minutes, just staring at her, before I woke her up. She was just so peaceful, and when my lips kissed her hair, I felt that odd pull inside me again.

There was such need to hold her in my arms just like the night before. To sit there with her head on my chest, feeling the rise and fall of her chest. I had never felt so content in my entire life. I continued to sit there the previous night, long after she fell asleep in my arms. My body and mind were not ready to let her go.

It's only going to be a matter of time before she realizes who I really am, and she won't want anything to do with me. *How can she love someone that could never love her back?* I am brought back to the present by some of the cadets laughing and pushing each other around. I glance down to make sure that I'm good and thankfully I am; we should be going.

I cover the short distance back over to Leena. "Stand up." She gets to her feet and looks steady. "Any dizziness? Nausea?" She thinks about it for a second. *Shit, it isn't a difficult question.* I wait irritably.

"I think I'm okay."

Thank goodness for small favors. "Fine, let's head back. We will take it slow. Leena, do not leave Trent's side. As for the rest of you, I hope you learned something from this little incident." My face shows complete seriousness as I look around to each of them.

"Let's go!" I don't wait for the rest of them; I start toward the trail to go back, and everyone jumps up to follow.

I can't hold back a slight grin when I sense Nadi walking

beside me, and I gently brush my arm against hers to let her know that I'm aware she's there. Her response is a smile, which I spy out of the corner of my eye. I think back to the other day and remember being so amused when she shyly asked me if my tongue was pierced, but I never got around to letting her see it. It turns me on thinking about what I could do to her with it. I shake the memory from my mind before it gets me into trouble, and decide to have a little fun with her.

I also owed her one for that 'cold shower' scene. Granted, she was right, and I was a little surprised that she understood given her limited male contact, but I ached so bad after I left her on her bed that a cold shower was necessary to get myself under control. Making matters worse, last time I'd gotten laid was two weeks before camp starting, when I met up with Liz. Again, I was elated that the cameras weren't working, although Jake had come in to check on the wires while I was dressing. I knew it wouldn't take him long to figure it out.

Patiently, I wait until she looks at me. When she does, I casually reach up and stick my tongue out at her. I pull on the barbell holding it for just a minute as I look at her, without moving my head. I let it go and then bite on it showing her the ball on top. It is clear, but you can see it quite easily when it isn't in my mouth. Her eyes go wide and she looks at me in shock. I let it go and sink my teeth into my bottom lip. Lust instantly crosses her eyes as she looks down, attempting to control herself. She changes the way she is walking for just a second, and it's clear I hit home.

Keeping the grin off my face is impossible. I seem to have such an effect on her body, and that thought alone brings me pure joy. Most girls swoon at my good looks and my well-toned physique, but I never give it a second thought. However, when I see the effect I have on her, the lustful thoughts are hard to keep at bay.

"Jerk." She says quietly, with a smirk.

"I never said I wasn't." She looks up at me, rolling her eyes. My grin turns into a full-on smile that thankfully no one else can see. It's almost painful that I haven't been able to spend any time alone with her since then. Granted it isn't from a lack of trying. I have been thinking over and over in my head, trying to find anyway but there haven't been any opportunities, and Paulo is already watching me.

The night we had our impromptu meeting at the gym, Paulo just became more suspicious. He already knew something was going on with me. Of everyone here, he is the only one that knows me, even if it is just a little bit. The day she confessed her secret to me and subsequently pushed me away had upset me more than I care to admit.

I went back to my dorm, leaving her on the stage, pulled up the camera, and just watched her. Paulo had picked up on my foul mood after a couple of hours and had tried to talk to me, but I had no desire to do so. I let him know I was going to the gym and got up, leaving him without another word. Once in the gym, I continued to watch her until she went back to the dorm. I had so much anger and confusion that I started hitting the bag and didn't stop until Paulo texted me that she had freaked out.

I rushed back, and he told me what happened. All the while, he was eyeing me curiously after he noticed my hands; they were red and bleeding. Even though I was wearing gloves, the chaffing of the fabric over several hours had done a number on my hands. I shrugged it off as if it were nothing, leaving quickly to take a shower and avoid further questioning. My actions during that week as I tried to stay away from Nadi, just furthered his suspicions. Partly because I didn't just withdraw from Nadi; it was from everyone including Paulo.

Then all the sudden I was okay. Paulo knew something was different. I think the icing on the cake was in the gym. He always listens to his music loud – I usually do too, but I'd forgotten my headphones. That night, he told me that he had seen me laugh at something she had said and that he had never seen me smile like that. He begged me to tell him what I was laughing at, but I wouldn't budge. He is naturally growing more and more suspicious.

I figured he'd seen me laughing, which is why I tried to pretend that I was correcting her. Although, I would be lying to myself if I said it wasn't also because I wanted to touch her again. After he had confronted me, I knew I must be more cautious of my actions – and not just around him. The last thing I need is more people picking up on my odd actions toward her.

After the note I left for her on her toothbrush; I didn't chance it again. I just hope she got the ironic connection to the little nickname she'd gave me her first weeks here.

As we close in on camp, I put more space between us. Honestly, I don't think Paulo would care or say anything, but I would rather be safe than sorry. Her smile falters at my actions. Unfortunately, this is for the best.

Please understand, I plead silently. I need to find some time for us to be alone. I want this to work, but I'm not sure how we are going to achieve it. We reach camp, and I whisper quietly, "Princess," as if saying goodbye, and the smile reappears on her face. Composing my own features, I stop to wait for Trent before escorting Leena to the infirmary, so Terrie can check her out.

When we walk in, Luther is already there waiting, and instantly irritation rises in me. "Everything is fine, Luther."

He gives me a pointed look. "Really? Then how did a cadet's tracker manage to go off?" His reaction is so typical.

"She's fine," I say, trying to reel in my frustration. I guide her over to the medical chair and then go outside, not wanting to finish conversation.

Luther follows me, and we go to his office. Once we are inside, he starts up again. "So, what the hell happened?"

"Trent wasn't watching his cadets. They tried to sneak off to have a make-out session and got too far away."

I know he is going to ask it before it is even out of his mouth and I already have an answer waiting. "And where the hell were you?"

I smile inwardly at my accuracy. "Watching my own cadets."

It's technically correct; I was looking at one of them, at least.

He looks at me, still irritated. "Are you okay, Aerick? You seem to be distracted lately. If you need some time, please tell me, because if you are here, I need you to be one hundred percent. It is our responsibility to take care of these teens, and I take my job very seriously."

Rolling my eyes, I shake my head; even he has noticed. There is no point in trying to deny that something is wrong. "I'm fine, Luther. I had an issue and resolved it. I'm good." I hope he believes me, because I don't want to take time off.

After a minute, he shakes his head. "Alright. I expect a full written report of today's incident on my desk by tomorrow."

I go to walk out. "You got it, Luther."

Before I close the door, Luther stops me. "Aerick. I need to see you tomorrow evening to go over Saturday's events." Nodding my head, I close the door.

Shit. This girl is making me weak. Get yourself together Aerick. You're stronger than this!

CHAPTER NINETEEN

(Saturday, July 4th)

I DON'T WANT to get up today. This week has been dragging on and on, partly because I haven't gotten to spend any time with Aerick; it's driving me insane. I hope his distancing is just him being cautious.

I've also been bothered by his ridiculous mood swings. First he's happy and playful, then he's irritable and cranky. Sometimes I feel that warm connection with him, and then other times he just seems so cold. It's extremely frustrating.

His reacted Wednesday when Leena set off her tracker, baffled me. He seemed pretty pissed off and had no problem letting Leena and Joseph know exactly how he felt. Then on the way back, the feelings that built up inside me when he was playing with his barbell and showing it off to me. It was pretty clear he did it to get me all riled up, and that's precisely what happened.

However, since we came back from the hike, he seems more distant, and I wonder if he got in trouble for what happened. It wasn't his fault, but nothing else explains why he's barely acknowledged me the last couple of days. It almost seems like he is in full instructor mode, in a camp where I don't exist. I've been wondering if maybe I did something wrong, but there is nothing that I can think of.

"Come on, Nadi. Where's my pushy little girl?"

I look up at Jeff, annoyed. "Little girl?"

"Okay, so maybe you're not such a little girl anymore," he says with a sheepish grin. I roll my eyes; I'm not in the mood. I drag myself out of bed and make it up super quick. We go out to the stage where Aerick and Luther are both standing on the stage. *Great. Now what?* Once we're in formation, Luther steps forward.

"Good morning cadets. Because today is the Fourth of July we will be doing things a little differently today. The rest of the world celebrates the Fourth, and so it's only fitting that we do so as well. After your evening classes, we will be taking a field trip to town to join into the festivities. There is a festival on Main Street during daylight, and then a big firework show at night. You will have a regular schedule until your last class, and then we will be boarding the bus to go to the town, where you will be able to roam around and join the festival. Now, we have a good relationship with this town, and I expect all of you to be on your best behavior. I will not be happy if we end up banned from this in the future."

"Also, don't get any ideas. Your trackers will be set to go off if you stray too far from your instructors or staff members, and by now I'm sure you all know what that means. All instructors will oversee their own groups, and additional staff will be teaming up with them, while Ayla and I roam around providing assistance as needed. This is meant to be fun, so everyone behaves, and we will all have a good time." Luther finishes his speech, and everyone is instantly buzzing.

I want to be happy, but I'm not sure what today is going to bring. We're hanging out in groups, which means zero chance of getting to spend some time alone with Aerick. As I walk back to the dorm, I glance over at Aerick; he's concentrating hard on his tablet. I should just be happy. At least I'll get to spend this evening with him – even if it is with a bunch of other people.

✳ ✳ ✳ ✳

Instead of hiking today, we climbed the big rock wall behind the gym, which was kind of exciting. The stray from our regular routine can't be due to the weather. It's a beautiful and warm day, not a cloud in the sky. I figure they just didn't want any more problems right before we leave. The day has gone by quicker than expected and I'm a little more excited to be going on this field trip. At least we're getting to go out and do something fun, and, I love fireworks.

Sitting here in our technology class, the last class of the day, it has turned into more of a tell-all from Tia about what to expect. She explains they have all kinds of food-stands and booths that we will be able to explore, and there are even a few rides. I haven't been to a carnival since I was a kid. It sounds way better than our typical night here.

Aerick helped me in and out of the climbing harness during our class earlier, which has also improved my mood. His hands lingered a bit longer than needed on my hips and legs and the contact sent chills through me. When I went to leave for the next class, he had given me a sly wink and I couldn't help the warmth it sent through me.

Tia wraps up class and tells us we have fifteen minutes to get ready to go. "Can I take my iPod?" I ask at the last second.

"Yes, that's fine, but I would be careful not to lose it." I give her a nod of acknowledgment and walk back to the dorm with the rest of the class.

John is walking to the side of everyone. I've been meaning to talk to him but haven't had a chance. I don't want to have enemies here, and Liz told me I should talk to him. *Now is as good a time as any.*

I make my way over to him, trying not to draw any attention to us. "Hey, John."

He looks up curiously. "Uh, hi." My presence seems to shock him a bit.

"You know, we never talked about what happened the other night." I am hoping we can just get past this. He doesn't say anything, so I continue. "We have to be here for another few months, and it does no good for us to sit here and be upset with one another." He finally stops as we near the dorm and looks at me. There's still a hint of faded coloring on his jaw, but I try to ignore it and look him in the eye.

He takes a few deep breaths as if he's trying to get up his courage. "You're right. I was a prick for trying to kiss you like that. I suppose the alcohol got the best of me. I've had a hard time talking to girls in the past. I kind of liked you and didn't know how to tell you." He rubs the back of his neck, seemingly nervous. "I promise that I never intended to take it any further, I just wanted you to know that I liked you."

I give a small chuckle, only because I'm thinking of what happened after I left. "Well, I'm sorry for hitting you. It was just a reflex. In case you haven't heard, I really don't like people touching me."

He finally smiles. "I have heard, or should I say now, I've felt." I smile and see Aerick watching me from the office. "So, does this mean we can be friends now?"

"Sure, but let me be clear. I'm not interested in anything but friendship."

He puts his hands up in defense, "Hey I'll behave in the future, promise."

I give him a quick nod. "I have to run in and grab some stuff. I'll see you later."

"Okay, see you later."

We turn our separate ways and head off to our dorms. Before I walk in, I look back at Aerick and he's still staring at me, looking almost angry. *What now?* I push the thought aside and go to grab my iPod and use the restroom before we leave.

Jeff and Patrick walk with me to the front of camp. There are a bunch of people standing in front a small bus that says, 'Donnelly Bootcamp' on the side. There are three people I've never seen before spread out between the staff. They're all wearing the camp uniform and they all have matching black backpacks. Luther steps up on the bus and waits for everyone to be quiet.

"Good afternoon. Listen up, because I will only say this once, as I am sure we are all excited about this trip. Quickly, I would like to introduce you cadets to our extra staff for this outing. Jack and Shannon here are ex-instructors who still help out occasionally." The older guy nods his head and looks at us all. The girl looks about the same age as our instructors. She's beautiful, and seems extremely confident.

"Then we have Laura. She is the camp's on-call instructor, who lives here in town." Laura gets a proud smile on her face, and Tia says something to her to make her chuckle. She looks barely out of high school. "As I said earlier, all cadets will stay with their instructors. Tia and Andi will be joining Brand's group, Jake and Shannon will join Trent's Group, Terrie and Jack will join Paulo's, and Brayden and Laura will join Aerick's group."

My eyes find Aerick, but I cannot figure out the expression on his face. Maybe something between happy and annoyed. "Once we leave here, no staff member should be responsible for more than one cadet at any given time. Cadets, I know you shouldn't have to be told, but I will say it again, *do not stray* from the staff. You are on a short leash, for lack of a better word, and if one person's tracker is activated, the night will be over. Is that understood?" We all nod our heads.

"Good. Everyone on the bus." He gets down, talking over his shoulder to Jack, "I'll follow you," as he starts to walk over to where there are some cars parked.

We all fall into a loose line and start getting on the bus. Jeff and Patrick are in front of me, and Aerick moves in behind me. Jeff goes to the back of the bus where there are several open seats together. Jeff gets into the middle one and Patrick sits in front of him. I'm about to slide in next to Jeff when Aerick pushes me forward a little, so I'm forced to walk past, and then nudges at my hip to sit in the seat behind Jeff. Everyone was walking so close together; I don't think anyone else saw what he did except Jeff and Patrick, who give me strange looks.

Aerick sits down beside me, and I roll my eyes. "I guess I'm on a really short leash," I say quietly, trying to justify his actions to my friends, and I hear Jeff laugh as Aerick glares at me. I guess my attitude and everything I've done has gotten me a bit of a reputation, because no one seems surprised that Aerick sat next to me.

There are exactly enough seats for all of us. Jack sits down in the driver's seat and we pull out of the parking lot. Everyone is chatting away with excitement. Jeff, Patrick, and Huck are talking about football. I just kind of tune it out and stare out the window.

I'm nervous about how this afternoon is going to go. I'm still a bit confused with our situation. My heart jumps as I'm startled by Aerick's hand finding its way to my thigh, causing me to go still. I hadn't realized that my leg was bouncing, and it must've been annoying him. I look up at him and he's still looking forward, pretending not to be paying attention to me. His backpack is on his lap hiding his hand.

"Relax," he says under his breath. He leaves his hand on my leg, moving his thumb back and forth on the inside of my thigh making my heart continue to race. I take a deep breath, put in my earbuds and lean my head back on the seat, looking out the window.

I'm pretty content just sitting with Aerick. The bus is small and so are the seats. Aerick and I fit perfectly in it with his hip pushed up against mine. After a few minutes, between us sitting so close and his hand on my thigh, I feel better than I have in the last few days. A smile spreads across my face, and I assume Aerick sees it because he squeezes my leg gently. I don't move to look at him because I don't want anything to change in this moment. This is the closeness I've been craving, and I want it to last as long as possible.

We get into town, and it's overflowing with people. The bus goes down a side street since most of Main Street seems to be closed off for the festival. About half way into town, we pull over and park on the edge of the road.

Ayla gets up. "Alright, staff. We will be going to the BBQ tent for dinner. Get the cadets sat down, and Luther and I will be bringing dinner over." We all stand and get off the bus.

"Stay together!" Aerick shouts at our group as Luther and Ayla walk ahead of us. Jeff and Patrick come to stand next to me in the back of the group, and Aerick backs off just a little to walk behind us. I feel a little disappointed, but my mood has improved significantly.

"I hope we get some French fries," Patrick says. I have to say; I would love some too. The food at camp is good, but it's also mostly healthy food; a good dose of greasy food sounds fantastic. As we turn onto a street with more people, the staff automatically creates a loose circle around us. They lead us to a large area that has tons of picnic tables, and several very large BBQs, behind a long line of tables with people taking orders.

We all sit at four of the tables, and Aerick sits next to me on one side while Jeff sits on the other. "What did you do to piss him off this time?" Jeff whispers in my ear.

"I don't have the slightest idea," I tell him and Aerick eyes me. I roll my eyes, and he pushes his leg against mine, keeping me at ease.

I look around, taking in my surroundings. On the other side of Main Street, there seem to be some fair rides, but none that are too big except a very tall pole-looking thing. There are lots of lights hung everywhere; people are walking around us, smiling and laughing like there isn't a care in the world. Kids are running around, and I see groups of teenagers messing around with each other.

A few people stare at our group. I'm sure our black uniforms stand out when you have twenty-four of us, but mostly they just smile and keep walking. A few even nod their heads to say hello. People here seem pretty friendly, despite who we are; this would never happen in Chicago.

Luther and Ayla walk up to us, each carrying a stack of to-go plates while several people follow behind them carrying even more. They hand them out to everyone, then Luther and Ayla sits down to join us for dinner. I open my plate. It is stuffed full of wonderful smelling food. It's complete with a pulled pork sandwich, baked beans, potato salad, a small corn on the cob, and a piece of cornbread. *Wow.*

"This place has the best pulled pork and cornbread," Luther tells us, and Aerick nods his head in agreement, as he's already eating his. I pick up my sandwich and take a bite. It's mouthwateringly delicious.

I eat the whole sandwich and a few bites of everything else before setting my fork down "Damn, that was good." Aerick smiles a little, but when Patrick grabs my plate to finish it he glares at him. Internally rolling my eyes, I ignore it.

It doesn't take long for us to finish and when most of us have finished eating, Luther rises. "Alright, staff, you are welcome to go off with your groups. Have fun but remember your responsibilities. We will meet back at the bus at ten o'clock to go over to the firework show. Ayla and I will be around if we are needed. Enjoy yourselves."

Brand and Trent get up and call over their groups. "Hey, Aerick, what are we doing first?" Laura asks. "I want to go browse the booths. Paulo, how about you?"

Terrie speaks up before Paulo can answer. "I want to go on some rides." Paulo gives Aerick a little shrug. Apparently, he isn't calling the shots.

Rides do sound like fun. "Man, I want to go on rides." I put in my opinion, hoping Aerick will let us go, too.

Paulo laughs at me, "Really... bet you wish you had some money!" My face falls at the realization that we don't have money to do anything, which will definitely put a damper on our fun.

"Jerk," I mutter in irritation as I look down at the table. Paulo laughs and gets up, calling his group over,

"We are going over to the rides, see you later," he tells Aerick. Jeff gives me a sad smile, pouting that we aren't joining them.

As they walk away, Aerick leans into me. "We have money for you guys to go on rides, he was fucking with you." His words instantly lift my mood back up.

Everyone has left except for our group. "Let's go, Aerick," Brayden whines.

Aerick rolls his eyes. "Fine, listen up. We are going to walk to the booths. You guys, do not go walking off. Brayden and Laura, I know it is your first year as leaders, so you need to make sure you are watching the cadets at all times. If you want to stray just a bit that's fine but I always need to be able to see you, and you need to keep a cadet with you. Nadalynn, no problems, and don't leave my side for any reason."

I'm about to say a snide comment until I realize that this was his way of keeping Laura and Brayden from taking off with me. I just nod my head; Huck and Mike look at me sympathetically. *Geez, do people really think I'm a troublemaker or what?!*

"Yeah, okay, you already told us all that. Let's go!" Brayden is impatient, but I see he's irritating Aerick, who rolls his eyes.

We get up and start walking to Main Street. There are so many tents to the left, just like an open flea market. To the right, there are tons of game booths running down the street. Straight in front of us are all the rides, and I hope we get to go on some.

We turn left and start looking at all the different things. There's so much stuff: clothing, jewelry, wood carvings, and trinkets. It's all so cool.

Not thinking, I stop and look at some animals carved out of wood. There's a beautiful one of two dolphins jumping out of water; it's completely stunning and I gently run my hand over it. "Can I help you with something, my dear?" The old lady smiles at me.

I return her smile. "Just looking. Thank you!" Aerick touches my back, and I realize the others have continued ahead. I look around to see if anyone can see us.

"Don't worry, Brand and Trent will be playing games most of the night, and Paulo is over on the rides." He smiles. "Come on, let's catch up to the others." He keeps his hand on my back until we are right behind them. Laura has stopped to look at some jewelry, and the guys are patiently waiting.

My eyes catch the beautiful pieces and I join her; Aerick stays at my side. They have hundreds of necklaces, bracelets, and anklets that have all kinds of ocean wildlife. "These are all so beautiful," Laura says to me.

I smile. "Yes, they are." My eyes find the many different dolphin-charmed ones. I love dolphins; they're such smart, beautiful animals. What's not to love? I always thought it would be cool to swim with the dolphins. It's on my bucket list.

"Check these out." Laura pulls me out of my thoughts and I turn to the other side, walking to the other wall to see. There are a bunch of different pearl bracelets; every color you could think of, and opal ones, too. I could never afford something like this, then again, I don't wear a whole lot of jewelry, either. Growing up broke you don't typically have an affinity for it, unless you don't mind stealing it. I have my ears pierced, but that's it.

"Okay, can we go now?" Brayden asks. "Hold on; I want this one." Laura shows the booth-keeper a gray pearl bracelet with matching hanging earnings. The booth-keeper takes it out of the case as she pays for it. It's so beautiful, and I can't help but be a little jealous. I go to step back, but Aerick is behind me and I run into him. I apologize quietly and walk over to where the other boys are waiting. Laura comes out, and we continue looking.

When we get down farther, Laura stops, buying both of us

girls a exotic feather with beads that we clip into our hair and I'm glad I left it out of its bun and brushed it down before we left. Putting it up in a wet bun the night before made it beautifully wavy, and it now falls just below my chest. I'm grateful it's cooperating for once. The feather she gives me has deep green beads that match perfectly to my eyes.

"Thank you, it's gorgeous," I tell her.

Aerick and I have been staying behind the others. He keeps putting his hand on my back guiding me around, and I almost forget that we're here with the camp. As we continue to walk Aerick leans down and whispers in my ear. "You look beautiful tonight. I love it when you wear your hair down."

His complement makes me blush as I look down and thank him. Butterflies begin to flutter in my stomach. Laura stops at another booth and Aerick pulls me into the one next to us. The surprise on my face doesn't faze him.

"I can't wait anymore." He grabs my face gently and kisses my lips ever so softly. Even though I know we only have a few seconds, he takes his time, kissing me slowly like we have all the time in the world. He pulls away and smiles with the biggest grin. "I have been waiting for that for a week." My smile is so big it's painful, and I try to slow my heartbeat.

Brayden say Aerick's name and I turn around to pretend I'm looking at some tourist shirts so I can compose myself. "Yeah, just a sec, we're coming," Aerick tells him as he quickly grabs two of the black shirts that say, 'Roslyn Café'; he and pays for them before he pulls at my wrist to join the others.

When we catch up, Aerick slows to stick the shirts in his bag. "Can we go on rides now?" Huck asks politely.

Aerick tries to act annoyed but I can see otherwise. "Fine, but if you go on a ride, one of us has to go on it with you," Aerick tells him. "Luther gave me enough for each of us to go on a few and after that, it comes out of our own pockets." He looks at Laura and Brayden, and they nod their heads.

We make our way over to the rides area. After a little debate, we agree to all go on the Gravitron first, and then we go over to the Scrambler. Pairing up, we get into the seats and of course, Aerick sits with me. As the ride starts up, he puts his arm on the back of the seat behind me. It starts going faster and faster so that I'm pushed snug against him, but neither of us cares. A laugh escapes him, and he seems so carefree for just a moment.

When we get off, my eyes again are drawn to the large pole I had seen earlier. There's a basket with three people in it that's climbing to the top. I watch it go up and feel Aerick move to stand right behind me. There are two people connected to each other, and as it reaches the top, the other guy opens a gate. After a minute the couple jumps. I hold my breath as I watch them fall toward the huge air bag below and right before they hit it the cord slows them and springs them back up.

"Have you ever bungee jumped before?" Aerick asks curiously.

"Nope, you?" He shakes his head 'no' but then a sly smile

crosses his face, and he raises an eyebrow. "You brave enough?"

I mirror his expression; he probably thinks I won't do it. No way I'm backing down to him. "Are you paying?"

He looks slightly surprised but recovers quickly, letting out a chuckle. "Only if I get to go too; that shit is expensive!" My eyes follow his to the sign at the booth and my mouth drops. The pricing lists eighty dollars for one person, or a hundred to jump tandem.

"Nadi, are you kidding? You're going to do that?" Mike asks, shocked, and I turn to look at him. It escaped my attention that the rest of our group have joined us, but I ignore that and turn back to the sign.

"Aerick, I can't let you spend that kind of money on me," I tell him, still suffering a bit of sticker shock.

It's too much money, but he looks insulted at my refusal. "It's my money. Are you scared?"

The guys giggle, and my courage explodes. "Absolutely not!"

"Good, because I have wanted to do this for a long time. Laura, Brayden, stay right here with these guys."

"We aren't going anywhere. I want to see her chicken out." Mike laughs.

"Fuck off!" I say, shoving his shoulder.

"Come on." Aerick grabs my forearm, pulling me back from Mike, and we walk over to the ticket window. "We would like to jump tandem, please."

"This is really expensive Aerick."

He rolls his eyes and pulls out a credit card. "I can afford it, trust me."

The guy hands us a waiver to sign and then stamps our hands. We step behind him to the other guy, who helps us put on the harnesses that will connect us together. We then move to the basket, where another man helps us in and puts our feet in the harness that connects to the bungee cord.

We shuffle back slightly, and he closes the gate. In front of us, our group watches with curiosity as we start going up. I'm getting nervous now. "Breathe," Aerick tells me.

The basket operator checks our feet again and then stands to look at me. "Facing him or away from him?"

I look confused and before I can answer Aerick does. "Facing me."

He smiles at me. "Gives me a chance to hold you in public," He explains looking into my eyes, and a grin spreads across my face.

The man eyes him but doesn't question Aerick's response. "Alright. Face each other and stand as close as possible." We do as he says, Aerick holding one side of me while the guy reaches between us, hooking our harnesses together.

"Make sure you hold her tight as you go down. To keep from hitting each other, you need to either lean your faces away from each other at the bottom or keep your head tight on his shoulder as it snaps back up." We both nod and he moves back so I'm able to look down. We're unbelievably high, and all the air leaves my lungs.

We come to a stop, and the operator tells us to move to the rail. Aerick pulls my chin up, so my eyes meet his. "Ready?"

I just nod my head because I'm too nervous to talk. The guy opens the gate. "You going to chicken out?" Aerick asks, and I glare at him.

"No!"

He chuckles and tries to hide his smile. "Okay."

We move to the very edge and I hear people below me yelling, but I can't make out what they're saying. Aerick wraps his arms around me tightly.

"I'll count down from ten, and you jump on one," the guy tells us, but we don't acknowledge him. He starts counting.

Aerick's joking face transforms as he looks deeply into my eyes, and everything else falls away. "Ready?" He says more seriously but looking thoughtful.

"Yes," I whisper and put my arms around him. He leans toward the inside of the basket and kisses me twice on my neck before his lips stop at my ear. "Be brave."

I hear the guy say, "Jump," as I press my head to Aerick's shoulder, keeping my eyes open; his arms tighten around me as we both push out.

For a moment, time stops and I'm completely spellbound, with nothing but him holding me in his arms, weightless. It seems like we stay like that for hours and then all the sudden I feel us snap back up and my stomach drops. "Oh crap!" I yell, and

Aerick's chuckle rumbles against my chest. We bounce around a few times and I grab him tighter, if that is even possible.

"Wow!" I say as I feel them starting to lower us. I can't believe we just did that. I'm so proud that I pushed off myself, not him pulling me off.

He pushes me back slightly so I can see his eyes. "You... are... amazing!" He says each word slowly and with so much conviction. "I really wish I could kiss you right now." He confesses.

The feeling is mutual. "That makes two of us."

CHAPTER TWENTY

(Saturday, July 4th)

WE REACH THE bottom, where someone unhooks us. That was by far the craziest thing I've ever done. My body is absolutely buzzing on its own natural high. We walk out of the gate, and I quickly notice that our group has been joined by Paulo's.

"Holy shit! I can't believe you did that." Patrick says to me, while Jeff just looks at me, speechless.

"Geez, thanks for the vote of confidence," I say with a laugh.

Paulo slaps Aerick on the shoulder. "Dude I can't believe you just took her up there. Luther would have your ass if he found out!"

He shrugs indifferent. "What? She's eighteen now. Besides I didn't think she was going to do it. I figured she would chicken out. Guess I was wrong." It takes all I have to keep from smacking him in the arm, even though it's obvious he is trying to play it off as meaning nothing.

"Well anyway, we're going to meet up with Ayla. I'll see you in a bit." They turn and walk away, Paulo still shaking his head, and I'm secretly glad because I don't want to deal with Jeff and Patrick's questioning looks right now.

A sudden spell of dizziness hits me and I reach out grabbing Aerick's arm for support, not even thinking about the repercussions. Concern immediately fills his eyes until he remembers himself and masks it quickly. "You okay?"

Letting go quickly, I stand up straight, realizing what I just did. "Ugh, yeah, I just got a little dizzy. I'm fine."

He shakes his head in disapproval. "It's the adrenaline rush. Brayden, Laura, stay here for a few minutes with these two. I'm going to take her to the restroom real quick just to be sure. I don't want her puking everywhere." He grabs my upper arm and starts leading me away before I have a chance to object.

He leads us around the corner and into a family restroom that's thankfully unoccupied. As soon as the door shuts behind us, I try to explain I'm fine, but I don't get a chance. I'm pressed up against the wall by his body and his lips are on mine, feverishly moving, so full of need. My body instantly reacts, and my hands are in his hair as he kisses down my neck. He mumbles as he continues to move across my neck, kissing and lightly biting. "You are the smartest... bravest... most incredible woman... I have ever met."

Desire explodes within me, and I'm completely overwhelmed

294

by emotion. I pull at his face, bringing his lips back to my own, fulfilling my own need. It's an interesting feeling, moving his barbell around with my tongue. His hands tighten on me as he bites my lip, and my need for him grows even more.

The feelings coursing through my body are so intense they almost scare me. I want him so much. I've never wanted anything so much in my entire life. "I need you, Aerick."

He lifts me up and turns to sit me on the counter, so I'm almost at eye level with him. My legs wrap around him as he continues to kiss me. Hormones race through me at a mile a minute, and it's so hard to contain the emotion.

As his hand reaches up, moving under my shirt, the ache between my legs gets stronger. My legs loosen a bit to give myself room as I undo his belt and unbutton his pants. I'm not sure where this bravery is coming from, but I'm too caught up to care. I slide my hand between his pants and boxers to rub the growing bulge. He's larger than I thought and a shiver runs through him as I massage his hardness.

"Christ. Is there anything you can't do, princess?" His voice is low, broken, and full of lust.

I know it isn't what he meant but my mind flits back to my objection to touch, and I'm brought down a little from the clouds. His hands feel so amazing on me. I can't believe I've found someone that I'm able to be with; the broken must be attracted to the broken.

Thoughts about what he said that night as we sat outside

come to mind. He doesn't think he can love and my heart aches because I think I'm falling in love with this man. *How can I love someone that won't love me?* The thought is saddening.

A single tear escapes my eyes and falls between our joined lips. The motion of his lips stops in confusion, and my head drops low as I pull my hand out of his pants. Our moment is ruined.

He pulls my chin up to look in my eyes. Why does my head have to screw up everything?

"What's wrong?"

It's not you; I'm just fucked up in the head. "Nothing, I'm sorry." My eyes cast down in embarrassment, but his fingers still resting on my chin prevent me from lowering my head.

He looks concerned, and he's not going to just let it be. "Hey, we have to be honest with each other if this is going to work."

His tone is soft but this week floods back to me and irritation grows in me. "Is that so? Is that why you ignored me most of the week?"

His eyes move away and he takes a deep breath, "It isn't so simple for me."

"And what, you think it is for me?" My words bleed with frustration. He can't possibly imagine how much I crave the simplest touches from him. Something I've never been able to have, but always wanted. I'm the fucked up one. *How could this possibly be simple for me?*

"Nadalynn you don't understand." Now I'm just downright pissed. It's obvious he's holding something back.

I take my hands off him, cross them on my chest and raise my eyebrow. "Then explain."

He huffs and pushes back from the counter walking over by the door and leaning against it. "Shit," he says as he hits his head against the door.

"I believe you just told me we need to be honest." I remind him.

He takes another breath as conflict spreads across his face. "This is not me." He pauses, and it's clear this is it. I knew it wouldn't last; better it stops now before it can go any further.

"I am a very calculating person. I like routine; I like knowing exactly what is going to happen and when. I love the control I have over my own life. It is something I never had when I was younger."

My heart sinks. "I get it; I'm messing that up." The hurt bleeds through my words, and I look down, not able to look at him any longer.

My body is itching to get out of here and away from him. Jumping down, I head for the door, grabbing the handle, waiting for him to move off it. "It's fine; go back to your life. I'll leave you alone." I try unsuccessfully to open the door. I need to be alone; I don't want him to see me weak. I pull at the door again, but he doesn't move, effectively blocking me from leaving.

"Hey, it isn't that. Stop. Please, I don't want you to go." Confused, I look up at him, not understanding. He just told me I am ruining his life; we need to let it go and get back to our lives –

simple.

"It's just that, around you, I am so distracted. I'm not used to it. It's making me sloppy at my job, and it's like I am confused all the time about my feelings."

Confused? I know that feeling but what is he talking about? My hand falls from the handle and I lean up against the wall next to him, curious. "Feelings?"

He huffs again, "Yes."

He pauses until I turn to look him in the eyes. "Nadalynn, I have never wanted someone as much as I want you. I wish I could hold you all the time, to sit with you in my arms; it makes me angry that I can't. I see you hanging out with your friends, and it frustrates the shit out of me that we can't have that. The way the guys fall over you, it makes me jealous, and that's not something I normally have to deal with. It makes me confused."

It's strange to process what he's just said to me. Everything he described is mostly mutual, so it's in part understandable. "Aerick, don't you realize that I feel the same way? I've never been able to be so close to someone. This is so new to me. I've a hard time processing it all, and your mood swings don't make it any easier. You seem so cold towards me sometimes, then you do a complete one-eighty and want to be playful. It's hard to keep up. I feel all that, just like you. Well, except for the jealousy. I think you're overreacting on that point."

He finally lets out a small chuckle and reaches over, pulling me in front of him so he can hold me against him. He tilts my head up so can I see his raised eyebrow. "Really. Mike, John, Jeff... should I keep going?"

I shake my head and roll my eyes at him; that's absurd. "Jeff and I aren't like that, but that's beside the point. In fact, none of them matter. I don't want any of them." It's my turn to hold his face to keep his gaze on me. "I want you; I'm just unsure how mutual the feeling is."

Something crosses his eyes. "Hey, I promise you the feeling is mutual. There's just some shit I need to work out in my head, so my feelings for you don't affect my job. There is also the need to find some alone time because the longer I go without you, the crazier my mind seems to get. It's causing me to screw up a lot, and I don't like that."

Relief spreads through my body. I smile up at him, allowing him to kiss my lips gently. "And for the record, I only stayed away because Paulo already knows something's up. I'm still trying to figure out what to do about that." *Crap.* Now I feel terrible for throwing that in his face.

"Next time, try telling me, so I don't have all these crazy thoughts going through my head."

More kisses pepper my lips. "Okay."

Someone pounds on the door, making us both jump. "Come on. We better get back." With one final kiss, we exit the bathroom as he buckles his belt back up, earning us a very dirty look from the lady waiting to enter with her small child. A laugh escapes my mouth, and Aerick struggles to suppress his amusement as she huffs past us.

When we get back to the others, I work to keep a straight face. "You okay?" Laura asks me.

"Yeah, I'm okay now."

"So, shall we go play some games?" Aerick asks, amusement in his eyes. Everyone agrees, and we go over to the games. We spread out just a little in our pairs, playing various games.

When we come to the 'Bulls-eye' game, I smile at him. "You want to play with me?" He looks at me surprised.

"Yep," I declare enthusiastically.

"Okay, but I am pretty good," he confesses, and I try unsuccessfully to keep the grin off my face; he has no idea.

He pays the guy, and we both pick up our rifles. My lips quirk up as I eye him.

"Eyes on your target," he says playfully. Looking over to my target, the bell clinks and we begin shooting, trying to remove the star on the target.

When the game buzzer goes off signaling the end, we have both completely shot out the star. "Well, aren't you full of surprises."

The guy tells us that we both can pick a stuffed bear. "Pick one," Aerick tells me. I point at the black one, and the guy hands it to me. "That's from me," he tells me with a mischievous grin. "But that means you have to give yours away." It's understandable, and I'm so smitten when he's like this.

I point at the white one. "I'll give it to Laura, for the feather she bought me.

"Actually, I will. Just don't take it the wrong way." I nod with a giggle, and he takes the bear.

✽ ✽ ✽ ✽

It's almost ten o'clock by the time we gather up the others. "You won, Laura?" I ask, as she has a cute floppy eared dog in her hands.

"Nope, Brayden won it for me. I see both of you did, though." Aerick looks at the bear in his hand. "Here. You might as well keep this one too. I don't have a need for it." He hands it to her, and her face lights up with shock as he tries to look annoyed. "Let's get back."

We walk back to the bus. Everyone else is already there. "Alright, everyone on the bus in your same seats so I can do a headcount," Aerick shouts over everyone, and we pile onto the bus.

Once we are sitting down, Jeff turns to me. "So, what did you win?"

I laugh playfully. "Who says I won anything? Someone could have given it to me."

Jeff looks over at Aerick and it's clear he's trying not to laugh. "Well..."

Before he says something that may get him in trouble, I give in. "I'm just playing. I won the 'Bulls-eye' game." Aerick's hand finds my thigh again as he takes his seat next to me, and there is the slightest smile pulling at the edge of his mouth.

"Yeah, that makes sense. You are truly a badass." He turns back around, but Aerick looks at me with a questioning look. I shake my head slightly telling him silently, we can talk about it later.

We get up to the school quickly, and Aerick stands up. "Listen up. This place is going to be packed; the whole town comes to watch it. Staff members, do not lose sight of your cadets. Cadets, do not move away from the staff. It will be easy to lose them, and it will not end well for you. Meet back here right when the show ends. Let's go."

We get back in our groups when we get off the bus. Aerick turns to ours. "Brayden, you are responsible for Mike. Laura, you are responsible for Huck. Keep them in front of you at all times, so you don't lose them."

We all walk over to the huge crowd of people who have gathered. There must be close to a thousand people here. We walk out on the field, and I have to watch my step as people have already set up their blankets and chairs everywhere. We head for the back of the field, and I'm not sure where the other groups have gone. Everyone slowly moved away from us as we walked and mixed in with the crowd. Once we're almost all the way back, Aerick stops. "Here is good, and I can see everyone." I turn, and Paulo's group is a little in front of us; the other two groups are more toward the front of the field. Our group starts to sit but Aerick slyly pulls me back just a little farther, and he sits behind me.

Everyone else on the field starts sitting down too as a voice comes over a loudspeaker, welcoming everyone and telling us to enjoy the show. Everything gets quiet, and I jump at the first pop of the fireworks. Then Ozzy Osbourne comes over the loudspeaker singing 'Crazy Train, ' and the fireworks begin to go off to the beat of the music. Aerick pulls me back against his chest and wraps his arms around my waist once he's sure everyone's attention is on the show, but I'm not worried because the bear that's on my lap is probably hiding his arms anyway.

"Happy Fourth of July *my princess*," he whispers in my ear. Today may have been the best day of my life, despite me freaking out earlier.

I lean my head to the side and look at him. "Thank you for such a great day." I smile at him and pull him down to kiss me. He gives me one of his half smiles, and we go back to watching the show.

After watching the show for a bit, he speaks up. "So, you going to tell me where you learned to shoot like that?"

I shrug. "My dad is big into hunting. He believes it's important for his children to know how to shoot and handle a gun. He taught all of us when we were kids. We used to go out and shoot at bottles and cans. I think he was proud I picked it up so quickly. He always told me I was a natural. When we got older, he would take us down to the shooting range." I smile at the memories. I was always a bit of a tomboy, helping fix cars and learning about guns; I never did like dresses and makeup. I'm sure my past had something to do with it as well.

I feel Aerick shake his head. "Amazing. You are just amazing." He kisses the top of my head, and we return our attention to the show until I start to shiver. With no clouds, it's getting very chilly.

Aerick shifts and grabs his sweater out of his bag. "Here, put this on. You really should have brought one."

I happily comply, even though it's big on me, and when I have it on, I inhale his scent still present on the sweater. It smells of the woods and cologne – a smell I instantly love. He looks at me a little strange but I just smile at him, and he returns it easily. I lean back against him again. So many of my senses: smell, touch, sight, hearing – all full of beautiful things; I wish I could stay just like this forever.

Unfortunately, it's over way before I'm ready. Aerick sits me up quickly and stands up. "Let's go, guys."

We get up and walk back to the bus. I notice several of the staff members are holding hands. Brand and Tia, Trent and Shannon, Jake and Andi, Jack and Ayla and even Brayden and Laura. "Are all these guys together?" I ask Aerick quietly.

"Pretty much, that is why Luther has them come up for the holiday. Ayla and Jack are married. Brand and Trent have been dating their girls for over a year. Andi and Jake have only been the last few months. Brayden and Laura are new though. Among others." He smiles at me and squeezes my hand quickly, then lets it go before anyone sees.

When we reach the front of the field, Paulo's group dissolves into ours. "Well, don't you look happy," Paulo says as he knocks his shoulders into Aerick's.

"What? I had a very exhilarating day. Am I not allowed to be in a good mood?" He questions. I'm still walking very close to him, and it makes me feel good knowing I was part of that day.

"Hey, man, whatever. I'm just saying. it's a good look for you. Hopefully, happy Aerick can show his face a little more often." I see Paulo look at me but Aerick just laughs; they must mess around a lot.

"Yeah, well, asshole Aerick is sitting close by, so watch it." I want to laugh at their carefree banter, but I hold it in.

"Okay, okay, I'll behave." Apparently what Aerick said about his suspicions is true.

Aerick orders us on the bus in the same seats for the head count. I know secretly he just wants to be sure he can sit next to me. We sit down and I set my bear in my lap, then pull out my earbuds and put them in.

I'm amazed at how today turned out. Leaning back, I look out the window, perfectly happy. Aerick's hand slides under my bear, so it's hiding under the backpack and bear. He laces his fingers with my own, and I close my eyes, not wanting to forget how I feel right now.

Our ride is over before I know it and Aerick shakes me a little. I'm not quite asleep, but I'm halfway there. Everyone is exhausting day. We quietly get up to leave the bus, but Aerick doesn't let me out until everyone has passed; then he gets up, and we start walking.

Before we get to the steps, he turns and smiles. "Night, Princess." His tone is so quiet I'm sure only I heard it. He turns and exits the bus with a straight face, but an almost unseen bounce to his step. I get off and find I'm unable to take the smile off my face.

Jeff and Patrick walk with me back to the dorm. Jeff seems upset about something. As soon as we get inside, Jeff stops me and I'm a little startled. "So, what the hell is up with you?"

I knew he was going to notice, but he has got to quit this. "What are you talking about, Jeff?" I don't give him time to answer. "You know what, I'm so tired. I just want to go to bed; we can talk about it tomorrow." I walk past him, grabbing out a pair of my shorts, and quickly take off my pants. The sweater goes down far enough to cover my underwear and right now I couldn't care less.

"Jeff!" I say as I notice he's still watching me. His face turns red, and he turns to his bed so I can have my privacy. I set the bear up on my desk and climb into bed, keeping Aerick's sweater on, snuggling it against me. "We will talk tomorrow," Jeff presses.

"'Kay. Night," I say with a yawn and I'm grateful to be able to put it off, but I am under no delusion that the conversation is over.

Who could've possibly guessed things would turn out this way? Even with my screwed-up past, I've managed finally to get past it enough to be with someone. Someone who can be close to me, someone who doesn't care about my past, someone who makes me happy, someone who apparently likes me just as much as I like him.

With my bad luck, I know it probably won't last, but be damned if I don't enjoy it as long as I can. He has me hooked and there's no way I'm walking away now. I breathe in deeply and fall asleep with Aerick's smile that he reserves only for me permanently etched in my mind.

CHAPTER TWENTY-ONE

(Sunday, July 5th)

NO ONE CAN keep the smile off my face today. I feel great, even with the lack of sleep. I get up and quickly change out of his sweatshirt and into a clean t-shirt. I don't want to ruin the smell of it with my sweat.

I head out to the stage with the guys; as I walk out, Aerick's eyes meet mine. He winks at me before putting his instructor face on. Luther starts in with his usual speech about things people did right and wrong, but I only pay attention to half of it until the ranking appears and I'm in the bottom three. I had a feeling that Leena and Joseph would be there, but I'm not sure what I did.

I look up to Aerick, and his face is impassive. Luther continues on about the importance of our educational classes and how he expects us to all participate with a positive attitude. Recognition suddenly hits me, thinking back to last week. I had been in a bad mood at Aerick's irritable behavior, and it may have projected out a little when I was in class. I did give Tia a bit of a hard time. Well, there's no one to blame but myself.

We continue with our stretching and begin our run. I start to run next to Aerick, but he pushes a little harder than normal. I have to try hard to keep up, but it puts a little distance between us and the guys behind. "Work harder!"

I look at him, and he seems a little pissed. I suppose he has a right to be mad. "I do not like having to put you on the bottom, but when I get reports like that from Tia, I don't have a choice." My thoughts are confirmed.

The part that bothers me the most is that he's disappointed in me. I bite my lip, trying to keep him from seeing me frown. "Yeah. Okay." Unintentionally, I sound a little defeated.

My eyes glance at him, and his anger seems to fade away, almost as if he feels bad. After a moment, he smiles and raises an eyebrow. "You want to rephrase that, cadet?"

I know his game, and it cheers me up again. "Yes sir – Aerick sir!" He smirks at my response.

We finish our workout, and I go in to take a quick shower since I didn't get a chance last night. I'm also secretly trying to stay away from Jeff's obsessive questioning. I gather my clothes in the bag and hang them for the laundry, but I make sure to leave Aerick's sweater out. I don't want it to lose his scent. Folding it, I put it in my clothing chest before going to brush my hair. After Aerick's comment yesterday I debate whether to put it up, but decide to leave it down since it's been up all week. By the time I'm finished the guys are done, so we head out to breakfast.

The mess hall seems loud today, and I'm sure it has to do with the awesome day we had yesterday. Most of them are mirroring my smile. As I go to sit down next to Aerick, I hear that I'm the topic of conversation at our table.

Royce looks at me. "You really jumped?" Looking briefly around, I quickly lower my head, not wanting all the attention.

"She sure did. Or maybe Aerick just pulled her over." Mike speaks up.

"Fuck off, dickhead, I jumped." I know I just told myself that I was going to behave, but I couldn't help it.

Brand puts his fork down. "It's true! Seriously, Aerick; you took her bungee jumping? Are you completely out of your mind?" He must have dismissed it as rumors. *Great – here we go again.*

Aerick stops eating and looks at him. "What? I have wanted to go for a long time, and she said she wanted to as well. Honestly, I thought she would chicken out when she got up there. Apparently, I underestimated her bravery. Besides, like I said yesterday, she's eighteen, it was her choice, and I went with her. We were within the rules, so back off." He says the last part with a bit of malice in his voice. Everyone stops to listen to Aerick's explanation, and when Brand doesn't say something right away, they go back to talking about how cool it would have been.

A few seconds later, Brand leans forward with a lower, serious voice. "And what about if she did chicken out, three seconds after you jumped? Her tracker would have activated." Aerick is getting irritated by Brand, and I wonder why they are constantly at each other's throats.

"Actually idiot, I have the ability to disable her tracker. It isn't like she would have been able to run, so I suggest you mind your own business and worry about your own cadets." I'm shocked. I didn't know he could have deactivated it. I look at him to ask questions, and the look in his eyes say it's not the appropriate time.

When he's sure I'm not going to say anything, he gets a sly smile on his face and looks back toward Brand. "What's the matter, Brand? You afraid this little thing over here is going to show you up because she just did something you would never do?" *Am I missing something?*

"Bite me, Aerick." Brand stands and leaves.

Trent shakes his head. "You don't have to be a dick, Aerick."

Aerick lets out a sarcastic laugh. "Whatever. It's not my fault the little pussy is afraid of heights," he says, answering my thoughts.

Trent stands up. "You're no perfect angel either."

He shrugs. "Yeah, but I never claimed to be." Trent walks off like a mad girlfriend.

"Geez, are they a couple or something?" I say before my mind can tell me to stop.

Aerick laughs a little, and Paulo almost chokes on his eggs. It takes him a second before he can speak "Wow, woman, you've got some balls!"

I lean in, "Quiet; you're giving away all my secrets," I joke. He shakes his head; Aerick continues eating trying not to smile.

We finish up our food, and I get a few more compliments on my bravery yesterday before I excuse myself and go to clean up so I can get my homework done. Slacking off last week, I have a ton of it to get done. Aerick was right; I need to try harder.

* * * *

Watching Leena and Joseph putting their hands all over each other is getting annoying, and I can tell Andi is getting quite annoyed as well. She has yelled at them twice already to get to work. I've done a bunch of the work and because of it, we're almost done. I grab the garbage, needing to get some fresh air. I walk out of the back door to throw it into the dumpster.

"Hey!" I hear him say in a muted voice, startling me. A smile spreads across my face, and I look over to him as I throw the bag away. Aerick is standing up against the wall with one foot on the wall and seems to be playing with something in his hand.

"Come down here so the camera can't see you." I obey his request, trying to hold in the giddy feeling that's pulsating through my body. As I come to a stop in front of him, I'm a little surprised he's risking doing this since he's been so cautious lately. I give him a questioning look.

"I just wanted to kiss you good morning." His lips lightly press against mine. "This clever mouth of yours."

My grin is massive as his cuteness peeks through. "Is that so?"

He lets out a small chuckle. "I also just got done reviewing last night's dorm camera footage, and I have to tell you, my pants became very uncomfortable when I saw you strip off your pants, showing all those guys these delightful legs of yours." He looks at my legs, dragging his fingers along my thighs and then looks back up at me as he bites his lip, driving me crazy.

I smirk at him, "Well, you're going to keel over when you find out that after I had got into bed, I removed everything else that was under that sweater." He closes his eyes and growls; suddenly he spins me, so he has me pinned up against the wall.

"I happen to know that isn't true but thank you for that visual." His voice hits that spot between my legs, and his lips crush to my own. I grab his neck, trying to pull him closer. These little impromptu make-out sessions are creating so much sexual tension; it's driving me insane.

He presses the hardening bulge in his pants against me, and I don't' know how much more of this ache I can take. "Fuck, Aerick."

"Keep that up, and I swear I am going to take you right here. I don't care who shows up," he says, continuing to kiss and biting my neck.

It's maddening, I can't take it anymore, "I accept that."

He stops kissing me and looks at me with a sly smile. "So bold!" He kisses my jaw and starts working up toward my ear. "What's the matter?" He moves back down to my neck, and I lean my head back on the wall to give him better access. "Getting a little impatient, are we?"

He bites the top of my shoulder, causing a moan to escape me. "Is that ache down there becoming unbearable?" His hands start roaming near the edge of my pants. My hands freeze on his neck, and I feel his smile on mine. His fingers slide under the front of my pants, and my breathing gets heavy with desire.

I pray that he doesn't stop and my prayers are answered when he undoes the button on my pants. His lips move back to mine, and he deepens the kiss as he moves to the side just a little, using his foot to take my leg with him. My legs are now spread apart with one between his, giving his hand better access. It slips inside my pants, and his fingers slowly rub over my underwear all the way down between my legs. My mind clouds over, and I don't care that we're doing this outside where anyone can walk up on us.

His leisurely pace is driving me nuts as he rubs over me again. "Aerick..." I breathe.

"You have to tell me if you want me to stop. Okay?" He whispers on my lips.

The lust in his voice pulls at me. "Please, don't stop." I feel his smile once more as he continues kissing me, moving down my jaw. Tilting my head back again, I'm lost in pleasure. His hand slides inside my underwear, and his fingers find my sensitive spot. The feeling is so intense; I hold onto his neck tighter as he continues biting and kissing away down to my shoulder. He puts his other arm around my back and clutches my side, pulling me close to him, so I can't move as he starts moving his fingers in circles.

I moan at the unimaginable pleasure I'm feeling. The sensation is so much more than I thought it would be. Feeling Aerick grow hard against me just adds to the intense feeling. "I want you so bad right now, but this is going to have to do."

He slides his fingers farther down between my legs and pushes one finger into me, causing another noise to escape me. "Hmm, so wet for me." My legs are getting weak, and an unfamiliar pull builds in me as he slides in and out while rubbing his thumb over my most sensitive area. His lips are working their magic, sending shivers down my body.

The feeling gets even stronger as he adds a second finger. My body tenses and my legs weaken. I don't know how much more I can take. "You are going to have to enjoy this for both of us, for now."

I've never felt this before; it's too intense, and I'm not sure can handle this. "I can't Aerick... it's too much." I barely whisper.

He brings his lips back to mine, "You can do it I know you can." He kisses me deeply as he continues. "It's okay, don't hold back, just let go." His words push me over the edge as my body is overwhelmed like nothing I've ever felt before. He covers my mouth with his own to quiet my moans and holds me almost painfully tight to himself.

He doesn't stop until my mind begins to clear the fog. He pulls his hand out of my pants, wrapping it around me as he leans his head against mine. It takes a minute to catch my breath, and I finally open my eyes.

"Hey." He smiles sweetly at me sounding a bit breathless himself. "Feeling better?"

"Hmm," is all I can get out. "Wow is my princess speechless? That's a first." My lips turn up in a grin.

"It sucks we have to cut this short, but I have to go, and so do you. I believe you have work to do." I frown at him but it is so hard to feel any kind of sadness right now. "Hey, none of that. You just got the best end of this deal. Not that I'm complaining, that was incredible!"

He kisses my neck again. "I can't wait to do that again," he whispers in my ear.

"Me either."

"I am going to step back, okay?" He loosens his grip on me and my legs feel weak but I'm okay, so I nod my head.

"Give yourself a little time before you go around the guys, or they will know," he says as he buttons my pants, with a smirk on his face. "I will see you later." I'm not sure what else to say. He pulls me to him by my belt loops, kissing me sweetly one last time before he walks away.

"Hey Princess?" I'm still leaning against the wall, and I turn my head to watch him. He's almost around the corner, with an evil grin on his face. "Next time I promise to show you the purpose of my tongue piercing." Then he puts the finger that was just inside me in his mouth and sucks on it. My mouth falls open, and he smiles proudly as he goes around the corner.

Holy fuck! I can't believe he just did that. I stare up at the sky in complete awe of what just happened. It was crazy, spontaneous, and just unbelievable.

I have no idea how long I stand there before Joseph comes out and gives me a strange look. "Hey, you alright?" I've calmed down mostly, but I'm sure I still look a little off considering I've never felt anything like that in my life.

"Uh, yeah I just was feeling a little sick." I lie and hope it's convincing enough.

"Well, Andi told me to check on you since you've been out here so long. We finished, so you can take-off if you want. I can let Andi know."

Nodding, I take a deep breath. "Thanks. I think I'm going to go lie down for a bit." He gives me an apologetic smile and goes back inside.

Careful to avoid the guys, I walk around the outside of the cabins to the dorms. Coming around the corner, my eyes glance over to where they're all out in the courtyard. No one is paying attention, so I quickly move from behind the cabins and go inside the dorm. My feet carry me into the bathroom and I look at myself in the mirror, still trying to come to grips with what just happened.

Shaking my head, I splash some water on my face. I do look a little flushed, and thinking of what we just did feels so surreal. I grab a paper towel and just hold it to my face.

"You okay?" Brand is standing behind me. *Shit.*

"Um, yeah. I was just feeling a little off. I'll be okay." Based on the look he's giving me, he thinks something's up, but he doesn't say anything else. He gives me one last look and then leaves without saying another word. I take a few breaths, glad he let it go. Deciding I can't put it off any longer, with one more deep breath I head to get my homework and iPod before going out to face the guys.

When I get out to the grass, I sit cross-legged near Jeff and Patrick and settle in to get my work done. I have English and Math tomorrow, and my game plan is to do my assignments in the order they're due. I finished my Math already, so I pull out my English. Thankfully it's just an article review.

"So, can we talk now?" Jeff asks. *Wow, that didn't take long.*

"Sure, Jeff. What's up?" I'm not mad; I just don't want to get into this with him. He knows me better than anyone and usually knows when I'm lying.

"Don't be irritated. I'm just worried about you." He scoots closer to me. "You've been really moody lately. Well, I mean, more than normal."

I look at him pointedly. "Jeff, I'm a girl. Mood swings are part of the package." He's not buying my explanation. "I don't know, Jeff. This place can just be overwhelming you know?" Well, at least, someone in it.

"I guess that's understandable. I just worry about you." I glare at him to stop right there.

"I'm fine, Jeff."

"Then why does it seem like you're hell bent on pushing Aerick over the edge? The way he looks at you sometimes, it, you know, worries me. Then you go and pull that shit yesterday with him. What in your right mind convinced you to do that? I mean, did he make you?"

My head snaps to look at him. "No, of course not. The other guys kind of egged me on but I wanted to do it."

He looks down. "I don't know. Seeing his arms around you like that. I've never seen you let anyone do that besides me, Patrick and your family. I guess I'm sort of shocked."

Patrick is looking at me expectantly now. It's probably safe to assume they've already had this discussion. Honestly, I didn't think about how to explain the fact that he can touch me.

Annoyance boils up in me but only because I have no explanation and I'm not ready to tell them the truth. "So now you're complaining that I let someone touch me?" I don't give him time to answer. "Forget it. I… uh… don't know. Maybe the adrenaline kept me from freaking out. It was either that or chicken out, so I just did it, no big deal." I've clearly become pissed, even though he's just looking out for me, but I don't like lying to him.

"Hey, don't be mad. I'm sorry. Just, please, promise me you'll be careful around Aerick, okay?" I take a few deep breaths, trying to calm down.

I don't want to cause problems between us. Today has been incredible, so put on a smile. "Okay, Jeff. If I have a problem with

Aerick, you'll be the first to know. Are we done with the interrogation?"

"Maybe. Will you to go with me next time?" He jokes, lighting the mood.

Laughter fills my chest. "We'll see about that. Okay, seriously, look at all this work that needs to get done. I refuse to be at the bottom two weeks in a row." I pick up my notebook, put my earbuds in and start reading the article, but I have a hard time concentrating because my mind keeps floating back to Aerick.

By lunchtime, I've finished Monday and Tuesday's work, and I'm happy with my progress, but frustrated when realizing I must have left my workbook in Health class on Saturday, so I can't do it yet. We put our stuff away and head to the mess hall. It sucks having to clean after all the meals today and, to make matters worse, I had to go in to clean the bathroom earlier while Brayden was busy doing god knows what instead of supervising us. I don't know how much more of those two I can handle.

I'll admit I'm a little nervous to see Aerick after what we did, but he's not there when we get in the hall. Disappointment builds in my chest. While I'm nervous to see him, deep down I want to. Jeff pushes me toward the line, and I smell the homemade pizza we're having for lunch before I see it, while Patrick hoots his approval beside me.

As I sit down, Trent turns to me. "So Nadi, I hear you have a question for me," he says with amusement. Heat runs up my neck remembering this morning.

"I'm sure I have no idea what you're talking about," I tell him as a matter of fact and Paulo laughs.

He must have been the one who informed Trent of the conversation after he left; I look at him with frustration. "Hey don't look at me like that, you're the one with the mouth, little one."

"Something tells me she isn't so little." I hold my breath at his voice behind me. Aerick sits down next to me, and I know what he's referring to. My cheeks turn pink with embarrassment. I just hope everyone else thinks it's because of his compliment.

"She has already shown she is courageous, which is more than I can say for some," he says, holding in a laugh, although most probably think he is just being smug. His leg pushes against mine and I relax a bit. These nerves are ridiculous. There really is no reason to be so tense around him. Mentally, I try to shake out my limbs and act normal.

"Aerick, don't start again, he's been pissy all morning."

Aerick shakes his head. "I can't help that he can't take a joke." Everyone quiets down as Brand comes over to sit down.

"You all up for a bit of football later?" Huck speaks up, changing the subject. Patrick, Jeff, and Mike agree right away.

"Fearless one?"

I roll my eyes at him. "Actually I have to get caught up on my homework, but if by some chance I'm able to finish, yes, I'll join you." He seems satisfied by that and goes on trying to recruit others.

I'm eating my pizza and I feel Aerick nudge me with his leg. I glance sideways at him and he does the same as he starts licking the pizza sauce off his fingers. I choke on my pizza in shock. *I can't believe this man!*

He pats me on the back. "You okay?" He plays it off like is completely unaware he's surprised.

I push his hand away. "I'm fine!"

He picks up his tray and leaves trying to hide his smile. *Asshole.* He did that on purpose.

* * * *

I'm finished cleaning up and need to finish my homework, but I need my workbook, so I decide to stop by the classroom on my way back. The counseling sessions are in the other room and the afternoon sessions haven't started yet, so I figure it'll be okay. When I get into the room I go right in; no one locks the doors here. My workbook is still on the back counter right where I left it. As I pick it up, a voice floats in from the other room. It's not my intention to be nosy, but the voice is familiar and I'm curious.

I stand by the door. "Trent said you needed me." I can clearly hear Aerick's voice. *I should leave now.* This isn't my business.

I go to turn, but her voice stops me. "Really… You don't need to sound so professional." It's Liz.

"I guess not. What's up?"

My curiosity gets the better of me. "It seems like you've been avoiding me the last few weeks that I've been here. Are we not friends anymore?" She questions.

"Liz, you are one of my very few friends. I have just had some difficult cadets this time around."

She laughs. "Yeah, you can say that again. Although I must say, it a real joy reading all of Nadi's reports. She sure keeps it interesting."

He lets out a quick laugh and she quickly changes the subject, intent now clearly in her tone. "So 'Pain in the Grass' is this next weekend on Saturday." *What the hell is that?*

"Really? Sometimes it bites being up here. I don't get any of the good radio stations. Who's playing?" *A concert?*

"Linkin Park, Theory of a Deadman, Disturbed, Three Days Grace, Pop Evil, and some other small bands. It's up at the Gorge again this year and lasts all day." *Wow, awesome bands!*

"Bad ass lineup." I love that he likes the same music as me.

"I was wondering if you could get Laura to cover you and come with me. It has been awhile since we went out." *Went out? As what, friend? Girlfriend?*

"I can't. We're doing the Lookout Trip that day." So confused again.

"Come on Aerick; I want to hang out," she says, but not whiny like most girls; it sounded more demanding.

"What do you want me to say, Liz? I can't."

"Fine. How about we go down to the Old Number Three for drinks next Sunday. Casey's already agreed to let me use the cabin all weekend because of the concert and work. I'm not heading back until Monday."

I don't like how this conversation is going. She doesn't sound like 'a friend.' I chance opening the sliding door just a hair. Without any noise, I'm able to open it just a tiny bit so I can see through. He's leaning against the desk on the other side of the room and she's standing in front of him, much too close for my liking. He's looking down, playing with something in his hand. All the hairs on my neck stand on end as my discomfort grows.

"I don't know. I'll have to check with Luther." Really, he's seriously considering going out with her?

She leans up against him. "Aerick, come on. I need a little release. It's been a couple of weeks since we had some real fun." She touches his stomach. He raises his eyebrow at her.

"Okay, okay. I know, not at work," she says slyly, and I can't believe him. My mind fights on whether or not I should go in there and say something or just walk the fuck away.

She laughs. "But we've broken the rules before." Her voice is full of lust as she grabs him between the legs.

"Dammit Liz, I told you I don't do this shit at work."

That puts me over the top! Unable to handle the scene playing out in front of me, I leave through the front door. I pause for just a second, not knowing where to go.

I will not cry, I will NOT cry!

My body is screaming to do something, anything. It's likely not smart to the go to the gym. Fuck, I should have known better. I put in the ear buds, turning it up loud, and go to the back field behind the staff cabins and start running around it where people won't notice me. *How the hell could he do this to me?*

* * * *

The running and loud music helps keep my head clear. When I finally look at my clock, I realize I'm five minutes late for my counseling session. *Shit!*

I stop and catch my breath. I've managed not to cry, but now I have to go and talk to this hoe. The problem is, my gut is telling me not to let her know about Aerick and I. *Why would I?* For what – so she can laugh at me that I actually thought he liked me? I start walking as I shake my head at myself.

How do I always get myself into these fucked up situations? As I'm walking across the courtyard, Aerick is walking out of the gym. He stops looking at his watch. "You're late," he says with disapproval, but he sounds a little off. I suppose he should.

"Thanks, I'm well aware. I'm going now." Continuing, I walk away toward the classroom and away from him.

Once in the classroom, Liz seems to not be in a great mood. *What's the matter, she couldn't get what she wanted today?* She sees me and perks herself up. "Hey, Nadi."

Sitting down, I don't bother to greet her back. "You okay today?" She asks, catching on to my foul mood.

"Oh yes, I'm just peachy," I say sarcastically.

I know I need to calm down and get through the next thirty minutes. "Is there something you would like to talk about today?"

Her chipper attitude makes me want to punch her in the face. I'm sitting here with her after she just pushed herself on my boyfriend, and he sat there like it was nothing. To make matters worse, it's obvious they do that sort of thing often.

Breathe! It isn't going to do me any good to hit her, as much as it would make me feel better. I take a deep breath, trying to control myself.

I'm more pissed at Aerick than anything. She probably doesn't know we're together; although, I don't think much of girls who sleep around. He should have never let her do that shit to him.

He could have easily gotten up and walked away from her at any point, but instead, he sat there all nonchalant. He didn't tell her he had someone and wasn't interested, or that he didn't want to mess around with her or anything. For Christ's sake, she grabbed his shit, and all he had to say was 'not at work!'

"Nadi!" Liz breaks me out of my thoughts. "Did you want to talk about something?"

My eyes unintentionally roll to the ceiling. "No, the last thing I want to do right now is talk. Can I go?" I tell her, trying to reel in my ire.

"Unfortunately, I have to complete the thirty-minute session. What would you rather do right now?"

Go a few rounds in a boxing ring with Aerick may make me feel better. "Listen to my music and exercise." She looks at me.

"Were you just doing that before you came here?" *Isn't she observant?* I'm sure I smell like sweat from running.

"Yes."

"So, this is your typical reaction when you get upset." It wasn't a question, so, I just shrug my shoulders.

"Did someone upset you?" *Didn't I make it clear I didn't want to talk about this?* Sitting here trying to get it out of me is just making me not like her even more.

"I don't want to talk about it. Period!" I'm very harsh, but hopefully she gets the point.

She writes some notes and shifts in her seat. "Okay. Well, let's go back to what we had been talking about the last few weeks. I would like to work on your issue with touch. From what I have seen in your records, this stems back to your preteens." *Shit!* I can't talk about this crap either. I close my eyes and try to breathe.

"But your doctor's records do not show any aversions to touch or possible causes, such as autism." *Is this bitch serious?* I look at her, irritated, trying to keep myself in my seat.

"Do you remember how old you were when you began you feel uncomfortable with touch?" *Of course I do, and I sure as hell am not telling you.*

"You know what, I've had just about enough of this shit today."

My body is up in an instant, moving toward the exit. "Nadi we need to finish our session."

Who gives a shit what she thinks I need to do. "Go complain to someone who cares. I'm sure you can find somebody!"

I'm out the door without another word. *Crap.* Why can't I control my ridiculous emotions? This isn't going to work out in my favor.

I walk back to the dorm and get my stuff to take a shower. As I go through my clothing chest, I see Aerick's sweater and it pisses me off even more. My fist slams it shut a little harder than I meant, causing Patrick to jump.

"You okay?" He asks hesitantly.

I wish people would stop asking me that. "I'm fine. Just fucking peachy." Walking toward the bathroom, I don't wait to hear a response. I don't want to see anyone right now and being here isn't going to make that easy. I turn on the shower as hot as I can stand it and get in.

I can't help it any longer; the tears began to flow as I let the hot water beat down on my head. *Can't anything in my life just be okay?* I'm so tired of being broken and weak. I'm tired of trying so hard, just to have it all torn down in an instant. I was so happy, and now I feel like the world's biggest idiot.

Why did I let him do that to me? I guess someone as broken as me, could never keep his attention. I was just something to pass his days here, something he could play with to bide his time.

As my tears dry up, I decide to wash my body. I can't cry about this anymore. Taking a few deep breaths, I try to put this in the back of my mind. I don't want everyone else to see me like this. I need to be stronger than that, and I've got to get past this. *I can get past this.* Shutting off the shower, I get dressed, resolved to move on.

Stepping out of the shower, my feet freeze in their place.

Aerick is standing against the wall, his lips in a line, clearly irritated. He looks up at me. "I just talked to Liz."

Really? Of course, that's who she would call. "Good for you."

I go to walk past him, but he reaches out and grabs my wrist. "What's wrong?" The irritation in his face is replaced with concern. Although, I'm not sure why he even cares.

"It's none of your concern anymore." Jeff walks in and looks at us. His eyes shoot down to Aerick's grip on me and then to my pissed off look. "I was just coming to get you for dinner. Ready?" His voice is full of hatred. He apparently put together that I'm mad at Aerick although it probably wouldn't take a genius to see it. Jeff reaches his hand out to me, and I take it, pulling out of Aerick's grip as Jeff and I walk out.

"Do I need to worry now?"

I shake my head at him. "I'll be fine, thank you."

I'm not hungry, but I can't deal with Aerick and I'm not trying to go back to our old arrangement, so I do my best. I sit down next to Patrick, and Jeff sits on the other side of me without me saying anything. He is the most amazing friend.

"So, are you playing football with us?" He asks me. Aerick sits down on the other side of Jeff, leaving a seat between them.

"Yeah, I'll play if it's flag football." I need to stay away from Aerick as much as possible. My eyes find him for just a second, and he seems to be concentrating awfully hard on his food. Hopefully he figures out I know, because I don't want to have to explain it to him.

I just need to stay with everyone as much as possible and away from him. He wouldn't dare talk to me with others around.

So, that's what I set out to do...

Coming Early 2019...

UNSTRUNG
Book Two in
the Donnelly Bootcamp Series

About the Author

Danielle Leneah is a person with limitless aspirations. Whether she is working full time to help support her family, designing web sites for fun, or writing books to calm her mind, she always puts her heart and soul into her work.

Her reading and writing ambitions started at a young age. By sixth grade, she was reading full Stephen King novels and writing short stories. Her first publication came when she was in high school. Her work was accepted to be published in a well known poetry book. Even though her dreams of writing were temporarily halted as she began to build a family, it eventually drew her back.

As she began writing, she remembered the peace and joy it use to bring her. In astonishing 50 days, she had the rough draft of the first two books in a her new series completed.

In her mind, if she can make just one person happy with her stories, it would have been worth it.

Danielle was born and raised in the suburbs of Seattle, Washington where she still lives with her husband and children.

To get the latest news and stay up to date, visit her website at:
www.DanielleLeneah.com

Made in the USA
Coppell, TX
28 May 2021

56489499R10187